Todd London's first novel, *The World's Room*, received a Milestone Award for fiction. It was hailed by novelist Lorrie Moore as "a stunning first book...written as if by a spellbinding and spellbound angel". His books include: *An Ideal Theater; The Importance of Staying Earnest; 15 Actors, 20 Years;* and *This Is Not My Memoir* (co-author Andre Gregory). The first recipient of Theatre Communications Group's Visionary Leadership Award for achievement in the theatre and winner of the George Jean Nathan Award for Dramatic Criticism, Todd holds an honorary doctorate from DePaul University. He heads the MFA Playwriting program at The New School.

Advance Praise for *If You See Him, Let Me Know*

"Within a few pages, I had fallen headlong into the world of the Friedkin Camp for Theatre Arts in Swallow Heart Lake Wisconsin. Todd London's incisively drawn portrait of young souls in 1974, stumbling amidst shadows of the Holocaust on their way to American adulthood, blew me away with its spot-on evocation of the feeling of aching dislocation that colored my own Midwestern-Jewish girlhood. This is a killer coming-of-age story: gripping and compassionate. I haven't stopped thinking about it."

– Lisa Kron, author of *Well* and the musical *Fun Home*

"With humor and uncommon wisdom, Todd London links the temporal agonies of adolescence with the ageless horrors of the 20th Century and shows us how we can't face these pains alone. A novel that harrows the heart. This one is going to leave a mark."

– Octavio Solis, author of *Retablos* and *Mother Road*

"In *If You See Him, Let Me Know*, Todd London creates an intricately woven universe drawn within the confines of one week at a children's summer theatre. As with London's brilliant debut *The World's Room*, the reader is deftly catapulted to a precise space and time—one generation removed from the Holocaust with Richard Nixon imploding and Bernadine Dohrn exploding—yet for Philip and most of the other young thespians of Friedkin Camp, the most pressing concern is authenticating themselves as Sharks and Jets. Still, larger issues manage to creep into the isolated utopia: acquaintance rape years before there was a name for it, white-collar crime and punishment brought home. The events of that summer of '74 and its long-term aftermath provide for the reader an engrossing journey, culminating in a denouement that is surprising, gratifying, and eminently moving."

– Kia Corthron, author of *The Castle Cross the Magnet Carter*, winner of the Center for Fiction First Novel Prize

"Todd London is a master conjurer of the lost—of lost youth, lost promise, lost Chicago, lost America. In *If You See Him, Let Me Know*, London has penned a memorably bittersweet and heartfelt love letter to a bygone age that feels both immediate and timeless, infused with both hope and regret. Populated by frustrated, frustrating and wholly believable characters and filled with clever, knowing theatrical references, it is at once an evocative road novel, a heartbreaking coming of age story, and an elegiac reflection on what America was in the 1970's and what it ultimately became."

– Adam Langer, author of *Crossing California* and *The Thieves of Manhattan*

Praise for *The World's Room*, Todd London's debut novel

"*The World's Room* is a stunning first book. Simultaneously warm-hearted and eerie-minded, it is written as if by a spellbinding and spellbound angel."

– Lorrie Moore, author of *A Gate at the Stairs*

"London offers a rich, nimble instance of the coming-of-age story, in which his narrator straightens himself up into life from the lurid psychological skein of family...With graceful nuance and subtlety, London's tale is a melancholy success, a cleanly written, emotionally credible debut that tamps its pathos with a firm, generous clarity, and so eliminates the hazy lilt of sentimentality."

– *Kirkus Reviews*

"The book [is narrated] with a wry, knowing wit, leaving the reader to marvel that such a sad story can be told so beautifully."

– *The Washington Post*

"London...has a magnificent sense of character and ear for dialogue....This engaging and crafty debut establishes London as a writer to watch."

– *Publishers Weekly*

"London's novel dramatizes the power of the written and the spoken word, not only to reveal truth but to conceal it....Nothing I've read recently except poetry conveys the language of yearning the way this novel does....The author uses his double vision to make us laugh and break our hearts and the same time."

– Citation for Milestone Award, Vermont Book Professionals Association

"For Todd London...whose first novel has the meticulousness of a memoir, this age of Banlon, Joni Mitchell, and divorce is as fascinating sociologically as it is rich in narrative."

– *Los Angeles Times*

"While this bittersweet tale of love, loss, and identity may be what [the narrator] calls 'the kind of collage that memory, imagination, and twisted feeling assemble,' it's one that will linger long in the reader's mind."

– *Library Journal*

Todd London

IF YOU SEE HIM, LET ME KNOW

AUSTIN MACAULEY PUBLISHERS™

LONDON • CAMBRIDGE • NEW YORK • SHARJAH

A CIP catalogue record for this title is available from the British Library.

ISBN 9781528950671 (Paperback)
ISBN 9781528972765 (ePub e-book)

www.austinmacauley.com

First Published (2020)
Austin Macauley Publishers Ltd
25 Canada Square
Canary Wharf
London
E14 5LQ

For Pearl

"A place belongs forever to whoever claims it hardest, remembers it most obsessively, wrenches it from itself, shapes it, renders it, loves it so radically that he remakes it in his image..."

– Joan Didion, *The White Album*

Chapter 1

Jerry Rosen drives his life.

From the near South side of Chicago into the farmlands of Wisconsin, the landscape changes like time. He drives past the depression, wooden houses built for single families, each housing several families, slammed together on the gray street. He loops the Loop and pictures his father selling silk stockings out of a one-room office with metal filing cabinets, the color of putty. Heading North towards Rogers Park, he passes the two-bedroom on Montrose where his sister was born. It's the world Roosevelt built, WPA bricks and mortar, elevated tracks, the umber apartments everyone was meant to afford. He cuts up and down the streets of West Rogers Park where he places someone different on almost every block, people he hasn't thought about in years, guys now maybe alive or dead, girls he once would have killed to kiss, now probably fat and prosaic. His ex-in-laws' former house on Kedzie: everything has slipped into a state of past-ness, of used-to-be or once was, until it seems to him that there's no such thing as the 'eternal present'. The past is the only thing eternal, and it keeps retreating further into itself, disappearing into its own folds.

The war ends, and his city turns to redder bricks and cleaner corners, the modularity of the American future—what can't we do? *Keep moving*, Jerry tells himself, as he goes suburban: Skokie. *Don't look behind*. His zig-zag through time hits punctuation. On the main streets, he stops every four blocks at shining traffic lights; on side streets, at every corner for a bright red sign. He was happy here among the pillbox ranches with their eighth-of-an-acre lawns, single picture windows looking out on streets lined with newly planted elms. Happyish. $45,000 for a mortgage in 1955, the same to add a swimming pool and garage in '68.

No longer new suburbs lead to old towns, the grandeur of water views on the northern shores of Lake Michigan. The old money of Evanston, Wilmette and Highland Park—*WASP money*, he thinks, picturing a swarm of white hairs flying back to hive, toting Monopoly-style money bags—leads to newer towns with newer money and bigger names: Arlington Heights, Buffalo Grove, Libertyville. Edens Expressway leads to I-87. He crosses the Wisconsin border and breathes out. He has left his life behind.

His ex had a saying, one she'd learned in a meditation class at Oakton Community College: "Every wall is a door." It seems backwards to him. Every door is, in the real world, a wall. As proof, he notices that no sooner has he shut the door on Illinois and the nearly fifty years he's spent there than he's hurtling into a world from which he can never drive far enough. The steaming breweries of Milwaukee loom. In their bricks, he sees the depression, he sees Germany, he sees his father's placid face, he sees his mother: fierce, unforgiving and cold as a block of ice hauled off a truck.

When he's out of the city, it's as though somebody turned down the sound. The wind has nothing to stop it, and neither does the eye.

The smell of cow shit settles over him, driving top down in his Triumph. The car is a killer, a Pimento Red Spitfire, bought new and shipped from the factory in Coventry. It's as out of place with the corn and hops fields and dairy farms as he is. No Jewish farmers, he half thinks. Jews don't dig dirt. He notes with what ordinarily would have been pleasure the play on the word 'dig', literal and groovy.

He makes his way through the yellow-greens, the open fields strewn with straw—acres of pick-up sticks. There's a cloud around his brain, a peripheral storm waiting to invade and break, burst and flood, flood and carry him away. "Gentile-man farmers," he mumbles, reflexively swinging after another pun. "Landed Gentile-ry."

His left wrist is resting on the inside of the steering wheel, and his right hand instinctively gives a tug on the brim of his suede cap. He wants to secure the hat against the wind, naturally, but he's also making sure the toupee stays put. It's a recent addition, since the divorce, as is the moustache, spiked handsomely, or mockingly, with gray.

His eyes flick up to the mirror and wince away. Usually, he likes what he sees. Today, he can't look. Brown barns, beer signs, arrows to CHEESE and the Wisconsin Dells, a billboard for Oktoberfest (though it's just August), and Holsteins patched black, brown and white—he checks these out instead. *"Vilkommen to Visconsin,"* he says out loud. "Grow potbellied *mit us, Bitte.*" His mind, used to concocting ad slogans, is dull today. Words like clods of earth. No joy in Mudville.

He'd better call soon, better find a phone.

Again, his hand moves without thought. He's touching his stomach. The hand reminds him that the potbelly remark could come back to haunt him. I'm rubber, you're glue. Yes, I'm getting fat. *Nu?* Jesus. It's the least of my worries. Where's a goddamned pay phone? And for a moment, he hates all farms and all farmers. *Fucking Nazi farmers*, he thinks.

It doesn't occur to him to slow down, to pull over, catch breath. No, you push through it, close the door, take the pain. The storm clouds squeeze in. This time, he catches his own eyes in the rearview. Grim him. Everything hits at once—the hot air, cow stink and the thought of what tomorrow might bring. *He's at summer camp. I'm taking him out of summer camp to tell him.* This time he does pull over.

There's something pleasant about the smell of manure. It's a rich, sweet smell, different from, but reminiscent of, the stockyards he'd smelled every day—especially every night—during his childhood. Something homey, warm about it. We come from earth and return to earth kind of smell, a smell that, if you didn't know its source, you'd swear was calling you somewhere forgotten.

God, the way his mother was about the yards. As always, talking out of both sides of her mouth. Peasant mom, half the time she didn't even notice the stench, so much like the old country. "Gee, Ma, the cows sure are sweating it tonight."

"What? Och, no. It's nothing. That's nothing."

And then better than everyone, above them all. "Don't get settled here whatever you do. These are shtetl people, with their slaughter houses and their lunch pails. They are not for us." Who did she think she was? And who did she think he was? If she wasn't already dead, his latest news would kill her.

Now, the only heart left to break is his son Philip's. Where's a goddamn phone?

He carries a handkerchief, and now he's using it, blowing his honker nose while the tears come down against his will. He doesn't remember crying like this, not when his mother died, certainly never during the war. Once, maybe twice, in the life of his son, a sudden day in the hospital, the night of the divorce. At such moments, life seems a descent, a waterfall of events from pain to pain, each plateau lower than the one before. This time, he thinks, there's no lower, not until I heart attack and die. (Dying, in his mind, is inseparable from heart attack. He never thinks cancer or stroke or age. It's one thing, a verb: to heart-attack-and-die.) Again, without his noticing, the hand goes to his waist.

There's much he doesn't notice: the cars passing on his left, one at a time. A family of rabbits cutting in and out of a field of tassel-shot corn. A man watching him from a flatbed hay wagon hitched to the back of a standing tractor.

He swivels the mirror. He watches himself wipe his eyes. Every grief is a show, if only for one's self. He notes the jowls, tilts his head to study the deep dimple in his chin. "Philip," he says out loud. His brain goes over his script, or tries to, but keeps drifting, veering away from the lines he's rehearsing. He knocks the mirror into place with the back of his hand, then taps it twice to make it right.

He ejects a tape from the dashboard—the Fifth Dimension singing, "Won't you marry me, Bill?" and pokes around in a black vinyl case for another. He finds it, and pretty soon Yehudi Menuhin is playing Brahms from the eight-track deck.

He shifts into first, shoulder checks and pulls back onto the highway. As he goes, he gives the finger to the man standing in the hay wagon. "You thought I didn't see you," he mutters.

Jerry Rosen drives. The landscape refuses to change. He passes a hand-painted placard reading, "Where there is manure there is Christ. Christ!" he says out loud. "Holy shit!"

He laughs with forced vengeance. On the tape deck Menuhin saws against the roar of air.

He looks around. There is nothing of him here—no city, no woman, no place where this happened or that happened. He is moving through empty German fields, through empty space, and nothing will fill it, fill him. At the next gas station, the next restaurant, he'll call.

Chapter 2

The costume shop walls rise out of sight, hung floor to ceiling with clothes: Dorothy's gingham, the Scarecrow's denim and the body of a tin man made of silver lamé. Oklahoma farm girl frocks, Highland kilts, grass skirts and hoop skirts, minks and pearls, the uniforms of sailors from World War II, fifties gang-war dancewear—each costume crushes up against its clones, resized for children of every age. It's a dress-up box, a box of crayons. There's crimson, daffodil, periwinkle, shamrock, yellow-brick gold, the hush of bridal white. It doesn't smell like crayons, though. The air carries the tang of mildew, not unlike urine left to dry. Wafting through the screen door, other smells—half-fresh, half-rotting—lake smells: pine, moss and muck, whiff of cocoa butter riding alongside. This contradiction of smells is summer. This warren of rooms, cramped and fabulous, is the world—a maze overstocked with faked finery, fabric, dented hats, mounds of shoes—pageant, carnival, dress parade, garment district, Salvation Army, Ellis Island.

In the center of the front room, on a rolling rack, dangles a row of clothes from *Fiddler on the Roof*, as-if shtetl rags, inspired by Chagall and fashioned for teens—a dazzling poverty, made on the cheap. At one end of this rack, wearing a babushka of her own, Lila Sahlins (nee Friedkin) is teaching sixteen-year-old Philip Rosen to iron.

He's seen it before, only the last time she had no iron and no shirt. There was no ironing board either, and yet he saw it then as clearly as he is seeing it now. The way she flapped the cotton blouse and let it float to the board. The way she gently tugged the sleeve over the point of the nonexistent ironing board and smoothed the largest wrinkles with her palm. The way her other hand, veined and spotted, almost absent-mindedly reached for the black plastic handle of the steel iron, her eyes shifting at the last minute to keep her knuckles from banging on the hot surface of the metal. She hefted the iron then and, taking her right hand off the shirt, licked her index finger and popped it just so against the scalding bottom. He could have sworn he'd seen a puff of steam rise up in the middle of her pantomime, there in drama class that morning when, with the most precise animation, the whole act and apparatus of ironing had appeared before his eyes.

"You have to observe every detail," Lila had said. "See, hear, touch, smell, taste—*feel*—everything." And so she'd done.

And now, in the real world of muslin and padding and scorching metal, of sweat and taffeta, of one mosquito dive-bombing his left ear, she is doing it again. For real. And he is watching, listening, smelling, almost tasting the metallic air. She puts a motherly arm (or a grandmotherly—bubbe's—arm) around his shoulder, pivots the handle towards him and says, "Now you try."

He lifts the iron, surprised by its weight. He touches it to the shirt and begins switching it around. "It won't burn," she says, "as long as it doesn't sit too long in one spot." She guides his hand, smoothing the cotton with the steel.

There's nothing wet about her touch, even in this heat, nothing sweaty. Just a silken care, the slightest suction, nestling on the back of his uncertain, nail-bitten hand. He feels a pulsing, a quick vibrancy, as if life were a barrage of electrical charges and she a conductor.

Philip presses one shirt on his own steam and begins another, a tunic that will be worn by Motel Kamzoil, the tailor. The basket at his feet brims with clothes that will cover the bodies of his friends. He begins to chatter, impressively he thinks, about why it's urgent for him to leave for college early; after junior year in high school, why he can't wait, why he needs to get out now, to cultivate the means to express himself now, to find, as he calls it, my life in art. "In the meantime," he says, "I'll be living with my dad this year. Just the guys."

"Hmm," Lila murmurs, hardly seeming to hear. Her concentrated gaze urges him to pay attention to what he's doing and leave the future to the future. "Now," her eyes say, "now is right in front of you." Philip monologues on, avoiding her look, attending instead to outside sounds, filtering through the screen door.

Voices that have been faint and sporadic grow louder. Girl voices. Exclamations of astonishment and disdain. Philip tries to identify them as they pass by the costume shop. Lila gives no sign of registering, but, of course, she does. She never misses a trick, a whisper of a trick. The mosquito that has been fencing with Philip's cheek comes in for the kill. It jabs the inner cup of his ear, thrust and suck. He whacks the side of his face. Lila tilts her head to look, cocks an eyebrow.

Philip hears shrieks and laughter outside and again he wants to know their source. She sees it. "Pay attention to what you're doing."

Now he's Hans Brinker, free skating the iron in graceful arcs across a sleeve.

"Don't get fancy," Lila tells the boy. "Don't show off." Is she talking about ironing? She's right, of course. He thinks about the birds he's seen dropping from the towering trees on the lakefront. They shoot straight down as if falling, as if dead. Then, pop! They land, 180° south of where they started. The shortest distance between two places, and they know it. If anything could make a boastful loop-de-loop display, it's a bird. But they don't. They go where they're going, with the bird-god's grace.

A small speaker above the costume shop's horse-stall door crackles. "Philip Rosen, please report to the office. Philip Rosen to Anatevka." The boy stares at the speaker, forgetting to keep the iron moving. The voice on the speaker belongs to Uncle Bernie, the camp director. Bernie is careful never to say, "You've got a call," because he doesn't want to make homesick kids sad. "It's the same as saying, 'Little Johnny, your parents have forgotten you,'" Bernie explains when he teaches teenagers to operate the P A. But, of course, Philip is being paged for a phone call.

13

"Give me that," Lila says, reaching gingerly around Philip for the iron. She tucks a strand of hair into her babushka and with her artist's eye, absolutely cold, absolutely compassionate, watches Philip leave the costume shop. She backhands a row of dresses, and the hangers shriek across the metal bar.

Philip crosses the parking lot and mounts the porch of Anatevka, the camp's main building. The lobby air is musty and familiar. There's a stone fireplace he's never seen used. In the summer of '71, they posted the lottery draft numbers on the lobby bulletin board, and, despite being years too young, he was jolted with relief to see his own birthday was 285. Now the bulletin board banner says, "Friedkin Camp for the Theatre Arts" above "Thursday, August 8, 1974". A piece of paper is tacked up: "9:00 p.m. President Nixon Speaks to the Nation. Silver & Gold Divisions. Anatevka Lobby."

Philip walks into the program office and over to the gray metal desk that occupies most of the room. The desk, a heavy metal chair with swamp green vinyl upholstery, one gray filing cabinet, a wall covered with a handmade calendar—eight weeks of activities blocked out in magic marker and a rainbow of colored index cards—these things fill the room, these things and Philip. He's on the ground floor of Anatevka, and through the slatted blinds he sees, on the massive front porch, a wicker rocker, painted to blend with the forest pines.

Weekly calls from home used to be a major event at camp; now they're neither weekly nor major. Sometimes, they aren't from home. Anyone might be calling—a Broadway producer, someone looking for an extraordinary teenage boy to interview for the *Tribune*, looking to catapult him into a spectacular new life. Something about summer makes him believe that every new encounter holds the chance of changing his life. It's what he thinks of when he sings 'Something's Coming' in *West Side Story*, that feeling that any minute someone could step unexpectedly out of anywhere and remake your destiny. Just around a corner. Underneath a tree. He picks up the phone.

Chapter 3

Jerry Rosen stands clenched in place, his jaw tight, eyes squinting. Just behind him, the steel tip of an air hose bangs in the wind. A thin, blond man in oil-stained service station blues watches through the window. Jerry stands there, holding the phone, for too many minutes, real minutes. He doesn't look at anything; there's nothing to look at. He wishes he had a drink.

Finally, he hears, as if through a wire strung between tin cans, the voice of a young man, a voice he recognizes, his son Philip's voice:

"Hello? Hello? Anybody there? Hello?"

"Hello?" he speaks from the dark side of a cave, a cave that might cave in.

"Dad, is that you?"

Jerry clutches onto the phone, his eyes narrowed against the glare of the sky. He can't remember it ringing. How did Philip know how to reach him here at a gas station in the middle of nowhere?

"Hey, Buddy. Yes, yes, it's me."

"Hey, Dad."

"Hey," repeats the father.

"Where are you? You sound weird."

"Where?"

"Weird. I can barely hear you." Philip raises his voice against the white noise coming from the phone.

"I'm here. I'm here. It's a Gas-N-Go."

"You're in Glasgow?"

"I wish. No, a Gas-N-Go."

"A gas station? Why are you calling from—"

"—Hold on a sec," Jerry says. He brings himself into focus, takes a breath. "I need to fish out some coins."

He has coins. What he fishes out is a cigarette. He flicks a silver lighter, embossed with a Chrysler/Plymouth logo, and lights a Camel. He sucks it in, pulling himself together with the drag, and lifts the dangling receiver.

"Sorry," he says. "I'm at a Gas-N-Go somewhere near Sheboygan. I'm in the neighborhood."

"For real? What're you doing there?"

"Thought I'd drop by. See my kid at camp."

"For real?"

"Really real. Thought I'd take a guy to lunch."

"I just had lunch."

"Well, you can have another," Jerry says.

"Really?"

"I shit you not."

"No way they'll let me out."

"I got permission."

"For real?"

"From the big boss himself. Uncle Boiney." It's been Jerry's joke since Philip started camp, Uncle Bernie pronounced in a little Jewish voice.

"No shit?"

"I got papal dispensation."

"Is the Pope Jewish?"

"Pope Boiney is."

"Is that a smear?" Philip puns.

"Is what what?"

"A papal smear. Get it. It's a joke, son. Joke, Dad."

"Funny, funny." Jerry sounds half there.

"Don't laugh too hard."

"No, it's funny," Jerry insists. "I'm laughing inside."

Dave Mecklenberg, the camp program director, walks into the office where Philip stands, leaning against the desk. A Jew from San Marcos, Texas, Mecklenberg is the only Vet at camp. He'd been a Green Beret and done two tours of Vietnam, the last ending in '72. This is his second summer back. Everybody calls him Tex-Mecks.

The good soldier squeezes past Philip, who flashes him a peace sign and jockeys away, pressing into the corner of the double window. Tex-Mecks reaches into a desk drawer and pulls out a clipboard, then angles out again.

"You okay, Dad?"

Jerry releases a gust of smoke. "Yeah, sure. I'm fine. I'm not dying or anything. Just want to have lunch with my kid."

"Really? He said I could go?"

"Really, really. I'll be there within the hour."

"I have class. Rehearsal."

"I got permission. She said the rest of 'em need a few days to catch up with you."

"Uncle Bernie said that?"

"Lila. Lila said not to worry."

"You talked to Lila, too?" Philip asks, confused.

"Sure, sure. It's all cool."

"Dad?"

"Not to worry, sonny baby. Just want to have lunch with my kid. So save room."

"Should I meet you?"

"I'll pick you up at the gate. Two, two-fifteen."

"Wow."

"We'll go to Injun Joe's for steak."

"Steak. Great."

Static and silence. Jerry finishes his cigarette. Philip pokes at a stack of folders in a tray on the desk.

Finally, he speaks. "I think I want to repaint my room, maybe put the bed on the floor."

"Sure," Jerry says.

"Do you think black lights are too adolescent?"

"However, you want to do it." Jerry's choking.

"Yeah," Philip says, "I really want to make it mine, even if it's only for the year before college."

"Uh-hmm."

"I just don't want it to be cliché. You know, 'teen boy living with his father.'"

"No," his dad says.

"You know, my version of mid-life crisis."

"Sure."

Jerry misses the 'mid-life crisis' crack, and Philip notices it. Did he hurt his father's feelings? "I mean I'm really looking forward to being there full time. And you know it'll be where I come back to when I go away."

"Fine, fine. We'll have to talk to your mom about that."

"She won't care. I doubt she'll even stay in Chicago. If she even comes back."

"We'll see…"

"I mean, Mexico…?"

The whole conversation wrenches, but Jerry won't let the boy go. "How's camp?" he asks.

"Good, good. Great. We're doing *West Side Story*."

"Terrific. How's the girl situation?"

"Fine, you know, good."

"Okay, Flipper. See you in a few."

"Flipper's a dolphin, Dad."

"You were Flipper before he was a dolphin."

"Right."

"See you in a few."

Jerry keeps listening on the line, even after Philip hangs up. He listens for echoes of his son's voice. He listens for the hiss of silence that will follow the echoes. He listens for a miracle.

Chapter 4

Philip hangs up the phone. Before he has a chance to register his confusion about the call, he hears Tex-Mecks on the PA summoning everyone to fourth period classes.

Even after nine years at Friedkin, Philip still gets butterflies at the end of rest period as he joins the jittery convergence of 250 bodies crisscrossing camp. As the end of the summer gets nearer—there are only eight days till the final parents' weekend—everyone is more animated than usual. He sings to himself, "Something's comin', I don't know what it is—but it is... gonna be great." He swerves to avoid some little girls, dressed in swimsuits and carrying towels, padding along behind their counselors like excitable ducks. One of the girls smiles all her teeth at him and flaps her hand in a wild wave.

He catches her enthusiasm and mirrors her flappy greeting. He calls several of the other girls by name, gently tapping them on their heads, "Duck Duck Goose." He passes the 'Stage Door Canteen' and steps out the back door of Anatevka, headed towards DeMille, the dance studio, named for the woman who choreographed *Oklahoma*.

DeMille is attached to Anatevka, juts out from it, a kind of butt-end annex. It looks out on a concrete volleyball court with benches on two sides. Here he meets up with Kathy Klein, a girl he's known since day one, eight years ago. She's smudged with ink, as usual, tending to a little kid, one of Friedkin's broken birds. Kathy's sitting sideways on a bench, brushing and braiding Suzie Shinder's hair. The other nine-year-olds in My Fair Lady have been picking on Suzie lately, joking about her frizzy pigtails, her missing front teeth, her nocturnally loose bladder. Kathy has her smiling and jabbering. Suzie hopes there's an Israel team at the camp Olympics. She has an uncle who lives on a kibbutz!

Philip admires Suzie's hairdo, *"Trés fashionable,"* he says, to her delight. "It goes with your new freckles."

"On your way, Pippi," Kathy says planting a kiss on the top of Suzie's head. Suzie kisses her back and skitters away.

"You've got the touch," Philip marvels.

"Making the world safe for outcasts," Kathy admits, standing. She bends down and scoops her notebook and another book off the bench, *The Diary of Anne Frank.* Thumbed to hell.

"Don't you every get tired of it?" Philip asks, indicating the book with his chin. "I mean, how depressing."

"It's the opposite of depressing," she counters.

"And you wonder why everyone calls you 'Anne Frank'," he says.

"I don't wonder," Kathy says. "I rejoice."

"You're a nutjob."

"And you love nutjobs." They are both looking at the dark-haired girl's face on the book.

"My dad's coming to take me to lunch," he tells her, as though this were a question she had the answer to.

"We just had lunch," Kathy says without judgment.

"He's coming to take me to yet another lunch."

"That's bad," she posits.

"No, no. He says he's not dying or anything."

"He said that?"

"Pretty much those words."

"He found it necessary to pre-empt your fears for his health?"

"I guess."

"That's even worse, Philip."

"You think?"

Kathy goes quiet. She studies Philip's eyes. He glances slightly downwards, inwards. This visible reflection is a rare preserve in the land of Philip. His eyes—baby browns, as she thinks of them—are always so quick and curious, offering help by letting you know he's with you every step. The eager eyes, together with the spray of freckles on his cheeks and the overlap of his front top teeth, give his sweetness a young cast. Why is she always the one to point out to him the half of the glass that isn't full?

Kathy leans towards him, twisting a little from the waist until her shoulder gently bumps his opposite arm. "When you get back from yet another lunch," she says, "I'm here."

They reach De Mille only seconds before the rest of their group. They enter to see their teacher, Markie, a wiry, high-strung man in perfect fitting Danskin pants walking through lifts with an imaginary partner. Today begins work on the 'Somewhere Ballet', the culminating dance in *West Side Story*, a final, imaginary oasis of happiness before the play's tragic end.

Philip feels like dancing as he leaves Kathy and moves through the overcast afternoon. He drums a roll on the wood siding of Anatevka. He passes two swarming volleyball courts and two tennis courts where pixies with giant rackets run every which way while balls fly every other which way. Philip flashes V fingers as he goes. Frags of Peter, Paul and Mary songs explode from a dozen kids hunched over a dozen Kay guitars on the Anatevka porch. Daredevil ten-year-olds crash land round-offs and handsprings on the grass. He shouts out encouragement. He's got an inner soundtrack going. "Mambo!" He makes a little Jerome Robbins leap.

Anne Frank's words come back, "He found it necessary to pre-empt your fears for his health? That's even worse." He wishes he knew what his father is doing in Swallow Heart Lake.

A tall fence barricades the campground from the world outside, though its gate is now open. Of the many singular rituals of this place, the most singular is the one that results each season in a new stretch of cement running along the front of Anatevka. In each patch of cement, the prints of hundreds of small hands and feet—and slightly larger ones and larger still—are embedded. In Friedkin's ever-expanding version of Grauman's Chinese Theatre, everyone's a star and every step is star-studded. A right hand marks the camper's first year, a left one the second. Right foot, left foot, two hands, two feet and so on up the chain of years in increasingly algorithmic combinations. Under each set of prints a name is written—a tombstone in reverse: testimonials to life, present life, continuous, growing, incipient life.

On the final night of summer, this year as every year, before the parents arrive to see their children perform and, over the course of a weekend, spirit them home, the magic of summer will be sealed around these same handprints. With their tear-streaked faces illuminated by flares, the whole Friedkin Camp family will remember their season together and, in a terrifically moving ritual, forever bind their hearts to one another. This year's handprint ceremony is still eight days away, and the summer's cement has yet to be poured, though the ground that will hold it has been measured and marked.

Walking the handprints, you can travel forward or backward in time, from 1955 through 1973, and as you travel, you can track the progress of a living soul as told by the lengthening of fingers, swelling of toes, solidity of impression. Philip gazes out over eight years and imagines himself at seven crouching, pushing his little clover hand into the wet cement for the first time. Young as he is, Philip already has a sense of legacy. He keeps a journal and saves his letters. He thinks of his life as a life to track. His handprints belong to him, but also to the future. Philip Rosen is a boy who contemplates 'posterity'.

1967, 1968, 1969. Philip steps over himself once. When he gets to the gate—two fortress doors of thick, rounded pickets—he takes a couple of steps out and to the left, so he can wait against the fence without being seen from inside camp.

The road is so empty it's hard to believe that it's ever seen a car. Up the street to the right is the entrance to Schwartzkopf's resort. Straight ahead a steep flight of stairs leads down to the lake. Voices drift up, young, squealing voices. Whistles blow now and again, and each time the voices die for a beat. Other direction: fencing, pine trees, more of the woodsy roadside that drops off about two stories to the waterfront where a boathouse sign warns—in Red Cross red—"Never Swim Alone."

No Dad.

Determined to heighten his senses, Philip tries, from time to time, to do without one or another of them. How would camp feel if I were blind? He closes his eyes and listens for engine roar. The wind clatters and shushes up in the trees. You don't get much sound off the water; the lake here is so still. At best, in a wind like this, you hear slapping on the underside of the metal pier. Swallow Heart Lake is hardly more monstrous than a big, friendly dog licking the grassy shore.

Summer washes over him: the sandy heat of asphalt, the vaguely rotten must of lake mud, the fresh water scent. He's amazed by how many smells carry simultaneously. *This is what it must be like to be fully alive*, he thinks, aware, as if for the first time, of the sensual density of a moment.

He opens his eyes and, for an instant, there's crystal clarity to everything he sees. The shivering of the trees, the wavy heat rising off the road, the white broken line becoming a solid line as he stares out. Even the air seems to have edges. A couple days ago, a man walked a tight wire between the World Trade Center towers. Could he walk these electric wires, stretching to the horizon?

A car is moving towards him from the direction of the highway. It's a brown Buick, and the off-white seats are visible as it passes. A man with 1950s hair drives with the windows rolled down, his wrist balanced on the steering wheel, a man who is not Philip's father. The car disappears around the bend towards town, and the natural quiet returns, quiet made of more sounds than he can count.

He starts to hum, "Maria," flipping back and forth between the prayer-like beginning of the song, which he keeps under his breath, and the little falsetto high notes at the end. He noodles his romantic hymn under the shade of the camp's border pines and doesn't notice his father's car sneak up until it's practically parked on his toes.

"You sleeping or praying?" his Dad asks from the convertible.

For an instant, as embarrassment burns off Philip's cheeks like fog, the man leaning over from the driver's side isn't his father; he's just a graying man with a pudgy face, large pores, garlic bulb nose and a suede cap. Philip wakes up to the face. "Hey Dad."

He climbs down into the sports car and hugs his father. He knows that something's terribly wrong, but he doesn't know he knows it. Only later, when he plays back over the scene, does he flag things. He remembers the stale smell of cigarettes and decay as Jerry kissed him awkwardly near his mouth. He remembers his father bending forward to eject some classical tape and shoving The Beatles' *Let It Be* into the 8-track deck, saying, "Bought this for you." He remembers the bloody cuticles on several of his father's usually manicured fingers. How his dad's bloodshot eyes flicked away when Philip met them.

At that moment, though, he reaches behind him for the seat belt and straps himself in. "AWOL," Jerry says stepping on the gas.

"A wall," Philip says.

"All's wall that ends wall," says Jerry.

Chapter 5

Nothing Native American has ever graced Injun Joe's. A cigar store Tecumseh stands in the grassy parking lot, towering next to a wagon planted with pots of pansies. A sign in the back near the kitchen points a finger to the rest rooms: "Potawatomi This Way." Wood-carved plaques on the toilet doors read Chiefs and Squaws. A six-foot photograph of Jim Thorpe, part Potawatomi, part Sauk and Fox, in his football gear, greets customers by the hostess stand. Without the kitsch, Injun Joe's might be any family-run steak house in the rural Midwest.

White tablecloths are laid at a quarter-turn over maroon tablecloths. The chairs and décor have western ranch-style spindles and curves. Stainless steel serving dishes hold celery sticks, ripple-edged carrots and radishes. The water goblets and saltshakers are crystal-cut glass. The whole square dining room has the air of a middle-aged Lutheran couple, grown children living one town over, dressed up for a Rotary Club dance.

The bar, on the other hand, partitioned from the dining area by a paneled half wall made whole by a series of lathe-turned pilasters and shrouded by hanging plastic ferns, has a rec-room feel—a well-stocked bar in someone's basement. There are always men sitting there, day or night, not the same ones, but similarly dressed. The man who sells insurance out of a small two-room, A-frame on the corner of Kiel and Main; the manager of the John Deere; the pharmacist, Mr. Mueller; the town clerk. These are the white-collar men of Swallow Heart Lake, the men with wives at home getting dinner on.

For the young farmers and auto body guys, the shop mechanics at Deere, and the custodial staff at Swallow Heart Lake High and Schnee Elementary-Middle School, there is The Shed by the railroad crossing where Main meets Route 17. The Shed is a beer drinker's bar, a watering hole for blue-collar guys and Ag-workers, with Miller, Old Style and Bud on tap. If you want something fancy, you splurge on a shot of Tequila and dump it into your beer.

The lake boys—the ones who run ski boats and staff the beaches of the four camps and six vacation hotels that dot the lake—hit the resort bars. There they find girls from somewhere else, summer girls looking for watery fun at night. A landlocked surfer culture plays out between lean, cocky boys with monosyllabic vocabularies and German names like Schuler and Ballschmidt, and Midwestern co-eds, bright-smile blondes who freckle up in the sun and glow pink with successive Tequila Sunrises or fizzes made with Sloe Gin.

But Injun Joe's is the place for the middle-class thinking man, the small business owner, the guys with a track record and professional course certificates framed on their office walls. So what if Swallow Heart Lake is no Chicago, Injun Joe's no Gene & Georgetti? So what if the waitresses—Kay,

Virginia, Yvonne—don't walk with the whiff of possibility that city waitresses have? Every man needs a place to go where they know his drink. Where he can depend on a medium rare T-bone coming out medium rare.

Jerry looks down the bar at the cornfield faces, the pale button-down, short sleeve shirts, and he thinks, *Get used to it. There ain't no regular anymore.* He lays a puffy hand on Philip's shoulder, says, "When you gotta go," and heads for the Potawatomi.

The owner steps out from behind the bar and escorts Philip to a four-top in the front corner by the window. Philip stares at his menu. Nothing makes sense, not the words—Chippewa Chipped Beef, Sheboygan Burger—not the emptiness of the midday room, not the gray light from the picture window. It isn't visiting day, he's not on vacation, and most of his friends are in singing classes, mangling harmony on 'America'.

His father pulls out a chair without looking directly at him. "Bet you haven't laid your teeth on a good steak for a while," he says.

"Who needs steak when you got corn dogs?" Philip rejoins.

"Mmm," Jerry says. His menu, too, is a blur.

When the owner returns, standing over them with one hand on the post of Philip's chair back, Jerry orders a Johnny Walker Red on the rocks with a twist and a Horse's Neck for Philip. "Can't call it a Shirley Temple anymore; they'll think you've got a thing for little girls. Or that you're swishy."

"Dad..." Philip intones, an embarrassed, cautionary whine.

Jerry ignores the warning. "So how are all the little Friedkin Shirley Temples?"

"Dad..."

"Flip..." Jerry imitates Philip's cadence.

Mr. Lanhoff, the restaurant's owner, reappears. There's nothing 'Injun' about him. Jerry orders two 24-ounce T-bones, rare, onion loaf for Philip and baked potato for himself. "And I'll have another one of these," he says, lifting the scotch and, almost dutifully, draining it. He turns to his son, whose face is a billboard of confused expectation, and asks how goes his summer.

"I might be going out with Kathy Klein," Philip tells him.

"Might be?" Jerry asks. He's known Kathy since the kids were seven. He's flirted with her blowsy mom on parents' weekends. She is, in fact, the only girl of Philip's acquaintance whose name and face click in at the same time.

"She's a little weird, though. All she does is read and write in her diary."

"That's weird?"

"Yeah. Maybe if it was a different book. But all she does is read the Anne Frank book. It's like she wishes she was Anne Frank. Larry Dorfman started calling her Anne Frankenstein. Now everybody calls her Anne Frank."

Jerry's face goes pale. He's a hard man to catch off guard, but Philip can see he's been caught. His father's shock shocks him. He keeps waiting for a quip, a snappy Rosen comeback from the king of the inappropriate remark. But Jerry just sits there.

"It's like she likes it," Philip says.

It's ghastly quiet in Injun Joe's, and something's really wrong with his dad. Mr. Lanhoff arrives with the Johnny Walker, and Jerry doesn't even let him set it down. He reaches over and takes it from the snow-haired man's freckled hand, spilling some. It bangs against his front teeth.

An older woman in a chef's apron comes up behind Mr. Lanhoff, carrying two small, wooden bowls filled with iceberg lettuce and shaved carrot, topped with orange dressing. She hands them to him, and he sets them before Jerry and Philip. Jerry points to his drink and raises a finger to Mr. Lanhoff, signaling for another. His hand quavers, and the restaurant man looks at him for a long second, looks at the boy, bobs a laconic nod, and turns back to the bar.

"Dad? You all right? Should we talk about something else?"

Jerry tips back his drink. He crunches the ice cubes, shoots more ice into his mouth, crunches that. He's not looking anywhere.

"I buried her," he says, when the ice runs out, speaking in some other man's voice.

"What?" Philip asks, his head moving involuntarily, a rattle shake.

"I buried her. Anne Frank. I mean I don't know I buried her, but I've always thought I did. Since I first heard about her years later."

He still isn't looking in his son's direction. His pupils are contracted, his eyes opaque beads.

Philip knows little about his dad's time in the war, but what he knows—given has own pitiful grasp on chronology and history—makes the claim seem plausible. Jerry had been a medic, entering Europe in the final months of engagement. His principal duty, his principal trauma, had involved following the liberating GI's into the camps, treating the sick, feeding the starved, interring the dead. Philip had heard this on their, otherwise, silent afternoon in Yad Vashem, the holocaust memorial they'd visited two years earlier while in Israel for a friend's daughter's wedding.

The wedding was a dismal, back-to-the-land affair in the Golan Heights. (He suspects that the ecstatic kibbutz-farming bride wouldn't have described it the same way.) The day in Yad Vashem had annoyed Philip. His father went rigid and weird, walking past photos of bug-eyed children and cadaverous prisoners in floppy, striped clothes. No, for all his nascent artistic sensitivity, Philip just couldn't get into it. It's all old past, he'd thought. The world isn't like that anymore.

In the months following the trip, Philip rethought Yad Vashem, troubled by the knowledge that he'd missed a moment. Something in his father had moved forward towards him. He'd backed away, and it had retreated, never to return. Now, with his father shaking an all-but-empty rocks glass into his mouth, desperate for the chips clinging on the bottom, he knows he missed more than a moment.

"Have you ever noticed I don't drink bourbon?" Jerry asks, peering into his glass as though reading tea leaves on the bottom. He doesn't wait for an answer. "I can't," he says.

"The smell was so horrible, worse even than what you saw. I couldn't eat. For days I couldn't eat. Hell, I couldn't even breathe. Nobody could. But we had Kentucky bourbon. Rotgut stuff. Plenty of it, and I drank nonstop. Then I passed out. One day, I just passed out and I woke up in a field hospital I don't know how long later, hours, a day. I don't know. And I never drank bourbon again. Even smelling it in an empty glass makes me gag. You knew that." It's a non-question question.

"No," Philip says. "Yes. No. I knew something about the bourbon. I don't know what I knew. Dad..." he adds.

"We gave people our rations. This was before aid arrived, before the Red Cross. Until some of them died. They were so starved, our food killed them. We couldn't even feed them."

Philip notices the gold watch on his father's thick wrist. Its square face reads three o'clock. Singing class is about to begin.

"It smelled like the end of the world. Guy I knew called it 'the after-death'."

Mr. Lanhoff serves the Rosen men their steaks and sets another drink in front of Jerry. In his mind, he has decided to cut this man off, should he ask for another.

"That's not what I wanted to talk to you about," Jerry says, studying the sour cream and chives on top of his potato.

Ever, Philip thinks. *He never wants to talk to me or anyone about that.*

"I need to tell you something." The words hang. Philip waits. After several uncharacteristically deliberate mouthfuls of a meal he has no stomach for, Jerry reaches into his back pocket and pulls out an envelope, folded once. He unfolds it. Philip's name is on the front, in his father's graceful handwriting. Jerry rubs the ends between thumb and forefinger, as if making a decision. Then he places it on the table and nudges it towards his son. Philip stares at it, as though afraid it might move. He reaches out, retracts his hand.

"What is it?"

"For you," Jerry says. "Information." They are both fixed on the plain business envelope, avoiding each other's eyes.

"Dad?"

"Go ahead," Jerry says, "it's just some numbers."

Philip takes it up, wedges his pinky into the space in the corner of the flap. He slices upwards until the top is torn from end to end. He hesitates before taking the yellow lined paper out of it, a single sheet from a legal pad. It, too, has his father's lettering on it. There's the name of a bank, an address, a long set of numbers. There's another name, one he recognizes, "Mickey Brodkey," with a Chicago phone number. That's all.

When he looks up, his face scrunched in curiosity, his dad is holding out a key he's wrested from a ring of keys. "Don't lose this. It's to a safe deposit box at that bank. The number's there. You went with me last year and signed your name. Your signature's on file, so you can get in."

"But why would I need—?"

"There's nothing much there, a pocket watch, some papers. An insurance policy." Jerry won't look at him. In fact, Jerry's checking out the bar, then the ceiling. He's looking for anything that isn't his son's eyes.

Scared, Philip swallows. His father thrusts something else his way. It's a brown plastic wallet. The boy accepts it, fingers the contents: $2000 in American Express Traveler's Cheques. He's stunned, completely lost. Something's happening, but it's happening in an anxiety dream, symbols full of meaning and meaningless at the same time.

"Consider it allowance," Jerry says.

"But that's like years of allowance, Dad."

"You sign those at the top." Jerry's holding out a pen now. "Right at that top line. Then when you cash them, you sign the bottom. Remember, we used them in England?"

"Sure, Dad, I remember."

"Sign them now. I have to tell you something." Jerry's speaking hurriedly, as though someone might descend on them at any moment and rush him from the room. He extends the pen even further. Philip accepts, uncaps it.

"I can't write with fountain pens. It gets all smeary."

"Oh Jesus fucking Christ," Jerry exclaims, grabbing the pen back from his son and, in the process, staining his palm with a glob of ink. "Jesus," he says again. He's on his feet now, stalking towards the Chief's room where he washes his hands furiously and wipes them harder. He looks at himself in the mirror. He's got dark bags under his eyes. His face is blotchy red. He got up too fast, is reeling from the Scotch. Nauseous and sweating, he throws cold water on his face, splashing and rubbing his eyes with the back of his hands, avoiding his still inky palm. He has to get back to the table. He dries his face.

He borrows a Bic from the bartender and slaps it on the table beside his son. "Here," he says, not wanting it to come out as peevishly as it does. "Maybe this will do you."

"Thanks, Dad. I'm sorry about the pen."

Philip is trying to piece it together—interpret the strange dream of it—the bank numbers, the key, the pack of money. Allowance for what?

"I have to tell you something," Jerry says, sitting. He lights a cigarette, sucks in a chest full of smoke. He flicks the ash and, straining to be casual, begins, "I may be...I will probably be..." He inhales again, empties his lungs of smoke, and forces himself to look his son in the eye. "I'm going to prison." The Story of Bourbon is over. It's time for The Story of Dirty Money.

Chapter 6

Lila Friedkin Sahlins stands on the side porch of Anatevka, her cocker spaniel Miffed sniffing the painted floorboards around her feet. She's spent the day shuttling between acting classes and sewing tables, staging scenes with wooden ten-year-olds and hauling costumes up and down ladders, prodding slouchy adolescents to passion and pinning the hems of their waistcoats and pinafores. She is taking her first free breath. She is schvitzing.

The five o'clock sun slices through the trees surrounding Mary Poppins, the cabin for six-to-eight-year-old girls—the babies—nestled between Ollie's kitchen and the Friedkin family's private house. The splayed light hits the corner of the porch, bathing Lila's upturned face, burnishing the lids of her closed eyes.

On the other side of Anatevka, hidden from her sight, children troop back from the beach. In half an hour, two or three from each cabin will straggle into the dining hall to set long tables for dinner. For the moment, everything is quiet—tennis and volleyball courts, front porch, even the lobby, which at other times resembles the waiting room of a small-town train station at holiday time.

For all its beauty, this part of late afternoon floods Lila with anguish. When she idles, when the ceaseless activity finally ceases, the sadness rises up. She misses her mother.

Most years, this would have been exactly the time for them to sit together, mulling over the events of the day. At such times, Lila often thought of the closing scene of Cyrano, where, with the sun settling beyond the orchard, the heroic, disfigured Cyrano arrives for his weekly appointment in the convent garden, bringing Roxanne, his secret beloved, tales of life from outside her hermetic walls. He recites for her the goings-on in the world beyond, his personal gazette. That's how it was with Lila's mother, Della, except that gestures and facial expressions replaced words. Lila played the gazetteer for sweet, deaf, dumpling Mama.

Della Friedkin was an alternately fierce and playful little doughball of a woman who made sure her two daughters knew how to sing, dance, act, play the piano, recite, sew costumes, paint and debate socialist politics. She'd given birth to both of them at home, a short walk from Chicago's Maxwell Street Market, Lila, just as America was entering the First World War, and Sylvia, after the war's end. Though she'd been born a Rosciapowicz, somewhere in the ever-shifting Ukraine and been plopped down in the US at the difficult age of thirteen, Della was a determined American, a vulture for culture. She took her girls to lectures by the learned, plays in Yiddish at Glickman's Palace Theatre, the ballet, and concerts by great violinists from the old country, which they watched from the cheap seats in the balcony of the Auditorium Theatre.

Della sang a tune or two herself, most famously Dark Eyes, and was often called to the piano of the fellowship club, *landsmanshaften*, or union hall. She sang to raise money for Jewish and leftist causes—The Home for Jewish Friendless and Working Girls, the Wobblies—and was a regular curtain act for readings at Ceshinsky's Jewish Bookstore. By the time the girls had reached eight and five, Della was losing her hearing, and they were joining her for encores. She'd gather them around her knees like skirts and lead them in mournful old-world ballads or peppy showpieces with a couple of kicky dance steps. The girls would shine up at their mama, and she would wink down at them. In time, she pushed Lila and little Sylvie out on their own. Della would beam from the front of the stage, clapping along and mouthing the words, as the tunes she'd taught them grew faint.

Gramma Della, as she was known to the campers, lived more than forty years in near silence. She saw her eldest, Lila, marry a good, hard-working man named Max Sahlins. Her baby, Sylvie, married the more charismatic Bernie Levine. Together the four of them opened and made a success of Friedkin Camp. No one, least of all her children, knew how much or how little Della took in. She had died the previous summer, two nights before visiting day. Because it was so close to the end of the season, the family decided to wait before transporting the body back to Chicago. And so, for a long weekend, the shows went on— *Cinderella, Oklahoma, King and I, Fiorello*—while Gramma lay in a Plymouth funeral home, nine miles away. Nobody told the kids or their parents that death had come to the village. Bernie, Sylvie's husband, camp director and ever-sensible businessman made sure of that. And nobody told the rabbi in Chicago exactly when she had died. Della would have wanted it that way: Jewish law— get the body in the ground—trumped by the principal law of the stage—the show goes on.

Lila has little time for mourning, but she wears it like a winter coat in the dead of August. There has always been something of the past clinging to her, as insignificant as a headscarf and as deep as the suffering engraved on her face, the way historical memory is carried by some, while others, even those closest to them, seem by their very presence, to obliterate that memory. Now the past threatens to swallow her. She's grown old almost overnight, marked by loss. She's stepped into the role of Gramma.

Someone standing close would see the redness spread from her temples down her cheeks and neck, her chest rising and falling with profound, prolonged breaths, would spot the water pooling in her eyes and hanging there, as when a glass is overfull before it overflows. No one could witness this slow, palpable grief and not feel drawn to it, even as the late day sunlight seems to be.

When she hears footsteps crunching her way on the gravel road, she wipes each eye with the back of her wrist. She turns her face towards the sound.

"Yehudi," she says, betraying little emotion. "The boy with the violin."

"Auntie Lila," Jerry Rosen says back. He climbs the three steps between them, and plants a kiss on her cheek, hand under her elbow. He kisses her as you kiss someone much older.

Even in her sadness, she can see how subdued he is, how shaken. She smells whiskey on his breath and skin. She knows him to be a good-time-Charlie and, with a deeper knowing, the sort of intuition she's spent her life attuning, she concludes that he's in distress.

"I was just coming to thank you for letting me take Philip out today. I know it's not an easy call."

"I've known you from when you were a little pisher, Jerry Rosen, and I've known that wonderful boy of yours from an even littler pisher. If you tell me, 'it's important or I wouldn't ask,' I know it's important."

"You're a doll, Lila, I can't thank you—"

"Then don't. Don't thank me. Just follow me. I want to show you something."

She escorts him down the steps and across the road towards her house up the walkway of granite blocks with grass sprouting through it in tufts.

Jerry and Lila share the parental collegiality of people who love the same child, who see each other at regular, distant intervals because of that child. Lila is a stand-in mother for Philip's own mother, Jerry's ex-wife. Early in the summer, Philip told her that his mom is moving to Mexico, a place called San Miguel de Allende. Lila doesn't understand why the woman can't wait a year till her son leaves for college. A man, apparently. Jerry and Lila are parents by association, an association they never could have imagined in the long ago of their initial acquaintance.

Almost a decade older than Jerry, Lila had seen him weekly for years, before the war, on the seventh floor of the Fine Arts Building on Chicago's Michigan Avenue. Lila studied and later taught acting there; Jerry showed up every Wednesday at four for his violin lesson. She called him 'Yehudi' after the majestic Menuhin, or simply 'the boy with the violin'. He teased her back, greeting her as 'Sarah Heartburn' and 'Joan Crawfish'. Twenty-five years later, when Jerry and his then-wife came to camp to fetch seven-year-old Philip, Lila recognized him as the pisher, the boy with the violin.

Set unassumingly behind a couple of tall oaks, the family's private summerhouse, known simply as Friedkin's, possesses a commanding a view of the front gate, Anatevka, the dining hall, and, out its side windows, the costume shop. Lila leads Jerry inside.

They pass through a small foyer. Jerry enters the living room behind her. He is surprised by how homey it feels, how lived in, for a summer cottage on a campground, where the buildings seem to him like so many shacks, set up by tramps with a few planks to bang together. There's a fireplace, never used, he guesses, its mantel topped by a kick-line of photos, candles, Hummel figurines and a few hardbound books. The furniture is overstuffed, *hamish*.

The kitchen is a sixties kitchen, yellow Formica and chrome table, red vinyl chairs and well-stocked counters. Family photos clutter the available surfaces here, too. Production shots of Lila and her sister and camp partner Sylvie. Sylvie always singing; Lila in one costume or another. Lila grabs two mugs from a crammed cabinet, plugs in an electric percolator, and wordlessly plops a tin of noodle kugel down, cutting several large square pieces and arranging these on a cookie sheet. She slides this into the oven and spins the temperature dial.

Lila is bustling, saying something about a family recipe. Jerry is trying to gather his wits. His lunch with Philip went badly. His brain is sluggish, raw from lack of sleep and too much booze too early. He's hung over before there's been an overnight to get hung on. The worst thing about the lunch was that no matter how much he told, he still had to hold back the biggest part of all. He'd told Philip the story he'd come to tell, all that had gone wrong, all he'd done wrong. He'd warned Philip that his sentencing was scheduled for the following week, that he would go to prison.

"Your father's going to be a jailbird; we just don't know for how long," he'd said.

You'd think this was the worst thing a father would have to confess to his son, but it wasn't. The worst is yet to come, unexpectedly, and for the long haul. Jerry's going over the moment they said goodbye, the way he'd wanted to clutch Philip in his arms and just kiss and kiss his son's hair. He hadn't done it that way. He hadn't wanted to frighten the boy. He was conveying, "It'll be all right," while thinking, *Oh my God, I can't believe this is happening.*

And to see the boy's face crumble like that. "Where will I live?" he kept asking. "I'm supposed to move in with you," he'd said. "I was going to paint the room."

All he could come up with in the moment was, "We'll work it out. Your mom and I will work it out." But he's not so sure they will. The ex is planning to move in with some showboater in Mexico and won't budge. They haven't hatched any kind of plan for what to do with Philip. "Don't you get it, I'm going to prison," Jerry had shouted at Philip's mother on the phone.

"Then it's your problem," she'd said, "and it's your problem to solve."

He should have laughed at the part about Kathy Klein being called Anne Frank. Jerry prides himself on being able to blow off anything, but between the nerves and lack of sleep, the constant beating of his brain against his skull and the terror of breaking Philip's heart—no, that wasn't what he was afraid of. He was afraid that the boy would hate him, or worse, that he'd judge him, find him weak, corrupt, pathetic. He would be right, Jerry thinks.

Lila is still talking when she sets a cup of coffee in front of Jerry. He hasn't heard a thing she's said. He's fighting back a spasm of tears, fending off the image of Philip, their awkward, half-hearted two-step of farewell. It's a moment he'll never forget and always regret. He tries to focus, just as Lila sits across from him with two plates of noodle kugel.

"Thanks, Lila, it looks delicious."

"Eat, eat. It's what I give the kids when they're homesick."

He isn't hungry, but he takes a bite. It does. It tastes of home. "How's your mom?" Jerry asks. "I didn't see her before."

Lila stares at him, stricken. Only then does he remember what he knows: that Della died last summer.

"Oh my God, Lila. I'm so sorry. Of course, I knew. I've been in my own world. Of course, I knew." Jerry reaches for the cigarettes in his shirt pocket. "How are you?" He smacks the pack against the side of his hand and grabs the cigarette sticking out the farthest. Lila watches him set the box down, flick open his lighter and suck at the smoke as if for air. "I'm sorry," he says again, on the exhale.

"The days are hard" is all she says.

"Sure. Your dad? Is he still—he's not, right? We'd know. This is such a family business."

Lila stands and crosses over to a shelf of recipe books. She takes a frame down and walks towards Jerry with her arm outstretched. "He didn't see any of this." She hands the photo to him. Jerry stares at it. "He was so handsome. Aaron."

"Dashing," Jerry says.

Lila nods, satisfied. "He died just before the war. Sudden."

"What did he do?"

"What did any of them do? He sold. First, he sold chickens at market, then he sold insurance policies. Finally, he got a job selling men's shirts at Mandel Brothers. Passed away a few months later just as the store was opening for the day. Every time I measure a sleeve—which is everyday—I think of him."

She accepts the photo back, drinks it in for a moment and replaces it on the shelf. Suddenly hungry, Jerry shovels kugel with the same hand that holds his cigarette. Did he eat any of his lunch?

"What about your folks?" Lila asks him, hanging back by the counter.

"My dad's still around, retired to Palm Springs with his wife. Mom died when I was in Germany. Nothing sudden about it. She took forever to die," he says, sounding peeved. "I couldn't get a leave. I'd already had one before I shipped out. Actually, I didn't know till months after. No news is no news."

Lila trains her eyes on Jerry. He looks away. She takes his plate and slides another piece of kugel on it. "He's a good boy, yours," she says, setting the plate in front of him. "He's something real."

"Yes. I don't know how that happened," Jerry says, earnestly.

"You must have done something right," Lila offers.

"I've wondered if it wasn't you and Sylvie did all the right things."

"Oy, no. We just finish 'em up a little."

"You underestimate."

"Maybe you do."

"Lila, listen." Jerry hesitates, draining his coffee cup, instantly sober. "Just keep doing what you're doing. Take good care of him, okay?"

Lila's eyes narrow, as though she's reading a face across the poker table. She can't make out what she sees. "The hard thing about losing Mama," she says, "is realizing every day—every day for the first time—that she isn't coming back."

Jerry glances down, fumbles for his cigarettes, lights up off the one he's finishing and stands.

"Did you want to show me something, Lila? I should get going."

"Just the kugel, Yehudi. You looked like you could use a bite of kugel."

Chapter 7

It's almost dinnertime when Jerry steps out of Friedkin's and heads down the walkway towards the front gate and his car. A stream of children has begun to feed into the mess hall. They pass like extras in a movie street scene. He stops at the foot of the path and distractedly surveys the faces. He realizes that he's looking for Philip. *I can't see him again*, he thinks, and hurries forward.

He is almost to the front of Anatevka, the main building, when a whispered voice calls him, "Mr. Rosen."

It doesn't register, and he keeps going.

"Mr. Rosen." Kathy Klein appears beside him. She brushes his sleeve with her inky fingers. "Hi."

He lifts his head and shakes it a little, no, no. His focus gathers like a camera lens shuttering in. "Oh Kathy…" he says, without conviction.

"Philip told me you were coming," she beams.

"Sure," he replies, unsure. "How are you?"

"How was lunch?" Her question tumbles over his.

"Fine," they both say.

It occurs to him that this is the girl Philip was talking about when their conversation went wrong, when he lost control over lunch. "Anne Frankenstein," he says without meaning to.

"An adolescent joke," she says, disdainfully. "I'm sorry Philip *stooped* to tell you." Kathy often emphasizes words she considers particularly juicy.

"No," Jerry covers. "No, it just came up. I asked how you—"

"Larry Dorfman thinks he's God's gift to satire—and women."

She is saying something, but Jerry isn't following.

He wants to get to his car. He wants to drive away.

"It's sheer hypocrisy," she is saying.

"What is?" he half-asks.

"What isn't!? Exactly! All of it!"

He grabs his Camels and flips one into his mouth. Without thinking, he holds them out to Kathy, who startles, almost imperceptibly, at his audacity or, better, as she phrases it to herself, his 'insouciance'.

"No, thank you," she says, "I quit." Then before he can withdraw the pack, she slides a cigarette out and into the pocket of her shorts. "Oh, what the hey," she says, with a sophisticate's toss of the head.

He lights up. She watches him.

"Where are you going?" she asks. "May I escort you?" She's adopted an easy air. She does this all the time, perambulates with older men, natural as morning.

"Sure. Just to my car." Let her come along, anything, just to get the hell out.

Kathy slips her arm through Jerry's. He wants to break for the gate, but he'd wind up dragging her. She's such a scrawny thing, he realizes, matchstick arms, no breasts to speak of, good bones in her face the way girls who starve themselves have. Is she one of the ones Philip told him about who eat and then stick their fingers down their throats? She could be.

"Philip was so excited you were coming," she is saying. "He told me you were just up for lunch."

"I can't make visiting day," he says, "so, I thought…"

"Oh, that's all. What a relief. We were worried about you, you know. Unexpected visit. Bringer of bad news."

"I didn't mean to worry him. I told him not to worry," Jerry has stopped at the mouth of the front gate and turned towards Kathy.

"Now who's worrying?" Kathy asks, a light, silly boy tease in her voice. "If everything's all right, then it doesn't matter, does it?" She taps his sternum with the flat of her hand and takes it away.

He studies her face, shadows under her eyes, smudges everywhere, as if she daubs her makeup with typewriter ribbon, wide white smile of Chiclet teeth, several of them overlapping. Her hair is shaggy and fine, a lovely honey color, but it's oily, strands sticking together.

Jerry Rosen thinks about his son and wonders how he'll navigate. These strange girls, appealing and repellent, tortuous and tortured. Here's this awkward, angular kid, so pretty, so messy, pretending to be something out of Auschwitz, flirting like frigging Blanche DuBois.

A gang of teenage boys smashes past them, chattering. Someone calls out, "Hey, Anne Frank!" He hears another ask, "Who's that? Is that her dad?" Kathy ignores them. Jerry flashes his eyes over the crowd, fluttering in his chest at the thought that Philip might be there. He's not.

Kathy tugs gently on his arm. "Where are you parked?" she asks, as if the town were full of parking lots. He half-lifts his arm in the direction of his car, standing guard in front of the camp, shiny and pert as a new toy. Ashes from his cigarette blow onto Kathy's V-neck shirt.

"I'm sorry," he says, as she brushes herself off.

"No big deal," she assures him. "Half my clothes have cigarette burns."

They step towards the Triumph. He moves to the driver's side, takes a last drag and flicks the butt into the street.

Kathy has both hands on the passenger door, as though ready to hop in and ride shotgun. "What a great car," she says. "Philip told me about it, said you got it in England on his spring break. He said you tooled around together over there before shipping it home."

"Yeah, it's a fun little ride. We had a good time."

Jerry keeps popping the lock up and down. He's ready to crawl out of his skin.

"Wow. That must have been profound for you connecting with your son that way."

"Profound," Jerry repeats, leaving Kathy uncertain whether she's being mocked.

"What do you do if there's more than two people?"

33

"Someone sits on that little shelf in back. It only works like this when the top's down." He sighs and climbs down into his seat. "I'd better hit the road," he says, adding, "Jack."

"I'm relieved to hear there's nothing to worry about," Kathy says. "I know how close you and Philip are."

Jerry sits curved over, about to turn the key in the ignition. He stops moving. "He's a great kid. I love him a lot," he says.

Kathy's face clouds again.

"Tell him that, okay? Not that he doesn't know."

"Sure, Mr. Rosen. I'll tell him," she says, hovering between rekindled concern and full-out foreboding.

The car revs. Kathy starts to lean over the door. Even with the window rolled down, it is a little too far to reach Jerry. She just means to kiss his cheek, but she teeters like a seesaw and sprawls forward over the transmission. He reaches to help her, grabs her upper arms. As she recovers, they jut their faces forward to peck each other's cheeks. She tips forward again and winds up momentarily plastered against the side of his face. She smells smoke and liquor. She feels the warm corner of his lips against the edge of hers.

She rights herself and slides back to standing. "Take care, Mr. Rosen. Drive carefully, okay?"

"Sure, sure," he says, checking his mirror. "Bye, hon."

Kathy steps back onto the grass along the high fence. Jerry swings the car into a U-turn and scuds up the street, gathering speed. Though she doesn't notice it at the time, the engine sounds louder in her memory whenever she recalls this moment, and the faintly pleasing smell of exhaust becomes more acute.

Her left arm wrapped behind her back, holding onto her right elbow, she watches him go. A few seconds too late to make a difference, she releases her arm and raises it in a goodbye.

A last call for dinner comes over the PA. Kathy pats her pocket for a pen, but all she finds is the cigarette Mr. Rosen gave her. She catches a glint off the car's rear bumper.

The horizon opens up and swallows him.

Chapter 8

Evening rehearsals end early. By eight o'clock, the kids in the red, white and blue divisions are off to bed, although the sky is incompletely dark. The lobby of Anatevka buzzes, bodies milling and jockeying for place, furniture being shoved, dragged and lifted around the room. Tex-Mecks, the program director, enters hefting a large Zenith black-and-white television. His arms are steel strong, military fit, his alignment perfect.

Everybody who can be here is here, everybody who isn't sleeping, courting sleep or watching over the sleep of others. The teenagers—campers and junior counselors—chitter and flirt; their hormones carom around the room like flashing dots in a hundred games of Pong. The counselors, older and wiser at nineteen or twenty, cede the actual seating to their juniors and lean against the lobby walls. The activities staff and theatre staff have come downstairs, gods from Olympus after a few drinks, ready for antic fun in the splendid mortal world. They mingle easily.

Lila, her sister Sylvie and Uncle Bernie, Sylvie's husband and camp director move through the hive, directing traffic. Lila grabs two folding chairs from a stack by the wall. Bernie helps position a couch and puts an avuncular hand against the back of a boy carrying a piano bench.

"Find a place to be," Sylvie calls out, her projection strong, her diction impeccable.

They plop down on pieces of floor, hoist themselves onto the deep window sills of the 'Stage Door Canteen' (which has been closed for this special hour), and drape themselves against furniture. This is one time Sylvie won't hassle them for lap sitting. She stifles her trademark harangue: "This is a camp, not a cathouse. Get off him." So, just about every adolescent girl has found some eager boy for a perch.

Kathy Klein arrives just in time. She's volunteered to read *Little Women* to the girls in the cabin My Fair Lady, part of her crusade to counter the superficiality the girls are exposed to in popular media. The counselors are pleased to have a nighttime ritual for their charges, a ritual that ends with Kathy closing the book and saying, "Remember, my little women, you are strong enough for anything."

"We're not little women," they chant. "We're fair ladies."

"You are both," she insists. "Now sleep."

She finds a spot on the lobby floor and sits Indian-style, spine yogi-straight, her head snug in the crook of the baby grand piano.

Dion Robinson, a junior counselor who nine years earlier was Friedkin's first black camper, positions a rolling cart under the television as Tex-Mecks

35

eases it down. Tex-Mecks thanks Dion and pulls the power knob; he clicks the dial to Cronkite. He and Dion step back. There's a lot of static, gray and white insects swarming the front of the screen. He turns to John Chancellor's news broadcast, which is clearer, and does semaphore with the rabbit-ear antennae. People shout out, "Good! No, there! No, go back the way it was!" Finally, there's an acceptable picture. A man at a desk reading. Two flags. Richard Nixon looks up, talks to the camera, to America.

He says something about his political base in Congress, claims never to have been a quitter, and then: "I shall resign the presidency effective at noon tomorrow."

A cheer goes up in the room. Pounding applause. Whistles, shouts, catcalls, stage-worthy sighs of relief. It is a moment of unanimity and difference, a shouting crowd and single faces in that crowd. Lila's old-world eyes are riveted on the screen. She holds a leash attached to the distracted Miffed, whom she seems to have forgotten, as she stares beyond Nixon's face on the screen into the sad interior of this ambitious world.

Tex-Mecks stands at attention, almost unblinking, his thoughts impenetrable. Nixon continues speaking, claiming to have ended the war in Vietnam, but the tightness of Tex-Mecks' jaw and the fixity of his eyes contradict the claim.

A girl named Jody Gold has her arms around the neck of a lanky boy with stringy hair down to his shoulder blades. She's making baby-baby eyes at him. World events like this are a great aphrodisiac.

Junior counselor Larry Dorfman calls out in a rich baritone and British accent, "Take that, you bloody bahstahrd," shaking an operatic fist in the air.

Fresh from a couple of martinis, Marty Ball, a theatre staffer who doubles as camp raconteur, leans over to Neil Roven, the prodigy pianist with a straw-blond, Beatles haircut, and confides, "I have it on the greatest authority that Nixon paints his toenails."

"Honest to God?" Roven replies.

"Scout's honor," Marty straight-faces. "Fire Engine Red. I know a guy who knows a guy in the White House. Nixon has this girl on staff who comes in three times a week for his pedicure. He found her in China. Brought her back on Air Force One."

"Honest to God?" says Roven, nodding profoundly, his fingers playing habitual runs on his thighs.

Kathy Klein studies Nixon's face, tries to memorize his words as he speaks them. The lobby hoopla fills her with disdain for the lack of seriousness, lack of consciousness on display. Something is happening, shifting in the world. She doesn't know what it is, if it's a shift for good or ill, but she's listening for it, and all the 'nattering nabobs' around her (yes, Agnew did one thing of value, coining that phrase) are missing the moment. She looks for Philip in the crowd and spots him leaning against the frame of the hallway to the program office. He uncrosses his arms to clap without taking his eyes off the president. He bangs his hands together and, in a fair imitation of the scowling, jowly soon-to-be ex-president, calls out, "I am not a crook! I am not a crook!" He seems to sense himself being watched because he is looking around the room, searching for something or someone, his eyes finally alighting on Jody Gold, his old girlfriend, curled up against the long-haired Jack.

So much happens, a maelstrom of clapping, whooping, slipping off to rendezvous, ambling into canteen line. Unanimity and difference. *Fifty people in a room celebrating*, Kathy thinks, *and fifty different realities*. Then Philip is staring right at her. His cheeks are burning, his eyes wet and red.

She gestures to him, a key in a lock. She mimes a woman singing. It's charades, a private game played in the middle of a crowd. Does he register?

Despite orders to meet back in the cabins at 10 or 10:30, despite Sylvie's brook-no-bullshit admonishments not to wander off, despite Tex-Meck's terse nods to the boys, as if to say, 'I'm watching you, so watch yourself,' there's a radical freedom in the air. The president brought down. This is better than levitating the Pentagon. Who has to worry about a camp curfew?

Three girls steal out the back door, giggling. Three boys go after them. Raconteur Marty Ball throws a wisenheimer arm around Lisa Climan's shoulder; she is beautiful, with hair as shiny and thick as the mink collar of a Tsar's cape. She is also fifteen years old to Marty's twenty-eight. Sylvie pounces. She points a finger at Marty, raises her carefully penciled eyebrows and says, "I'll cut it off." He removes his arm. "Run along, darling," she tells Lisa. "I'll buy you a can of mace in the morning."

Philip spots Jody Gold and Jack cutting out the side screen door and feels his heart twang. Kathy won't take her eyes off Philip; he's caught in her high beam lights.

A loud, raucous voice recites:
Bernadine Dohrn come blow your horn.
Your dynamite's lately in waiting.
And the Hoffman boys, where are they now?
Are Abbie and Julius dating?
The voice belongs to the strange Brian Kotlicky who's wearing a Nixon/Lodge button from 1960 and a winter hat with earflaps. Kotlicky wears thick, plastic glasses and has a voice that drips with dorky, superior irony. When he grows up, he'll either be a nuclear physicist or a serial murderer. Kotlicky seems intent on unsettling everyone simply by being.

Philip puts his head down, and knifes through the lobby, stopping down the hall, outside 'The Met', Friedkin's music library. He reaches to the lintel and palms a key. He turns the key in the lock and opens the door, switches on the overhead light. Closes the door behind him.

37

Chapter 9

Nixon's resignation, and the air of festivity surrounding it, loses the spirit of anarchy on the grounds of Friedkin. There are shadows everywhere: among the trees guarding the camp perimeter, in the fields where the red ash-glow of cigarettes mimics the wink from the thousand stars that pierce the black sky with thrilling light. The archery pit, train tracks, deadly butcher's house in the woods, arts & crafts barn (aka Plain & Fancy), waterfront copse, stacks of hay behind the cabin My Fair Lady—in these crevasses and others you can hear breathing, footsteps, soft laughter, feverish whispers. Teenagers galore, dispersed and dispersing, jazzed as bees and juicy as mouths full of fruit-striped gum. Bottles have been opened. Shirts have been unbuttoned. Lips are being kissed, souls bared and retainers stowed in plastic snap cases.

It's like something out of Shakespeare's Arcadian plays, where the young flit and dart, plot and become the objects of plotting, fall in and out of love and wait desperately, rocking on their heels, for some magic to touch their achy hearts. And all because Nixon is gone.

Tex-Mecks would have to be a wizard to wrangle them all. History has trumped protocol, and even the counselors have gone errant. They celebrate over beers in town or mill in clumps around Tobacco Road and Green Fields in the center of the campgrounds, talking excitedly. They were young teenagers when Nixon was first elected, and they recount rallies they attended and eulogize friends of friends who were arrested marching on the Pentagon or at the Dow Chemical protest at Madison. They pepper their conversation with phrases from Jefferson Airplane songs. In other words, they revel in the president's downfall because they helped make it happen, if not by direct action, then, at least, by their choice of clothes and tastes in music. No, tonight belongs to any dreamer willing to grab it.

* * *

Philip sits at the plank desk by the window of The Met room, piled with Xeroxed piano scores for *Most Happy Fella* and *Cinderella*. He nestles his head in his arms like someone trying to sleep.

There's tapping on the window screen. The tapping keeps on till Philip lifts his head. Kathy is standing on the porch, bouncing the edge of *The Diary of a Young Girl* against the screen, but she can't tell if Philip sees her, his eyes are blurred and uncomprehending.

She doubles back through the lobby of Anatevka and scratches on the music room door, a cat wanting in. Philip opens up.

Kathy enters mid-thought. "They don't even understand what they're seeing," Over her head, labelled shelves of master scores and scripts in brown faux-leather binders run the length of the room. "They're insensible, completely uncomprehending, completely unexamined. Cows chewing cud. Geez, Louise, get me out of Wisconsin!

"I mean the president of the United States—a crook, an idiot, a *Machiavellian plotter*. YES! But the elected president nonetheless—resigns right in front of them, and all they can think about is which itch they're gonna get scratched first and where! 'Man, politics are great for sex, don'tcha think, Jack?'

"'God, Dorfman, photos of the Oval Office make me so hot!' And Kotlicky—what the hell was that? Jesus, Philip, I think the kid's been talking to Charles Manson."

"I feel sorry for him. He keeps running away from camp. His parents keep bringing him back. All he wants is to go home," Philip says. "They should let him."

"You're way too nice. He's a menace—a one-man lunatic fringe! They should lock him up in the infirmary AND call out the National Guard. Doesn't it make you CRAZY?"

She bangs her head, Charlie Brown style, against a filing cabinet.

Philip is sitting on the plank desk, his feet dangling, his hands cupping the edge. "I kept thinking, this will change my life. Tonight. My life will never be the same. And I don't even know why," he says quietly.

"Exactly!" Kathy exclaims, hitting the 't' with precision.

They're silent for a few seconds. "Exactly," she says again. "We have to do something. Change our lives. Make some deep impact on this fucked-up world."

Philip nods.

"I mean you tell me who out there is going to do anything. Are there any artists in that lobby? Any thinkers? Anybody who thinks at all? My God, the president of the United States just resigned!"

Philip runs his eyes along the shelves overhead: *Paint Your Wagon, Pajama Game, Showboat, The Fantasticks*. Scores and scores of scores. He knows the lyrics to so many of them. Useless knowledge.

Kathy studies him. She wants to ask about his father. She reaches into her pocket and finds the cigarette Jerry gave her. It's bent but not broken. She straightens it, taps the unfiltered end on the top of a filing cabinet and puts the filtered end in her mouth. She leans over Philip, gripping his shoulder loosely, and reaches behind a stack of *Bye Bye Birdie* scripts. She pulls out a white ceramic mug with Pisces the fish painted on it. She pokes inside the mug and removes a battered red pack of Pall Malls and a small box of safety matches. She lights one of the matches, holds it to the cigarette from Jerry and replaces the matches and Pall Malls on the shelf, squinting against the smoke from the cigarette between her teeth.

"I thought you stopped," Philip says.

"I did. Your dad gave me this."

"Oh great."

"Yeah," Kathy says, "*corrupter of youth*."

Philip gnaws the cuticle of his index finger. Kathy inhales and aims a stream of smoke towards the overhead light. She holds the cigarette between her middle and ring fingers.

"Wait," he says. "When did he give you that? You said you got the cigarette from my dad."

"You're slow."

"I didn't hear you at first," Philip explains. "I heard it now."

Kathy flicks ashes into the Pisces mug. "I saw him leaving Friedkin's. He was lighting up a cigarette. He offered me one, so I crammed it in my pocket. Seemed impolite to refuse."

Philip nods. Kathy holds her breath, still not meeting his eyes. "We talked. He said to tell you he loves you." Philip deflates.

"He's going to jail. He said he's going to jail, maybe even Monday."

"Wait," Kathy says, trying to refocus, "who are we talking about, your dad or Nixon?"

"No, Nixon's not going to jail next week. My father. He's being sentenced Monday. He's been on trial; they found him guilty. They were bugging his phone and taping him. I didn't know anything about it. They were probably taping me, too. Two years."

"Wait, Philip. What are you talking about? Your dad? What did he do? What happened?"

"I don't know exactly. I couldn't completely follow. He has this client. The guy was gambling, and my dad sent him money. He didn't want to do it, he said. He knew it was wrong. Dad sent money to the guy in Las Vegas."

"What's wrong with that," Kathy asks. "Can't you lend somebody money, if he loses it?"

"I don't think that's it. I mean, yes, I think it was all right to send the money."

"So what's he going to jail for?"

"Something about the guy billing it back through the business. Like it was a business thing." Philip is trying to explain. "Like my dad billed him, and he paid it back out of his own business."

"Your dad was laundering money for a client with a gambling problem?"

"I think that's what he said. My mind was going a million miles. I couldn't even think to ask him anything. He said he didn't want to, but it was like a godfather thing. He needed this guy. He was my dad's biggest client. He's like the car stereo king of Chicago. My dad does all his advertising. He's known him for a hundred years. We all know him; he's a great guy. Like a father, my dad said. Like my father's father. Don Car-leone. He didn't think he could say no."

"No."

"But he didn't make any money. My dad. So he thinks they were just trying to get to this guy through him. He'd done it with other people, too. He's the big fish, my dad said. Dad's the—I don't know what—little fish. Bait. But now he's caught."

"How, if he didn't make any money?"

"This is the stupid part. This is the part I heard really clearly: he tried to bribe the IRS guy."

"No, what? Why'd he do that?"

40

"He said he was entrapped. Said the guy told him how he doesn't make any money, how his wife has to stay home with the kids, how she needs a new car they can't afford. Hell, my dad knows every car dealer in Chicago. But the guy says, no, he'd have to account for the car. So he offers the guy money. Says he was watching himself walk into this trap and he couldn't stop himself. Slow motion."

"Oh, Philip."

"They got it all on tape. Giving the guy money."

"What'd he have—a suitcase full of cash? Small bills? One of those bags with a big dollar sign on the front like in the old movies?"

"I don't know. I didn't ask. I didn't ask anything. I don't know."

"My God, Philip. I'm so sorry. I don't know what to say."

"Me neither."

"That's a first. Us with nothing to say."

"Yeah," Philip agrees.

Kathy snuffs the cigarette in the mug.

Philip had followed his father's story with a strange far-off feeling. Nothing sunk in. Jerry's explanation hung around his head like thick air. "It's okay, Dad," he'd said. "It's okay." He held his father's hand across the table.

His dad wept shaky, remorseful tears, snot running from his fleshy nose. The restaurant man came over to see if everything was all right, and Jerry waved him away, his hand in the air, pushing the air.

Jerry paid the bill in cash, escaped to the men's room—the Potawatomi— and stayed there a long time. He met Philip in the parking lot and tossed him the keys to the Triumph. "Here," he said. "Take a turn. Drive me somewhere. Let's see how you handle it." They drove to Kiel and back without saying much of anything.

"Judge is going to use us as an example," Jerry said. "It's Nixon time. They want to prove white collar crime is crime. I wanted you to be ready. I wanted to tell you myself. I should have told you a long time ago."

Philip concentrated on the clutch, on shifting without jump.

"Oh, Philip," Kathy says. "I'm so sorry. Your dad's such a great guy."

"Yeah."

Kathy stows the Pisces mug behind *Bye Bye Birdie*, and the two of them shuffle towards the door.

"Oh my God," she says, stopping. "What are you going to do? You're supposed to move in with him? Is your mom still leaving town? You can't go to Mexico. Where are you going to live?"

"He said they'd work it out," Philip says. "I don't know. I asked him, but I couldn't keep on it. I've never seen my dad like that. He said they'd work it out."

"Sure," Kathy agrees, despite a queasy certainty that no one's going to work anything out. "They've got to."

"I'm not spending another year with my mom. That's all there is to it," he says.

"They'll work something out," she offers.

Philip reaches out—to take her hand, she thinks. Instead, he takes the *Diary*. He studies the girl's picture on the cover, willing it to take dimension. He flips the book over and, as he reads the back cover, Kathy reads him.

"We have the same birthday," he says. "Me and her."

"I know," Kathy says quietly, taking the book he hands back to her.

Philip twists the top lock and opens the door for Kathy, checking behind to see if they've forgotten anything. He says, "President Gerald Ford. Makes you feel safe, no?" And flicks the light off.

Chapter 10

Philip walks Kathy back to her cabin, Brigadoon. He doesn't notice the revels in the shadows around them. They hug good night. She wants to hold onto him, to enfold and comfort him, but as is always the case with Philip, his hug says, 'I will take care of you.' "Later, Rosen" is all she says. And she's up the stairs and gone.

It's Kathy's contention that Philip couldn't find alone in a mirror. He's a people magnet, a people compass, not a social butterfly exactly but a social homing pigeon. He homes in on the largest mass of body heat, the crowd, the group, the town center. And people are drawn to him. Still, she thinks he's lonely, and maybe never more so than tonight after his father's visit. She wishes she could stay with him, that they could keep talking. *He needs kindness now*, she thinks. But he makes it very clear—he's dropping her off.

Philip may not be able to find alone, but he longs for it. Especially tonight. He's got so much to think through. The problem is there's no place to go. Or rather, there are many places to go, but no places he wants to be.

He walks a road he's walked a thousand times over the past nine years. Tonight, though, the ground feels shaky. If he were to put his ear to the ground, he might hear sounds under the earth, captured by the earth. In Swallow Heart Lake, he might hear drumming, the stamping of moccasins and the pounding of hooves. He might hear the scuffing of the boots of German settlers, the plowing of fields. He might hear children running, despite shouts for them to stop, and the offbeat beat of their dancing to Gershwin and Berlin, as adult voices call out the count. He imagines water rushing under the crust of the world.

When, in a theatre game, Philip circled the room and the kids in his acting class described his natural walk, they said he was a lion. Tonight, he is a something halting and timid, a boy treading on breaking ice. Water is rising around him, flooding the cracking ground.

In three days, his father will be sentenced, sent to prison for—God knows how long—a year? Five years? Jerry Rosen alluded to the possibility that they would not see each other for a long time, but Philip only half-heard.

Now the questions tumble through his brain: *Will I be allowed to visit? Will I be able to call? How much time will they let me spend with him? How often? Will I be body-searched? Will we talk through bulletproof glass? On phones from opposite sides of a window? Will he wear prison-camp stripes? Orange coveralls? Will I be able to hug him? Will they beat him? Will he be scared? Does my father get scared?*

Philip's violent imagery comes from movies and TV— blaring ceiling-hung televisions and long lines of angry inmates yelling to use the pay phone. Another question: Where will I live? His heart goes nervous, a low electric current humming through. He misses his father with a homesickness he hasn't known since that first summer at camp when he was seven, when he worried he'd never see his family again.

Marty Ball, the staff wiseass, once teased him about it, claiming that Philip had cried for two solid weeks, that Marty'd had to push him onto the stage. The minute the boy got in front of the audience, though, the crying stopped forever. He'd performed—in what Marty calls the 'No-talent Show'—a pantomime, a clown juggling (and dropping) way too many objects. Marty joked that it had taken three adults forty-five minutes to get Philip to finish the act, and that they, finally, had to drag him, waving and smiling, into the wings.

Philip remembers both feelings: the homesickness and the love that rose in waves from the audience over the apron of the stage, like steam off street tar in summer. The homesick feeling is back, and it aches everywhere.

That's the thing about homesickness. You miss other people, but mostly you miss yourself. The ship pulls out, your loved ones are standing on the dock, but you're the one at the rail of the ship, moving away, growing smaller. It doesn't matter whether a guy books the passage, pockets the ticket and walks up the ramp happy as a million bucks. A gulf widens, swallowing the life he knows and the people he loves. Swallowing him. A gulf, a gulp.

Philip knows he will grow smaller to his father. He knows that, separated, he will be forgotten because no one can hold another living being in his mind's eye for long. His dad may squint and strain to see him, but, eventually, he'll disappear.

Kathy is right: Philip has to be where people are. And he has to be alone, has to think. His cabin offers both solitude and the bodies of others. The bodies are all at rest, thankfully, including Philip's head counselor, the genial Terry Heisman, who, as usual, crashed early. Terry sleeps in a single bed at the front of the cabin without privacy, kids' bunks crowded around him. He's snoring steadily in stereo with Dr Dave, Philip's friend and fellow junior counselor, whose bed shares a narrow, partitioned backroom with Philip's. Their snores have the effect of cheap, raspy speakers, hung on opposite sides of the cabin. They're leading a chorus of eleven-year-olds growling, honking, whistling, slurping and horror-movie aspirating. Paint Your Wagon is a zoo at night.

Philip sits cross-legged on his mattress, separated from the campers by a thin wall that goes up eight feet but doesn't meet the beams of the peaked ceiling. He clicks on a small directional lamp clipped to the head of his metal bed frame.

Philip keeps a journal, a simple spiral book the size of a hardback novel. The book was a present from Kathy Klein the year before on his fifteenth birthday. Jody Gold, his on-again, off-again girlfriend, had thrown a pre-camp gathering in Evanston. Kathy, going by the nom de plume 'K' at the time, showed up with the little notebook in a flat green paper bag from the stationary store. A single piece of scotch tape held the bag shut, proletarian giftwrap. In it she'd written, "Even 'actors' need journals. Your loving pal, K."

It was a joke between them. Philip wanting to be an actor and Kathy running actors down. "It's a puny thing to want to be," she'd say. "A pale imitation of the real thing. Even a great actor, which, of course, you'd be." Kathy believed that he was more than an actor. She believed that deep down he was an artist, an artist who had yet to find his 'métier'.

"I don't know what that is," he'd say, "an artist. Or I do know. It's pretentious."

"You love it," she'd counter. And she was right. He loved being thought of as an artist, just as she loved thinking of herself as a writer. Even though he had to look up 'métier', he knew she was right. He didn't know his own.

Tonight, he doesn't know anything. His thoughts jump around, nervous and partial. He holds a pen in his hand, not knowing where to begin. "My father will be sentenced to prison next week" or "Nixon resigned tonight". He could write about the night outside his window with its weedy aroma and bright stars. He could write about the feeling that after tonight, his life will never be the same, the feeling he has of being called to something greater than himself. He can't get his thoughts in a row. As he did last summer, when he played the Scarecrow in Wizard of Oz, stuffing his clothes with straw for each rehearsal, he dances stiffly around everything that is painful inside.

"Positive boy," Kathy sometimes calls him, "the superhero with a smile." It's his one failing, she's let him know, his inability to think ill of the world. "If you refuse to look at the dark side, you'll never see it coming. You'll be blindsided by life."

"If you stare at everything that's wrong, everything that's ugly, you'll think that's all there is." It's their favorite argument.

Maybe she's right. He was blindsided today. He never saw it coming, never saw his dad as a man with troubles, as a man with wrongs. But there he was, swilling Johnny Walker and crying. There Jerry Rosen was: confessing.

Philip's stuck on the bourbon, even more than the prison part. His father. In hell. Burying young girls and sucking down bourbon. What does bourbon taste like? He doesn't know. "If I were really an actor," Philip thinks, "I could imagine it." He can't. He's never known anything like what his father described, like the stench his father called the 'after-death'. The sight of bodies in stacks, the roar of war, the sickness and disease. Almost thirty years later, a whiff of that particular whiskey brings it all back and makes his father gag.

In plays, when you can't conjure a feeling, you substitute something in your own life for the circumstances in the drama. There's nothing in his life substitutable. He's seen war on the news. He's seen images of black children set upon by firehoses, angry white mobs and police dogs—horrible, horrible images—but he's never known anything like what his father saw. He's never been at war, never been attacked or spit on. He was in the hospital at eight for appendicitis. There were a couple other kids in the hospital room, but nothing major. They'd played Mille Bornes on each other's beds. In seventh grade, some kid stole his bike.

In 1968, after Martin Luther King was killed, riots broke out in Chicago. Philip, eleven at the time, had nightmares of Molotov cocktails being thrown through the large picture window of his boxy little Skokie house. The window was a membrane...the only thing between him and the violence of the world. That night—for the first time—it occurred to him that the membrane was breakable. Tonight the barrier broke. The violence of the world burst in. It is taking his father.

There's a picture Philip carries loose in his journal, an image so hot for him now, so infused with irony and strange pertinence, he can hardly touch it. It's a postcard of Martin Luther King Jr. in the Birmingham Jail. Taken from the side, a little behind, King's chin rests on steepled fingers. He gazes out the bars of his cell, light shining on his face, shadow cloaking his back and shoulders. Why does Philip even own this postcard? Why does he keep it with him, tucked alongside his private thoughts?

When they'd read the *Letter from Birmingham Jail* in sophomore Social Studies, Philip had thought it the most astonishing thing he'd ever read. Now the memory of it deflates everything he's struggling with. Deflates his father. There is no majesty in that man. There is no purpose in him. He will go to prison and live inside without vision or meaning. No light shining on his face.

"My poor dad," he whispers. And he pictures himself swilling down a bottle of bourbon to shut out the horrible things he'd seen, as though he were his 'poor dad'. He can't get there. And yet he knows there's a connection, a line from that bourbon to the bribe that's sending him to jail. The connection is fuzzy. He's fuzzy.

Philip hides the journal in his underwear drawer. There's a letter sitting there from his mom. It's two pages of the usual nothing. His mother, who seems to him a seething waterfall of tears, is in a happy-happy phase. Mexico this, power of positive thinking that. She calls her boyfriend Eduardo even though he's a New Jersey Jew, whose real name is Eddie. "Jesus," Philip says out loud, before internally translating it to the Spanish sounding 'hey-zeus'. His forced laugh is uncharacteristically harsh.

In fact, much of what Philip feels about his mother is uncharacteristically harsh, a negativity he has earned. He's lived alone with her day after day, except for alternate weekends, for four years since his parents divorced. He's suffered her tirades against Jerry and her torrential crying jags. He's held her hand, wiped the snot running down to her chin. He's impressed her friends with his cooking, cleaned up after drunk boyfriends and walked on eggshells. Or maybe walked through a minefield, the minefield of Mom.

He glances down at her letter. "My first real chance at happiness..." he reads, and he knows that if she were beside him, he'd say:

"Of course, Mom. You've got to go to Mexico. You deserve to be happy."

"You're my closest friend," she'd say, "the only one who's ever understood me." But here, in this partitioned crevice of a bedroom, wedged between the creepy woods out back and the menagerie sounds coming from the kids on the other side of a wall, he wants to shout at her:

"GO! Go to Mexico! Don't come back!" Living another year with her, he believes, will make him crazy. If she's forced to give up Mexico, it'll be worse than 8th grade, after the divorce, when every night for almost a year, she cried herself to sleep in his bed, while he edged as far away as he could.

No, if Jerry goes to jail, he'll have to find another way. He'll live alone or stay with a friend, anything but back. He has to figure something out, and he has to do it before he talks to her.

He drags his pillow into the main room where Terry and the kids honk and purr. *This is our barracks*, he thinks. He tries to reimagine the two-tiered beds as the three- or four-level wooden bunks he's seen in pictures from the German camps. The room is floor-to-ceiling with starving, staring Jews wrenched from their homelands under threat of death. There is disease everywhere.

He can smell sleep breath in the air. He can smell mildew and urine, dirty clothes and half-wiped butts, sweat, old wood. Was this some whiff of what his dad's friend called the 'after-death'? How do you sleep in a stench like that? Where do go for fresh air?

He drops his pillow to the floor in the middle of the room, and he stretches out on the hard wood, inhaling, imagining. Surrounded by the thick, easy slumber of others, he seeks comfort in the unnatural sounds of the everyday world.

Chapter 11

Dion Robinson, a sixteen-year-old junior counselor for the little boys in Pippin, is alone. He stands on the hatch to the cellar of De Mille, weighing his options. This involves checking out the ground at his feet on either side of him and thinking about where to go. It makes no sense that he has found his way to the backside of De Mille. He hates dance. But nothing makes sense at the moment. The president of the United States has just resigned, and he can't figure it out. What will happen next?

Dion's been Friedkin's poster child for integration since the mid-sixties, when photos of him riding horses side by side with a white boy were splashed across brochures, ads, newsletters, and the Super 8 home movies Uncle Bernie showed to prospective families at homes across the suburbs of Chicago, Cleveland, Milwaukee and Grand Rapids. Dion, upright and a little bit brooding, focused straight ahead, like a guy riding somewhere important, determined to get there before sundown.

Earlier tonight, Dion studied the grainy black-and-white image of Nixon on TV, the way you study elders and enemies. He ponders what he saw there and concludes that Nixon's problem was what it had always been: an inner and outer ugliness. *The uglies,* Dion remarks to himself, with a slight smile, *will get you every time.* Then he gets serious, though without clarity, as if he's trying to work out strategy for a world that hasn't been born yet.

He makes his way along the pasture beyond Green Fields where the presence of a half-dozen scooped holes in the grass make up what's called The Golf Course. He sees bodies huddled everywhere. Matches flare. A couple of girls peek out over their boyfriends' shoulders and say, "Hey, Dion."

He says "Hey" back.

Finally, he arrives at the whitewashed fence circumscribing the horse rink. It's quiet and the sky, sparkling with the kind of stars he never sees at home on the south side of Chicago, comes almost within reach.

As he makes his way around the circle, he notices something agitated happening farther out. He picks out a retching sound and steers over to it. Jack is there, pacing and pumping his arms as though rehearsing an angry soliloquy. Near his feet is Jody Gold, quaking. Things smell like vomit. *Something is really wrong,* he thinks.

"Jack," Dion says, uncertain, "what's going on?"

"Shit, man," Jack says. "I don't know. I don't know. She's having a seizure or something, spazzing out. I don't know."

"Is she all right?" Dion asks. "Is she gonna be all right?"

"Fuck," Jack replies. "Fuck, fuck, fuck."

Dion looks for an answer from the handsome boy with long hippie hair. Jack always knows what to do. But Jack keeps moving, swearing, huffing and puffing.

Dion is pulling Jody up by the wrists, peeling her off the ground. His head down, his shoulder in the shivering girl's stomach. The Fireman's Carry. They learned it for *Carousel*. It's a surprisingly easy lift. Dion is compact, not very tall, so he doesn't have to get Jody up too far. For a kid who hates dance, he makes the lift with notable grace. He begins to run, loping at first, then breaking into a dash, carrying Jody out of the field, across the road and up the side porch of Anatevka in the direction of the infirmary, breathing deeply as he goes.

Chapter 12

Jerry Rosen is a planner. He plans his days. He plans what he's going to say before he says it—even days before. He plans how other people are going to react. As a kid, he planned his walk and his hand gestures; he planned how he would smoke. He plans meetings ahead of time, plans how he will play scenes, what emotion he'll draw on. For some time now, he has been planning to disappear.

It's not an easy thing, disappearing from a life you've lived for forty-nine years. Jerry couldn't arrange it in a minute. He needed to sign up for charge cards. He needed to buy things, open a bank account with a made-up name, get that name on a lease. He needed to deposit money in that bank account, money that couldn't be traceable back to Jerry Rosen or to anyone who knew him. He needed to create a paper trail and, simultaneously, cover his scent.

Travel and establish himself in places he's never previously been. Get a fresh driver's license in a new town. Make up history that's true enough to remember but fictitious enough to keep from being found out. Plan a way to survive for the rest of his life that doesn't rely on making point at craps in Vegas. Jobs: freelance ad man for the Missoula rodeo, selling space for the Shithole Daily Bugle or airtime for Schmuck radio, Des Moines. Jobs for a guy without a Social Security Card.

His son will try to find him. His friends and business associates will play parlor games over steaks and ribs, trying to figure out where he's gone. Somebody will play detective. The detectives his ex-wife will hire won't be playing. She wants her alimony to the last drop. Nor will the IRS be playing. The Feds will hunt him—he's been found guilty. He has it planned; they won't find him.

He had to want it—disappearance, thin air. He had to plan to never go back. He had to give up the idea of calling old girlfriends—to live a life he never got to live. He had to plan on things going wrong. To plan to keep moving. To pack his stuff again and again in the same fraying suitcases. He had to plan on scrapping plans and planning new ones.

Much as he tried, he couldn't plan for the emptiness. His old life would be over, everything in it. He'll look in the mirror—a smudgy mirror in a shabby motel off some rat's ass highway. The person staring back at him will have a different name, no family, no job, no past or present.

What was he thinking? *I'm a balding man with a stomach bulging over my belt? I wear a toupee that never looks like anything but a toupee? My scrawny legs? I look like a ham walking on chicken bones? I crave Johnny Walker Black and Beefeater Martinis. Now I'll have to buy bar brands?* Was he anticipating feeling haunted and hounded, knowing that he will be the one doing the haunting and hounding?

Was he thinking, can I do it, before he set a course he couldn't unset? Had he always harbored a wish to leave the big city for a small town in Washington State or North Dakota or—would he have the chutzpah—the city on Lake Superior where he was born and lived till the age of four? Jerry Rosen, born and died in Duluth. Duluth. Sounds like drowning.

He wound up in a parking lot in Green Bay, Wisconsin, a place he'd never been before, paid cash for a beater car he'd drive a few hundred miles then trade for another.

What was going through his mind when he stuck the keys in the ignition, stepped on the gas and backed out of the parking space? Did he pull over every time he crossed a state line—Wisconsin, Iowa, Minnesota, Kansas? Did he stop on the shoulder of the road to cry or retch? Did he think how Philip would react when he found out? He was always sensitive, Jerry thought. How does a kid like that live without a father? Or did he steel himself and shut off these thoughts at the source the way you turn off water deep in the basement?

An English sports car and a rental apartment, furnished with middle of the line Scandinavian teaks and low-slung leather chairs, were what Jerry Rosen left behind. And questions. They were all Philip, or anybody, would have to hold on to, to track the lost man, touch absence—to understand the laws of disappearance.

Chapter 13

Before class begins each morning, Lila examines Showboat, a little garage with a 6'-by-10' makeshift stage at one end. She fusses with the placement of the chairs, forces open the windows on two sides and fluffs a little pile of folded beach towels for her dog Miffed to rest on while he watches the children perform. She sits for a moment, taking deep breaths, as she anticipates the day. The walk from Friedkin's is short, a hundred yards at most, and she is usually alone, which gives her the chance to think through her classes. This late in the summer, creative dramatics and rehearsal are essentially the same thing, and she has prepared a schedule of scenes to work and run.

Philip walks Tobacco Road to meet her. He likes to arrive at Showboat before the kids do. He has assisted Lila since 1971 when he was thirteen and volunteered to sit in on her classes with the little ones and to assistant direct as many plays as he could. Lila took him under her wing, letting him observe, direct scenes, and, on occasion, lead a classroom exercise. She talks to him without condescension, about belief and imagination; she cares about the way things mean what they mean. If he could put it into words, he would call her his first 'artist-teacher'.

With Sylvie it's different. With her presentation is all. Watch her class in 1965 or '70 or '74 and, if they're working on *South Pacific*, for instance, she'll take the kids through the same moves, smack the same syncopation on the piano lid, bark out the same instructions on harmony and diction. Sylvie resembles nothing so much as a Kabuki master, for whom teaching means demonstrating traditional forms: the hand gestures for "Happy Talk" or "Honey Bun"; the dynamics of "Carefully Taught"; the obbligato line of "Bali Hai." You teach the form and the pupil fills it. Or not.

Lila teaches the pupil. He enjoys the pre-class time with her. He helps arrange chairs. He sweeps the floor and platform stage and questions her about character motivation, sense memory, inner action—all ideas he's brought to camp from his acting class in Niles North, the Skokie high school at which he's about to begin junior (and, for him, final) year. Today, though, the creatures nibbling at the edges of his consciousness warn him to stay alert. So much happened yesterday—a single day. It should be an ordinary Friday, but it, too, might hold anything: A call or message will come; bad news will arrive.

"Can I ask you a question?" Philip asks Lila, tipping the broom away from the wall.

"You just did." It's a running line with them, and usually Philip follows with, "Can I ask you another?" This morning, though, he drops his cue and goes right to it. "How do you imagine something you can't imagine?"

"Say more," Lila urges, giving him her attention.

"I don't know what I mean exactly," Philip hesitates.

"I think you do. I think you know exactly what you mean."

She waits for his response. Her waiting is, for him, like the sound of a loud clock ticking.

He plunges in: "You're acting. You're supposed to play a murderer or, like, a soldier. But I've never killed anyone. I've never been in a war. I've never even known anyone who died."

Lila, who conducts emotion the way a raw wire conducts electricity, twitches. Philip can't miss it. "I mean, I know people who've died. I knew Gramma Della. I'm sorry. But it's not like I was with her, you know, when she died."

"Point taken," Lila says with compassion. After a pause. "So you're asking: some things are too big, too foreign to your experience..."

"To imagine," he finishes.

"So how...?"

"How do you make that leap? I'm a killer, I'm starving to death, I'm sitting with my dying...I'm sorry..."

"No," Lila assures him, "nothing can be off-limits. Not in the world of feeling. Not if you really want to act. You must feel everything."

"I've heard you say that. But what if you can't? What if you can't feel any of it?"

She reflects and as she does, she straightens chairs. "You are asking me a big question. A big question—maybe two questions—about feeling and about imagining."

"I guess," Philip sweeps, trying to keep the broom soundless. He doesn't want to miss a flicker of sound from her.

"There are a couple of schools of thought about this. At least."

"Okay."

"There's a substitution school and an imagination school."

"Okay." He leans on the broom for a second, standing the way dancers do, when dancers lean on brooms, in *Oklahoma*, say.

"We've talked about substitution."

"My dog died."

"Well, that's one way to think about it."

"But that doesn't work. I don't have a dog. He didn't die. I don't know anything about anything. I live in Skokie."

"Skokie is full of stories."

"All boring."

"Skokie is full of survivors. Stories are all around you."

Philip hesitates at the word 'survivors'. "I haven't survived anything."

"We all have. By the time you're sixteen, you've done all the suffering, all the feeling you need to do. It's all in you. What fills you with joy? What makes you despair? It's all there." She points to his chest, the bull's eye that is his heart. They struggle, these children. No matter how beautiful the costumes, how simple the songs, she has no illusions about that.

"The stories are everybody else's. I flunked out of substitution school. What do you mean by imagination? I feel like I haven't got one."

"You need to be absolutely specific: What are the smells, tastes? What do you see? What happened to you just before you came on stage? You must arrive fully loaded, and you need to imagine every detail."

"I don't have an imagination."

"Oh, Philip Rosen, you do. You are one of the most empathic, intense, imaginative boys I've ever known."

Philip looks down at the dust mice clinging to his broom. He might overflow, but he doesn't know what it is that's brimming in him, pride at her words, sadness, confusion, what? "Tell me about smell. How would I imagine the worst smell imaginable?"

She purses her mouth and squints her eyes, looking at him with a twinkle of humor. He knows she sees through him. It's why, much as he's drawn to her, much as he loves her in this deep way—like a mother or grandmother, but more real, is the only way he can think of it—but as much as he feels, she still makes him itchy, makes him feel ever so X-ray exposed, fraudulent. He sweeps the spot he just swept.

She hands a small biscuit down to Miffed, who's curled now on his towels and says, "When Gramma died, I thought I would die. Everything I felt when my father passed away came washing over me like a tidal wave—even stronger because now both of them were gone. I kept washing my hands, as though if I washed them enough...as though I could clean their deaths away."

Is there a secret in her words? Philip holds still.

"We had started using a particular kind of soap. We had a bar in the bath, at the sink, in the kitchen—Irish Spring. You know Irish Spring?"

"Sure."

"It was the worst smell in the world."

He wants to understand what she's telling him.

"I have now thrown out every bar of Irish Spring in the house." She checks him for a response. Her X-ray vision. She always sees. And she is always deep within herself, that mix of absolute openness and absolute inwardness that marks the artist. "I will never again use Irish Spring."

"Bourbon," he says.

"Bourbon?" Lila asks. Something is stirring in him and, if they were rehearsing a scene, she would say, "Begin from where you are. Start to say your lines." Instead she asks, "Philip, where did you go just now?"

But before he can answer, the kids from Pippin and Mary Poppins bumble into Showboat. He turns his back on them, pulls himself together, wipes his streaming eyes. The children fidget and flitter.

There is another question he wants to ask her, one that just occurred to him. Or maybe it's a plea.

Another voice keeps him from asking, though, "Mr. Rosen, I'd like a word with you."

At the sound of Uncle Bernie's croon, Philip turns around. He wipes his hands on his painter-style jeans. "There's somebody here to see you." Bernie nods to Lila who frowns and touches Philip lightly on the back. Philip's stomach flip-flops. More bad news.

Bernie leads Philip past the dining hall and out to the street. There, parked along the side wall of Ollie's, is his father's red Spitfire. A guy he's never seen is lounging against it, smoking a cigarette.

When Philip and the man fail to greet each other, Uncle Bernie says, "Philip, this is Michael Kitzke—am I saying that right? Your dad sent him to deliver your car."

Philip stands, struck dumb. Uncle Bernie looks at him, then at Kitzke, who just smokes. "I'll leave you gentlemen to business," Bernie says. "I'll see you later, Phil."

"Sure, Uncle Bernie."

Bernie heads back the way they came.

Once he's gone, Kitzke flicks his cigarette butt into the middle of the road and says, "He your uncle, that guy?" Kitzke wears cut-off blue jean shorts and a yellow tank top. His moccasin-brown hair is thinning in front—though he doesn't look to be older than mid-twenties—and longish in back, down to his shoulders. He's skinny and tough, like a tendon come to life. His calloused fingers are black under the nails. One of them is purple at the root from being smashed.

"No," Philip says, "he's a fake uncle, a camp uncle."

Kitzke squints and nods, taking it in. "Right. Fake. All my uncles are fake," he says, like he thinks the whole place is fake. "You Philip Rosen?"

"Yeah," Kitzke's what Philip thinks of when he hears the word 'grunt'. "You in the army?" he asks. As soon as it's out of his mouth, he knows it's stupid.

Kitzke laughs and sure enough he's missing a couple of teeth near the front. "No way. I thought about going, but I didn't want to come back in a box. I got asthma anyway," he adds, lighting up a Tarreyton. "You want one?" he asks Philip, extending the pack.

"No," Philip says. "Thanks." He feels like a kid from Catholic School, in a blazer and tie, carrying his books home and running into a neighborhood tough. "Trying to quit," he adds, lamely.

"I'd rather fight than quit," Kitzke says, laughing at his own joke.

"My dad around?" Philip asks, approximating nonchalance.

"Around somewhere," Kitzke answers. "Not around here."

Philip nods, as if he's following. He looks over at the car and back at Kitzke. He hasn't got a clue where this is going.

There's something twisted about the guy, Philip thinks, maybe not bad, but badass, Milwaukee, high school dropout style.

"He said you might be surprised," Kitzke says.

"No. Not really," Philip lies. "Nothing my old man does surprises me." He sounds like a choirboy imitating a Bowery boy.

"I fixed it up, tuned it, changed the oil, rotated the tires, the whole shebang. Drives nice," Kitzke says.

"Where's your shop?" Philip asks.

This cracks Kitzke up. He chokes with laughter in the middle of streaming smoke through his own smoke rings. "Man, that's good. Shop. Don't even have a garage. Mostly a couple of cinder blocks next to a gas pump. Green Bay south," he says. "Shit Brown Bay."

Philip isn't sure what this last part means, but he thinks the guy is saying he lives in a shithole.

"Your old man have a lot of money?"

Philip flinches. He's got kidnapping scenarios running through his head, though he can't figure out who might have kidnapped whom, and why this Kitzke is asking him. "No. I don't think so. Not a lot. I mean he's okay."

"Gave me 200 bucks."

"Wow," Philip exclaims, in spite of himself.

"Yeah, just to check it up and drive it down here. Wanna see if you don't believe me?"

"No, man, I believe you. Sounds like something he'd do."

"Good guy, your dad."

"Yeah, he's great." Philip swallows. "Did he say anything else? Anything for you to tell me?"

"Not much. Just happy birthday and not to worry 'cause everything's all right."

"He said Happy Birthday?"

"Some birthday present, huh? Spitfire with 27,000 miles on it. I could use a birthday present like that." Kitzke doesn't say that he did use it. About a hundred of those miles came from his detours down the back roads of Wisconsin where he tooled around for an hour and a half longer than it takes to get to Swallow Heart Lake.

"Yeah, unbelievable," Philip agrees. His birthday was two months ago. "Amazing."

"Good father to have," Kitzke says.

"Nothing else?" Philip asks, "that's all he said? No... birthday card or anything?"

"Naagh," Kitzke says. "Just the tape—he took all the other ones with him—and Happy Birthday, everything is good, kinda thing. Enjoy the car. Like that."

Philip goes over to the Triumph. *Let It Be* is sticking out of the eight-track player. He pops the glove compartment, which is empty, except for the owner's manual and a silver tire gauge. Kitzke, meanwhile, unlocks the trunk for him, and Philip comes around. "Spare's new," Kitzke says. "Jack's under here." He lifts a rubber mat off the floor.

"He go back home?" Philip asks.

"Guess so," Kitzke says. "Had me drop him at a parking lot in Green Bay before I came here, said his other car was there."

"Sure," Philip says.

"Just took his stuff—tapes and suitcases out of the trunk. Made sure I knew where to go. Big guy for surprises, your dad, huh?"

"Yeah, loves surprises."

Kitzke lingers as though waiting for Philip to tip him. "Watch out for semis," he says. "Those things jackknife like a son of a bitch and never see little cars like this."

"Yeah," Philip says, "I know."

Kitzke circles the Triumph, reluctant to turn it over to a kid without a clue what to do with it. "Might wanna put the top up," he says. "Gonna rain. You know how?"

"Sure. Do it all the time," Philip lies again.

"Okay," Kitzke says. He tosses Philip the keys.

Philip wakes up a little. "You need a ride or something? How you getting back?"

"Naagh. Your old man gave me money for a bus. Thinks of everything, that guy. I'll probably just hitch back, though."

"Right. Hitching's prob'ly fastest."

"Why, you wanna give me a lift?"

"Well, sure, yeah, but I don't think I can right now. I gotta do some stuff back at..." Philip stops before the word. It sounds so fake... "Camp".

Kitzke laughs through his brown teeth. Philip feels like a drip. "Don't drive too fahst," Kitzke says, putting on a kind of 'upper crust' dialect. "Thank your dad for me," Kitzke adds, nonchalantly. "Tell him if he ever needs anything..." And he prowls off in the direction of the main road, hunching to light a cigarette on the way.

Philip can't take his eyes off Kitzke's bony silhouette as he goes, or, more exactly, he can't face the car, to think about what it means, why his father sent it, where he's gone.

Finally, he opens the driver's door. He loved this car the moment he saw it. Now, he can barely stand to touch the thing. He searches for a button that will raise the convertible top.

Chapter 14

Jerry's plan is as simple as it is delusional. He pays a kid $200 bucks to deliver his car to Philip. He has another car waiting in Green Bay, in a lot to which the grease monkey will ferry him. When he gets where he's going, he'll trade it for yet another. He's got a leather duffel with a shoulder strap, and a briefcase, as if he's just going to the office for the day or on an overnighter to Vegas or the Playboy Club in Lake Geneva with some chippie. In the low trunk of the Triumph, he's got the rest of it: a Samsonite hard-shell containing all the clothes he could cram in, including a pair of suede slippers with lambs' wool lining that Philip bought him some Christmas a hundred years ago, and, in the interior pouch, held tight with elastic, file folders—school papers his son wrote, letters home from summer camp, class photos. It's his get-the-hell-out-of-dodge bag or his march-them-to-the-ghetto luggage. He doesn't know. Is this a getaway or forced march? Is he cowboy or captive, free ranger or exile?

He's on the road in a flash, and it occurs to him that the grease monkey might have caught sight of the used Skylark before he left. Fuck it. The punk can barely read, and he's so dazzled by the thought of tooling Wisconsin in a shiny Triumph; his cow eyes are making circles in his head. But Jerry's a planner and trading the car in before he crosses over would be too risky.

So many kids have made this trip, so many of the hippies and yippies and dippies who wanted the hell out of this war that just 'ended'. Of course, he knows what they don't—wars never end. Even when the last troops bundle into cargo and the choppers disappear with the remains of the dead. He went to the University of Wales at Swansea on the GI Bill, two semesters of drinking. He dated women whose virgin strongholds fell with Germany. He spent 1946 carrying spears and practicing tongue twisters at the Pasadena Playhouse. The war didn't end. He got married, opened up an ad agency, had a son. And still the war didn't end. Why does anyone think Vietnam is over, just because they airlifted the last standing off a rooftop in Saigon?

But he's not running from war without end. He's running from prison. He's running from the humiliation of watching his life go up in smoke. He's running from a sentence. He's the subject of the sentence and confinement is the predicate. Prison is, what, the object of the preposition? *Who can remember grammar terms? Who can remember anything?*

Nobody will look for him in Canada. It took a long time to get to this plan. It took maps and days in the library. It took long drives, plane trips and tours of almost-towns. He knows he'll be safe there. He'll be gone. Simple: just the other side of the lake he was born on. He doesn't know how Jews ended up in Duluth or how they got to Lake Superior in the first place. He knows his father wasn't the only one by a long shot. Now, he's reversing their migration, maybe part of a new current of history, a backtracking stampede. The sound of that stampede: Thunder Bay.

It never occurred to him to dodge the draft in the forties, never occurred to any of them. Couldn't enlist fast enough. He considered lying about his age. In fact, he lied about lying. He told his son he lied to get into the war before he was old enough. When Philip does the math years later, he'll realize that this, like so much else, was fiction, Jerry translating his life to myth. He enlisted in '43 after he turned eighteen. Such exercises in 'bullfiction' will come to define Jerry Rosen's life for his son. "I was too smart for military intelligence," he told Philip, of his army IQ tests. "I spent the war years in Pigalle with the whores. I wrote the school song at Swansea. They still sing it there." Maybe one day he'll send a card from Thunder Bay: "I'm a fur trader in the woods of Canada." Delusional.

The novel that is Jerry Rosen's life will carry the title: *The Man Who Disappeared*. Or better, *The Missing Man*. Like those Air Force flyovers when a pilot dies, one plane gone from a perfect V formation. The pages will be full of blanks, and it will be up to the boy to fill them in. This is the way it goes, Jerry thinks. We fill in the blanks for our fathers. He doesn't know the half of it. God knows his own father is blank enough. Sam. Will he blink, this blank man, when he finds out? His son the convict, the escapee, his failed fuck of a son. Will he break? Will he go his bland way with his stolid wife of twenty years and grow forgetful?

So once again—and maybe for the last time—Jerry drives his life, the one he's leaving behind. And once again, it tails him. Not-so-hot pursuit. He wants to pull over. He wants to look back, but he knows how it goes: look back, pillar of salt. He wants to hold his son again, wants a second chance on the last goodbye. He wants to say more to Lila than what he said: "Watch after my guy, will you?" He wants to shake his father's hand, to look him square in the eye and tell him not to worry. He wants to weave the word love into all his sentences. He wants to do so many things, and he can't do one of them.

As he drove out of Swallow Heart Lake, only a day ago, he downshifted and, against his better judgment, glanced over his shoulder at the Lake itself, glistening through the trees. It was brief, this glance, but now it's blinding him. The sun bouncing off the water. Stretches of sand the color of oatmeal. Whitewashed boathouses with green trim.

Philip looks like this, too, in Jerry's mind, bright and glistening, just washed. The bright lake shines in this new-minted memory and beckons him somewhere he can never return to, somewhere he has never been. And he drove away from it, drives away from it.

Jerry knows better. Nothing is pristine in this world. Nothing he's ever known. But that's just it. He's never known anything like the camp life he imagines Philip living, this seventies childhood with its flowers and harmony and happy weed. And he never will, even through the eyes of his boy. This brightness will dog him to the end of the country. It will follow him across Lake Superior. This brightness, incompletely glimpsed as it was, will haunt him.

Fathers are supposed to haunt their kids. Isn't that the story of all those Shakespearean tragedies he read back in Pasadena after the war? Parents close doors and freakish things jump out from behind them to terrorize their children. How did it happen that his sixteen-year-old son, shiny as a Kennedy half-dollar, became his ghost?

Chapter 15

On the back of Anatevka, snaking up one side of the DeMille dance studio, rising another story to a battered, green door, runs a rickety wooden fire escape. Evoking images of the sketchy, temporary scaffolding in an archaeologist's cave or the untended balcony entrance of a segregated Bible Belt movie house; it's no place anyone would want to walk.

Kathy Klein takes the stairs two at a time. Nimble and stealthy, she appears unconcerned with the precipitous danger of the climb. If you want to visit the infirmary, if you want to sit and have your temperature taken and your throat sprayed with green, numbing Chloraseptic, if you want vague, inattentive comfort, aspirin, or a way out of fourth-period dance, if you want to make it to the infirmary in one piece, this is not the way to go.

But Kathy does make it to the infirmary in one piece. From the landing, she hears the noisy release of campers, sprung from breakfast. She slips, sylph-like, in the fire exit door.

Stock-still at the end of the long hallway, the girl blends into the dirty white walls the way a deer blends into the naked brush of late winter. There's movement and murmur down the hall, in a narrow waiting room with mismatched wooden chairs. Kathy knows it well. As part of what Philip calls her "Daily Broken Bird Tour," she often chaperones one or another hobbled child to the nurse. She views it from a distance now, from the other end of the telescope.

Five of the doors between Kathy and the examining room are open, spilling shadowy daylight into the hall. A sixth is shut. Nurse Aspillaga emerges from the examining room and vanishes into the office. Kathy tiptoes to the closed door. She turns the knob and ducks inside, backing against the door till it clicks.

Jody Gold is sleeping in one of the room's two beds. The other is empty. Pale and peaceful, except for a sprinkling of sweat on her forehead, she doesn't stir. Kathy remembers playing the scene of Peter Pan's arrival with Jody when they were ten. It was just like this, only instead of watching Wendy (Jody) from the door, she mooned down at her from the window's wide ledge, without interest in the two boys sleeping in the neighboring beds. When, as Peter, she'd found her shadow but failed to find a way to attach it to her foot, Katie (as she was known at the time) sat on the floor and wept into one thin arm, crooked at a right angle across her eyes. Wendy (Jody) sat up, hands folded primly in her lap, asked, "Boy, why are you crying?"

It was their single scene in the play, except for filling in as pirates and Indians on group numbers, but it was exquisitely done, a love scene of the sweetest order, ending in a triumphant flight out the nursery window, past the stars, and off to Never Never Land. (At Friedkin the flying is danced, as there is neither the apparatus for stage flight nor fly space above from which to wire it.) The performance sealed the deal on their friendship. They would forever after be best friends.

Until they weren't. Kathy and Jody have been in six plays and six cabins together since that year. Kathy can't remember the last time they had a civil conversation. And Jody is not sitting up in bed asking her why she's crying. Jody is lying on her back, breathing deeply with a small nasal catch, sweating. Last night, they were all together watching a president resign; this morning, she's watching Jody recover from God knows what.

They are no longer best friends, but Kathy still knows everything there is to know about Jody. She knows how sweet she can be and how hateful. She knows that her attraction to damage—in boys who drop acid and stick needles in their arms and men who are way too old to have sex with the likes of Jody—comes from her own very real damage. She's heard about the room where Jody's grandfather lives, windows blacked out against the Nazis, newspapers piled to the ceiling, cigar smoke hanging in the dim air.

What is it about Friedkin? It's the smilingest place under the sun, and it attracts kids who have real reasons not to smile. Maybe this is what amazes Kathy about the girl whose diary she carries even now: her power to radiate humanity in the midst of horror and suffering. She knows that Jody, for all her self-destructive ways, is drawn to music and God and goodness. She knows Jody's past and her future. The only thing she doesn't know—at this very moment—is her present, and how she got here.

Kathy grabs the room's only chair from the wall by the sink, a gunmetal office chair, and lugs it beside the bed. She turns back, lifts a thin terry washcloth off the towel bar, runs some water into it, wrings it out and carries it to the bed, where, poised on the chair's edge, she holds it against Jody's forehead.

Sleeping, Jody sighs as she accepts the wet cloth. It's quiet and early and time is in no hurry. Jody's eyes open. They are the only things about her that move, painstakingly surveying the vision of the girl before her, reaching over with a cooling compress.

"Hi Katie," Jody says groggily, her tongue, lips, and palate all dry and stuck together.

"Hey Jo," Kathy replies.

"How you doin'?"

"Okay. How about you?"

Jody snorts. Then she winces.

"What're you doing here?" Jody asks.

"Getting you water," Kathy answers, lifting the washcloth and going over to the sink where she pops a Dixie cup from a plastic dispenser next to the mirror, fills it with water and crosses back to the bed. She reaches the cup to Jody who takes it and, inching her head off the pillow, sips.

"You're not here to kill me?" Jody asks, grimacing as she swallows.

"Yeah," Kathy says, "like you need me to do that."

"You suck," Jody says, a statement of fact.

Kathy doesn't respond. Instead, she returns to the sink and rinses the washcloth. She wrings it out again and, sitting on the edge of the chair, ministers to Jody's forehead, after taking the Dixie cup from her hand and setting it on the windowsill.

"What'd you do, Jo?"

"Who wants to know?"

"I want to know."

"Why, so you can run around and tell everybody what a sick bitch I am?"

"Nobody needs me to tell them that, Jo."

"Right," Jody snorts. And again she winces. "My head feels like it's crammed full of wet cotton. Only the cotton's burning."

"Ouch," says Kathy, without inflection. "That must hurt."

"Did I say you suck?" Jody asks.

"Yes, I think you did."

"Good. I was afraid I forgot to mention it."

Kathy turns the cloth inside out, folds it back over and lays it against Jody's head.

"What are they saying?" Jody asks, avoiding Kathy's eyes.

"Nobody seems to know anything. You never miss breakfast and there you weren't. I overheard Marla tell our dear counselor something about driving at a crazy speed to Waukesha County Emergency Room and stomach pumping. Jack looked pissy and guilty, like someone had stepped on his hash pipe. But come to think of it, he always looks like that. Anyway, I put two and you together. Other than that, you know, mostly whispering and guessing. Just another morning at Broken Lake."

"Yeah," Jody says.

"What'd you do, Jo?"

"I like the way you say that. Not 'What happened?' or 'What'd he do to you?' Like you just assume I did something stupid or wrong."

"Okay, so let me rephrase: What'd you do, Jo?"

"You're such a bitch. A schizo bitch. Can't decide if you want to be Queen asshole of the century or Clara Fucking Barton."

"You know me so well."

"Damn right I do." Jody glowers. "Who sent you here?"

"As in 'who do I work for?' Well, Sylvie asked me to find out why you make yourself throw up after meals; Uncle Bernie wanted to know about the drug use; Tex-Mecks was wondering about the compulsion to sleep with people you don't like; and Jack wanted me to ask if you stepped on his hash pipe."

"You suck," Jody whimpers.

"So I guess I work for just about everybody. Oh yeah, Dr A said to check if you needed some Chloraseptic. How is your throat?"

"It hurts. I threw up half my guts last night. They stuck a tube down my throat."

"Poor baby. Everybody's always doing mean stuff to you."

"Yeah, they are."

"I said poor baby."

"I appreciate your concern." She fake smiles at Kathy. Kathy fake smiles back. They almost laugh.

"Nobody sent me here, Jody. I wanted to see if you were okay."

Jody doesn't say anything. She closes her eyes and tries to make the pain go away, the pains go away—head, throat, stomach, muscles, eyes—a jumble of pains, a throbbing room. Seeing Katie has her aching, too. There's no one in the world like this intense, scrappy sister of her heart. The heart is a muscle, and Katie Klein has been a tear in that muscle.

"Did they call your parents? Is your mom coming up?"

Jody shuts her eyes.

"Let me guess: Marla lied to the doctor and said your parents were already on their way. Anything to protect the purity of Friedkin."

Jody nods, eyes still closed. "I think," she whispers.

Kathy soothes Jody's temples, cheeks and neck with the washcloth. She dabs the moisture dotting her upper lip.

"So you wanna tell me or not. My time here is almost up. I have to get back to caring for the lepers." She tosses the washcloth into the sink and stands behind the chair, holding on to it, shoulders hiked up around her ears.

Jody glares at her. She knows that whatever she says will stay in the room. Katie is a total, judgmental bitch, but she is also the most trustworthy person Jody has ever met.

"Dion practically saved my life."

"That was nice of him."

"Yeah, he was so sweet. Unlike some boys."

"He's a gem that one."

"He was last night."

"I'm glad, Jody. I'm glad somebody practically saved your life."

Jody tries hard to read Kathy's eyes to see if she means it. As well as Jody knows her, it is always hard to tell. She has those melty Bambi eyes and that wiseacre, side-of-the-mouth delivery. Even when they were kids, she seemed to be saying numerous things at the same time.

"We were out celebrating Nixon and everything, and Jack decided that was a good time to tell me he had fucked Melly Barber. He's such an asshole. I was really messed up. I took a Quaalude, then I took some more. Then I got sick."

"Geez Louise, Jo."

"I know. It was a bad day."

"No, I mean, what are you thinking? Jack's an idiot. He'd screw anything that would let him, and Melly's not exactly Miss Chastity Belt 1974. Of course, he screwed her. Did you think he wouldn't? And didn't anyone tell you pills are 'hazardous to your health?' You stupid cow! What were you thinking?"

"Oh go fuck yourself. You're so superior, Kathy. You always do this. You just came here to pronounce fucking sentence. God, I hate you."

"You hate yourself, Jody."

"Ooo, now you're a freakin' psychotherapist! I'm okay, you're okay, so why is Jody Gold so fucked up? Well, fuck you, Kathy, Katie, Kate, K, Anne Frank, Clara sick bitch Barton. Get out of my hospital room before I tell the doctor you're trying to steal all the Aspergum. Get out."

Jody's throat is raw. She starts coughing which makes her head throb and her face turn red. She spins over and coughs into her pillow, furious with herself for saying anything.

"It's not a bloody hospital room, Jo."

"Don't you think I know that," Jody says, choking. It sounds like gargling.

Kathy dismisses her with a wave of one hand and bolts out the door into the hall where she slams right into Dr Aspillaga and his clipboard.

Chapter 16

Jerry spends the day circling Duluth in his Skylark. It's a place unchanged—the massive brown warehouses on the lake, white wooden homes, brick schools, oppressed by North Woods pine. Some places suit old photographs, and this is one: late 19th century industrial frontier, a study in sepia, even saturated with the greens of late summer. A few of the street names ring a bell, so he parks and walks around. He associates these streets with family, return addresses for second cousins, but he has no memories of the place. He moved away when he was three and visited as a boy forty years ago. Now he's staring down the throat of fifty, and he can't remember a fucking thing.

Duluth is one blank, Chicago another. It eats at him how little he recalls of his childhood there. He finds a coffee shop and orders a cup of black coffee. He stirs, as though the slow circling of his spoon can invoke this past.

When he was sixteen, America went to war. Jerry Rosen was living in a two-bedroom apartment on Kedzie with his mom and dad and eight-year-old sister. He took the sofa at thirteen, in an ass-backward attempt at privacy. His baby sister Phyllis became the only one with her own room. Mom insisted he unmake the sofa every morning. He stowed his sheets in a milk crate behind the sofa. His pillow didn't fit, so he had to stack it neatly on top. His mother had been sick for two-and-a-half years by then and would be sick for another two-and-a-half.

Her dying would, ironically, save his life. He was granted leave to visit her before going overseas. While he was on leave, his company received orders and shipped out for Okinawa. Nearly everyone he'd trained with was killed. He flew instead to Europe and, in the spring of '45, as his buddies fell to the Japanese and his mother lost her last battle, he entered Germany. He couldn't say exactly where he was when she died, since it was months before he got word. At least it wasn't Okinawa.

Before this, when the war was new, and he was too young to fight in it, he read all the papers he could get his mitts on—the *Tribune*, the only paper they had at home, the *Daily Times*, *Daily News*, *Herald-American*, the new *Chicago Sun*, and even, when he could, the weekly black paper, *The Chicago Defender*. Sports and the war—that's what he read, what they all read.

Sports and the war. He understood everything he needed to in the war news. The Japs attacked us; they were crazy, and they were cowards, sneaking up like that. He'd never heard of Pearl Harbor before they bombed it, and then it became the dividing line of his life and nearly everyone's. The Japs attacked and, when we went after them, the Nazis and the Fascists made war on us. They all wanted to take over the world. And they all wanted to kill the Jews. At least the Krauts did. What's not to understand?

He can picture the radio—brown plastic, Deco pattern on the dial—and he can hear that news anchor voice, nasal and portentous. The Nazis marching inevitably across Eastern Europe, mowing down one place at a time. Marching west and marching east, north and south, all around the town. He heard the news the way he heard radio serials, the way he watched movies. Capone and Ness, Dick Tracy and Flattop, Eisenhower and Goering. It was a story, a game: Cities and countries fell like tricks in a rubber of bridge. The tension around the fallen had a pumped-up feel, dramatic, not really real.

He played war in the streets and alleys. He took turns being a Nazi. He liked basketball better and trying to get under girls' shirts. His dad never talked about the war. His mom was always pushing him to do better in school and to practice his violin, her physical pain translating into a desperate push to make something of her son. He could cut classes from time to time, but he couldn't skip out on his violin lessons downtown because they cost extra and she'd know. "Yehudi Menuhin practices fifteen hours a day!" she would scold. (What was it about Jewish mothers and the violin? He'd once heard someone say that Heifitz was god, and Yehudi Menuhin was god's son on earth. Maybe that was it: Jewish mothers dream of giving birth to Jesus. That'll show everybody!) She'd started the PTA chapter at his school, and now he was making her look bad, being too wild. "Doctors don't have time for chutzpenik."

"Geez, Ma, talk English. I don't even know what you say half the time." But, of course, he did. She was saying he was an impudent fuck-up and he'd never amount to anything. Then she called him 'my son the doctor' to her few remaining friends, and always to her sisters. 'Jerome the doctor' this, and 'Jerome the doctor' that. Encouragement with a smack in the face. Jerome, Yehudi, Jesus.

By the time the war came, she was in bed most of the time. They had to bring her everything while she barked orders at them. She didn't have time for war talk. "Acch," was all she said, with that dismissive wave of the hand, always 'Acch'. The war was over there. Back there. "We don't go back," she said, and she proved it by dying without her son knowing she'd come from Vilna at the age of seven. "I'm from here," she would say, belying her familial accent, her atavistic caw. "Right here. Chicago. Acch." Even that didn't make sense, since Jerry'd been born in Duluth and, God knows, his mom didn't just hop a train north to meet a nice Jewish boy and get knocked up.

He began memorizing the names of towns in Germany, Poland, Russia and France. He was never good with Hungary or Czechoslovakia. Forget about Scandinavia, Holland and Northern Africa. He followed the war, and he followed the White Sox, Cubs, Bears, Black Hawks and the ever-changing basketball teams in the NBL. He checked box scores and statistics because you never wanted to get caught out when talk turned to who was best at what. Three things you needed in the neighborhood: your own smokes, a decent jump shot and facts at hand when some goyische smartass challenged you on the Bears or their Jew-boy quarterback Sid Luckman. Or four—a ready fist in his face.

They would all be soldiers. And Jerry couldn't wait to get the hell out of the house. He stayed away as much as he could and called it schoolwork. Mostly, he bummed around smoking cigarettes and, when somebody could get it, drinking whiskey or gin. They played pickup basketball outside Roosevelt High. He prided himself on being quick and cagey, even if he was a short-legged 5'8". They didn't talk future, except the war.

He finished high school in June '43, his ever-dying mother having forced a promise out of him that he'd start college, so he did a summer at the U of I, Circle Campus. Even the hypnotic stirring of his coffee can't stir up memories of that summer. When he finally did enlist, she yelled at him for not being made an officer, yelled at him, like he had anything to do with it.

This is all that surfaces, no other facts, impressions, smells or sights, except his mom's thick peasant legs and hard Lithuanian scowl, his father's bland smile, an indifferent hand patting him on the shoulder. He remembers his sister's quiet. He loved his little sister Phyllis and was glad when she got sent to their aunt's house during Mom's last year because nobody paid her a bit of attention, including Jerry. He just wanted out.

These hardly qualify as memories, but this is how the past presents itself to him, especially now that he's left Chicago. It's just narrative, boiled down. Chicago and childhood, from this distance, might as well be Duluth. A swath of brown.

One thing he's never forgotten. The good lie. He was on his leave, mother deathbed leave. His private's uniform pressed, kinky Jewish head shorn, face smooth. He held his hat in his lap, the way they do in the movies. Once he'd leaned over to kiss her. She even seemed happy to see him for a change. He was a medic, he told her, and when he shipped out for Europe, he would help the guys who got hurt. They'd taught him to give shots and blood; they'd staged emergency operations. A surgical technician is what they call him.

The sun washed over her face, and her eyes lit up like a fanatic priest running into God's arms. "A doctor," she said. "You're a doctor!"

"Yeah, Ma. I'm a doc."

And for the next twelve days, she told everybody who visited, "Jerome's a surgeon. The Army made him doctor." His good little lie, her hoity-toity.

Germany was the dividing line. Once there he began his own inevitable march, everything else, everything from before, browned out. Had he stayed at the 77th, it would have been bad enough. But they sent him out of the field hospital and into the field, and that's when the doors started closing. Bury the past, hell. The past was one big burial. Buchenwald, Nordhausen, Penig and Leipzig buried the past.

Chapter 17

Philip tries to sleep. Sights and sounds batter his brain. His father clanking ice cubes in a glass, Lila pointing at his heart, Kitzke ambling up the street. They picked up teams for the camp Olympics earlier in the evening, and he's been made a captain. Afterward, at Friday night services in Gershwin, Uncle Bernie gave a soaring sermon about a black man named James Meredith, who, having integrated the University of Mississippi, started a solo "March Against Fear" from Memphis to Jackson. While Bernie told the story of Meredith's courage, described him being shot multiple times and dragging himself to the side of the road, the Blue Division twelve- and thirteen-year-olds, arrayed behind a curtain made of scrim, whisper-sang "The Impossible Dream" from *Man of La Mancha*: "...that one man, torn and covered with scars, still strove..." Philip, like so many, wept. Then he heard that Jody Gold, who is never far from his thoughts, overdosed last night.

He fingers the plastic envelope of Traveler's Cheques he's stashed inside his pillowcase. In that awful country quiet before sleep, which to a boy from the suburbs isn't quiet at all, but the frightening press of unnamed things flapping and ticking against windows and walls—in that infested stillness, the crust of the earth breaks and up crawls all he dreads.

He sees his father's face. It is ghostly, Jacob Marley-like. Whispering something to him.

Outside is scary, but nowhere near as scary as this. He slips a work shirt over his football jersey, steps into his painter's pants and Adidas. He grabs his army jacket, which has the name Cruz sewn over the pocket, and tiptoes out. An electric clock reads one twenty-five.

Philip crosses Green Fields, staying in the light. Once he reaches the cabin Brigadoon, he raps a quiet, persistent beat on the screen above Kathy Klein's bed. Balanced on the ramped cellar door, he's about to knock again when Kathy's head crawls into frame. She's clutching a dog-eared copy of the *Diary*— *does she sleep with it, too?* he wonders—but has the droopy eyes of someone who's been sleeping rather than reading. Philip draws an invisible question mark in the dark. She clicks a flashlight twice, shining the light in his face, and holds up a finger. Philip loops around back.

The whoosh of the screen door. Kathy swings under the railing, over the edge of the concrete stairs, thudding to earth beside him. "Faster than a speeding bullet," she whispers. Whenever Kathy tries to be chipper, she sounds snide.

"Sorry I woke you," he says.

"It's all right. I was dreaming I was at camp. It was a nightmare."

"I hate to break this to you, but you are at camp."

Kathy lets out a bloodcurdling—silent—scream. Philip smiles at her Munch. When she's done mugging, she notes that his smile is *dutiful*. He is a dutiful boy, wouldn't hurt a fly; dutiful, even when he's *breaking the rules*. Philip will never be ordinary, she knows, will never go to work in a suit and tie, but he'll never give the world the finger either. Whatever path he takes will be a veer not a radical off-ramp. Coming for her at night is such a veer—no loud uprising, just a step to the side of the regulations. "When I'm the one trying to crack you up," she says, "something must really be wrong."

Kathy is at her gentlest right after waking, as though the camp's cheap sheets sandpaper away everything tough and knowing. "Oh captain, my captain," she says, "you look so sad."

Her impeccable aim. It's why he's here. She touches his shoulder, pulls him towards her. He starts to cry. "That's right," she says.

As Kathy's arms begin to encircle him, a flashlight beams from the direction of the flagpole. "Shit," she mutters, ready to tear into whoever it is, even though she's the one who's supposed to be in bed. Philip wipes his face, turning from the glare.

They expect someone walking ground patrol, but it's only Kenny Tannenbaum, the counselor from the cabin Golden Boy. He is ecstatic. His eyes zip around in their sockets. "It's not a drumlin!" he nearly shouts when he reaches them. He waves the flashlight as he talks. "They're not going to believe it!"

"Calm down, Kenny. Shh, shh." They're within hearing of the Brigadoon counselors' room and the last thing she wants is to wake them.

"It's not a drumlin," Kenny repeats. "I've known it for years. But in the back of my mind, you know? This little voice. It never made sense."

"That's great, Kenny," Kathy nods. She elongates her words, like she's lulling a frantic child or a maniac. "Now... what's...not ...a...drumlin? The drumlin? That hill out in Green Fields?"

"Right! Right! It's not. I knew it." He shoves the flashlight in his armpit and pulls a piece of crumpled paper out of the pocket of his shorts. The paper is crosshatched with measurements and numbers. He holds it out to them and snatches it back.

"Hey, Kenny, wow," Philip ventures, gathering himself. "D'you mind my asking what it is?"

"Get this," Kenny gushes. "It's unbelievable." He thrusts the paper towards them. "It's a turtle."

Kathy and Philip stand confused, somewhere between laughter and concern. Kenny has been at camp a long time, and so now he's a counselor, a function of age rather than fit. He's one of those distractible, preoccupied counselors, one of those hyperactive teddy bears the Friedkins always make sure is partnered with a steady, attentive co-counselor. Kenny has hovered around Uncle Bernie since the age of nine. He's Bernie's aide-de-camp, like Radar in Robert Altman's *M*A*S*H*, except he's a Radar without a homing device. Now Philip and Kathy fear Kenny has lost it.

He starts recounting days of study and calculation, explaining how he's matched his own measurements of the drumlin against photographs and drawings in books he checked out of the Sheboygan County Library on his last day off. He reaches into a different pocket for another sheet of stained graph paper with a blue pencil drawing of a turtle imposed over a scale diagram of the drumlin's dimensions. He's not making sense.

"Kenny," Kathy says, quieting down. "Are you okay? I mean, really?"

"I'm great!" His smile is a canoe. "I just discovered an American Indian Burial Mound." With that he stuffs the papers back in his shorts and careens off.

"Oh my God," Kathy says.

"Holy shit, Batman," Philip says.

"He was for real."

"Do you think he's right?"

"I don't know. I've only seen burial mounds at the Wisconsin Dells when I was little."

"How were we supposed to know he was making actual sense?"

"I thought he was tripping," Kathy says.

"I thought he was doing a Carlos Castenada thing—See the turtle…"

"I know, I know," she says, doubled over, laughter and shock.

"Do you think actual Indians are buried under camp?" Philip asks, suddenly serious.

"There are 'actual' Indians buried under everything in this country."

"I know," Philip says. "But I mean piled up, right here. In a heap?"

"Maybe. If anybody would know, it would be Kenny. I mean the guy takes notes on Uncle Bernie's sermons. He reads books on rocks."

"I never thought about it."

"I thought he meant a turtle-turtle."

"The whole earth is bone."

"Sure," the girl they call Anne Frank says, "I know." even though she doesn't know, even though this may be one of the least characteristic things Philip has ever said.

A light goes on in the Brigadoon counselor's room. They hurry around the corner, away from Green Fields, away from the turtle-shaped mound of earth that might mark Winnebago graves.

They scurry down to the waterfront, lit by the moon and a street lamp's vague blue glow.

On the banks of Swallow Heart Lake, the waterfront is grassy, except for a strip of mucky sand as long as the opening of a small proscenium. Tall pines ring the waterfront and line the coastline, which is studded with campgrounds, private homes and resorts. Swallow Heart Lake sits in a kettle, as the pits or small valleys are known in Wisconsin, cut long ago by the retreat of glaciers across this land. The ground rises steeply to the road above.

Nature is friendly here. The beach grass is mown. A bright white pier extends into the shallow water. And, as sentry at the foot of the pier, a massive, twisted oak overhangs the scene, dotted with bubble gum of every color in a spectacle of shapes—stretched, pressed, molded, buttons of chewed gum jammed into the grooves of the bark. Nailed to the Bubble Gum Tree, a red-on-white painted sign commands, 'Spit out Your Gum Before Going into the Water!!!'

They walk out to the end of the pier. They sit, a mirror image of each other, cross-legged, hands on ankles, hunched for warmth.

"Crazy day, huh?" Kathy says.

"Crazy."

She wants to tell him about her visit with Jody Gold in the infirmary, but she learned long ago that if she wants Philip to herself, she shouldn't bring Jody into it. Jody and Philip haven't been together for at least a year, as far as she knows, but he's still on her leash and only takes the smallest tug to heel.

"Hear from your dad?"

Philip tells her about Michael Kitzke and his dad's car. "He told Kitzke to say 'Happy Birthday'."

"Your birthday was two months ago."

"No kidding. What do you think he was trying to say?"

Kathy resists the urge to speak her mind. Under his likable-boy shrugs and half-smiles, he's about to boil over. She's also fighting the impulse to throw her arms around him again. *I'm not his mother*, she reminds herself.

"Read me something," he says out of nowhere.

"Sure," she says. She rifles some pages, straining to read them by the moon and the spillover light from the tower lamp on shore. She reaches into the pocket of her jacket and grabs the flashlight she stuffed in there when Philip came to her window. It's about the size of a cigarette pack and doesn't cast much more light than a cigarette would. She moves it over the words, as though searching for something.

Saturday, 11 July, 1942
Dear Kitty,

I expect you will be interested to hear what it feels like to 'disappear'; well, all I can say is that I don't know myself yet. I don't think I shall ever feel really at home in this house, but that does not mean that I loathe it here; it is more like being on vacation in a very peculiar boardinghouse. Rather a mad idea, perhaps, but that is how it strikes me.

She looks up from the page to check if Philip is listening. The pier itself is white-painted metal and bumpy, to protect against slipping. Philip is running his fingers over the bumps like someone reading Braille. "Go on," he says.

She goes back to the book; the flashlight hovers over it.

The 'Secret Annexe' is an ideal hiding place. Although it leans to one side and is damp, you'd never find such a comfortable hiding place anywhere in Amsterdam, no, perhaps not even in the whole of Holland. Our little room looked very bare, at first, with nothing on the walls, but thanks to Daddy who had brought my film-star collection and picture postcards on beforehand, and with the aid of paste pot and brush, I have transformed the walls into one gigantic picture.

Kathy glances up again. "How did he know to do that, do you think? God, my father would never have thought of doing something so nice." God no, she reflects, with three new kids under the age of seven—his new family—she's surprised her father even remembers her name. No response from Philip, still surfing the bumps on the pier with the tips of his fingers. "And how long did she have to go without her collection and postcards before they moved? She never explains. Hmm."

When he lifts his head, Philip is eerie quiet. Slow in a way he's never slow. Thoughts of his father seem unreal. Maybe he's blowing everything out of proportion. Just because someone gets sentenced doesn't mean he goes right to prison. Maybe there'll be a grace period. An appeal. *Maybe they can postpone his sentence for a year while I finish high school,* he thinks. *Dad should argue that he's a single* parent *of a son still in school. Who will take care of my son, while I'm in prison, Your Honor? His mother has relocated to Mexico.*

"Philip? Talk to me," Kathy says.

"I keep thinking my father's going to die," Philip says.

"Oh Philip."

"I see him dead."

"He's not dead, though. We saw him."

"I've never seen anyone dead," Philip says.

"Is that a bad thing?" she asks. No answer. "He's not dead."

"I've never seen anything."

For once, Kathy Klein is at a loss for words. It's true what he's said. It's true for him and it's true for her. They've never seen anything.

"It's like he's trying to tell me something."

"What do you mean? Your dad?"

"It's like he's coming back to tell me something."

Now, he's frightening her. This is not Philip. "Oh Philip. He's not dead. He's told you everything there is to tell. For now. Later—when you see him later—there'll be other things to tell."

"I don't believe he's coming back."

These contradictions drive her nuts: does Philip think his father's coming back or not? She stifles her impatience with his logic. He's in distress. She takes his hand and says the stupidest thing she can think of: "It'll be okay."

He puzzles over her face, as if suddenly confronting a Martian. "Okay?"

No choice but to defend her position. "Yeah, okay. It'll work out. It may take time, but he'll be back. You'll have your father back." His hand, so warm and right in hers, is snatched away.

"I've got to go." And then Philip does something she's never known him to do, this boy who makes everyone around him comfortable and happy, so they know he's there for them. He stands up and leaves her sitting on the pier. He stands up and leaves.

No, Philip Rosen doesn't just walk away, she thinks. Ducking out is everything he is not. But there she is, a pile of girl, alone on a length of white-painted steel with all the things she might have said. All the things she might have done to keep him with her. Her life, it seems at times like this, is distinguished by the things she might have done to stop people from leaving.

After a long while, Kathy rises and makes her way up the long flight of cracked cement steps to the road. She reenters camp by the path beside Ollie's Dining Hall, emerging near the Costume Shop. It's as though she can see her own life in summer camp musicals through the walls: Mrs. Anna's hoop skirt, Laurie's farm-girl picnic frock, the jaunty sailor suit worn by Nellie 'Cockeyed Optimist' Forbush. "Dress up," she scoffs aloud, detesting all innocence.

Before she knows it, she's at the Riding rink. She plants a foot on the bottom board of the corral fence and folds her arms along the top. Her head drops to the nest of her arms. If this were day, she'd shut her eyes and listen to the horses canter by. The horses are gone now, stabled for the night. All she hears is her own breath in the chamber of her skull. She shouldn't be here. She should be in Maine or California or wherever with her dad and Alice and the kids. It's always easy where they are. Why didn't she insist on going with them? Why, at the first sign of Dad's hesitation, did she throw in the towel? Why is she here?

Something rustles. Her heart jumps. "Oh. Didn't see you, Dion."

"I didn't mean to scare you, Kathy," Dion says. "I was trying not to move."

"You don't scare me, Dion. Didn't scare me. I just..."

"Your eyes were closed. I was trying not to move." They stand maybe six feet from each other, faces mottled with shadow. "I couldn't sleep."

"Me, too," she lies. They gaze over the fence into the circle of grass where the horses aren't. "Neither," she corrects herself.

"I sleep better in the city," he explains.

"Yeah, me too," she says. "Not that Evanston's much of a city."

"How you been? I haven't seen you much lately outside of rehearsal," he says.

"I've been wearing my invisible cape," she says. He nods.

"You seen Jody today?" he asks.

She purses her lips like a prisspot. Marian the Librarian. Then she remembers. "Oh my God, she said you saved her life last night."

"I just carried her back to Anatevka. She was sick."

"You're a hero. You might have really saved her life."

"I didn't save anybody's life."

Kathy lets his humility sink in. It's odd coming from him. Dion was for a long time the only black kid at camp, seven years old, eight years old. He has always seemed so brave to her, at least, bravely unselfconscious. He'd have to be, the way everyone treated him—just over-friendly and hyper-casual enough to make him seem like an unexpectedly clever space alien. And in a way she's right, he had to be confident, and he was. She hears fear in his voice, a pleading not to have saved a life, not to have done anything heroic or decisive or even noticeable.

"Was it because of last night? Jody? Was that keeping you up?"

Dion takes the pause to end all pauses. "I can't remember much of what happened. Jack was there. Here. I don't know what he was doing. Jody was on the ground right about where you are. Or it could have been over there," he says, pointing to the other side of the rink. "I carried her over my shoulder like a fireman. I thought she'd be heavier than she was." His eyes are pained. "What happened? Do you know?"

"She was in trouble. You helped her."

"Jack was there. Why didn't he help her?"

"Oh, God," Kathy grunts, "who knows? Jack's a jerk."

"Jack's a good guy. He's always been nice to me. We grew up together here."

"He thinks he's hot shit."

"He's one of my best friends."

"Everybody's your friend, Dion. Everybody at camp likes you."

He starts to cry.

Kathy goes to him. She can't remember ever seeing Dion cry. He's always so held together. She brushes his shoulder with her fingertips, afraid he might bolt. "That was so brave of you, Dion. You really helped someone. You did something real good."

Anne Frank brushes a tear from his cheek. She kisses the spot where the tear had been. It's like a scene from *Peter Pan*, she thinks. She's Wendy Moira Angela Darling, tending one of the lost boys. She strokes his cheek with the back of her knuckles.

Dion crosses his arms away from his body, as though someone's just slipped out of his embrace or he's trying to hug air.

"You helped her," she says. Stepping closer, Kathy rests her fingertips on his forearms and gingerly uncrosses them. Before Dion knows what hit him, she pushes her mouth against his, jams her tongue against his. Her braces scrape Dion's gums. She kisses the startled boy for dear life.

Chapter 18

Jerry has attempted to put Chicago behind him before. Almost as soon as he got back from the service, he laid GI money down on a new Plymouth Deluxe, spent a couple weeks visiting his father, who had already and regrettably remarried. Jerry drove his twelve-year-old sister Phyllis around the city, regaling her with stories of his wartime exploits and doing his best to ignore the pleading looks she threw his way. She wanted, needed him to stay, but he'd set his course: flight as adventure. "Have I spent my whole fucking life driving?" he asks himself, as he exits the Duluth coffee shop and unlocks the Skylark.

Winter of '46, as soon as he could extricate himself from the family drama he headed west to—where else—California. The Pasadena Playhouse. All these years later, he can't remember how the idea came into his head or how he applied, but there he was, one vet among many, one would-be hambone among many, taking classes morning and night, words tripping on his tongue, being called upon to remember feelings he'd never had.

What was he thinking? Actors are feelers and feeling was the last thing he wanted to do. Yet there he was, warming up his body, humming into the front of his face, reading scenes from plays by Sidney Kingsley, Robert Sherwood and Clifford Odets—that was the experimental stuff. Then there were the classics: Shakespeare, Moliere, a crazy chanted version of *Agamemnon,* sweating behind a moldy plaster mask. Feelings everywhere he turned.

He met some truly talented kids, some who went on to become stars. But, as Jerry was fond of saying, while he could carry a spear, he couldn't hold a candle. "You are up in your head, Jerry," his acting teacher told him. "You can't think your way through tragedy!" And so he thought his way home, almost as fast as he'd fled in the first place.

He had one foot out the door—and more than a few other body parts, as he'd later tell it—when he saw her. He remembers the first sighting. Judy was there to audition, and he lingered around a practice room door while she sang 'Swinging on a Star' to an empty chair, after giving herself a starter note on the piano. She was bright, expressive and charming—a ball of light. Judy passed the audition, and they started going out, first in clumps of students and then alone. "A regular little Shirley Pimple she was," Jerry would say whenever he told the story of their meeting.

And so he lingered. He kept going to classes for a while but soon gave up the pretense altogether. He hosted a nightly poker game in an apartment he shared with two other guys, both also, eerily, named Jerry. They distinguished themselves by being Jer, Jerry and Jerome, but with all the poker playing, whenever someone held three kings, it was said they had 'trip Jerrys'. Judy would sit at his elbow, and he would urge her to 'be a little less expressive' when she saw his hand.

But less expressive was impossible for her, as he would find out over time. She was the queen of expressive, poker or no, not a pleasant set-up for a guy trying to think his way through tragedy. But she was pretty. A looker in the forties style, blonde curls, desirous eyes, and a stage-light smile. Performing, she was dazzling, a nightingale with a rack. And for some reason, she loved him, thought he was a real somebody.

He left California for Chicago and a job selling cars for a friend's father. Judy stayed, living with some of the girls in Pasadena. Jerry and Judy wrote long letters, a pile of which he found (and tossed) when they split up in 1970. It was a sell job, his. He wouldn't let her out of the showroom without the latest model Jerry Rosen. Judy hailed from Chicago, too, and after almost two years of correspondence and long visits—during which time he continued to do every woman who let him—she gave up show business and, with it, everything that made her a lively, interesting girl.

Not that it was love. He never loved anyone, except maybe the boy. He didn't have that kind of love in him. You just did what you had to do, like get married and, up until a certain point (that point being 1970), stay married. Then it all looks different. The stage light eyes become black holes, hungry to suck everything into the drama of Judy. The nightingale seems like a vulture, and the confidence is just con. She's still a pretty woman, he suspects, and people tell her so, but he can't look at her.

What is she thinking now? He wonders, as he circles Duluth yet again. Why is he going over and over this? He's only miles away from Canada. His life is behind him.

You can't trade in the past like a car. Or maybe you can trade it in, but you can't put it behind you. He wouldn't anyway. He wouldn't want a life without his son, even though that's the life to which he's about to exile himself. Drive all you want, as far as you want. You will be followed.

Year after year, the temperatures in and around the North Woods of Minnesota register the lowest in the continental US. It is cool up here until it is cold, then it's cold for a long time. Today, though, it's hot, that pocket of sweltering summer before the early fall begins. The air conditioner in the Skylark merely mixes the hot air around, so he lowers all the windows. He wishes he was driving the Triumph, top down, but it's too late for that. I am, Jerry thinks grimly, driving the Failure.

He pulls over at a sign pointing towards a fish camp on Tofte Lake. Jerry doesn't know what a fish camp is, but he imagines it as a kind of lakeside slaughterhouse, fishermen in yellow overalls pouring their jumpy haul out of buckets onto tables covered with newsprint. Cleavers rising and falling. Fish heads tossed in kettles, knives wielded by rubber-gloved hands slicing and gutting still-wriggling lake trout. The squish and squirt of galoshes on blood-rich, entrail-thick ground. *More likely*, he thinks, lighting up a Camel, *it's a couple old geezers asleep in ratty beach chairs with their fishing rods stuck in the mud.*

Maybe that's the way to live, like some Canadian Pappy Yokum, sluggish and shiftless and catch-as-catch-can. Sun himself by the lake in summer and stare into the ashes of a fire the other nine months. Stop fighting, stop running, listen to the strains of old-timey music coming from the porch of the cabin down the road. Jerry would choose that if he could.

But even in Thunder Bay—or anywhere else to which he might remove himself—it won't be so mellow yellow. (He likes that turn: I have removed myself.) He'll have to work. He'll have to find people. He'll have to keep moving even once he's removed.

In this heat, on the verge of these deep, thrumming woods, it's all too real. He has no energy for any of it. New places. Want ads. Coffee with other solitary men. Chasing aging tail. Join a bowling league? What would a friend be, who didn't know a fucking thing about you? He has no stomach for any of it. He wants to lie down in the dirt and die. It's that simple. The thought of starting over stops him.

He planned and planned and thought it through, but here he is almost at the crossing. There is only forward and, not for the first time, he wishes he could stop for good. Why can't he? His life—as he's known it—is already over. Every pathetic thing he's built is over. He's washed up and about to disappear as it is. Why not finish the job. Dayenu. It would have been enough, and it is enough.

He's staring not through the windshield but at it, parked off road at the edge of the woods. He is minutes from the Boundary Waters that can be crossed by canoe. They might as well be ocean. Maybe he just needs a nap. He knew it would be hard, and it is. The thick August air. The wall of green. All's wall that ends wall, he'd punned with his son, and so it ends. Can't go over it, kids chant, can't go around it. Gotta go through it.

Going through this literal green wall would mean driving the car he calls Failure into Tofte Lake. Skylark going down. He pictures it: the dirt road ahead, the crack of tires on that road, the line of the shore, the water. The still, unpeopled lake. A new plan is forming. He feels the breathy excitement of a bold idea. Locked windows with enough space for the water to get in and too little for him to get out. How much pressure will it take to hold the doors against any attempt he might make to get them open? How long will it take? The car will sink, won't it? He will disappear.

It's a horrifying thought, but it doesn't panic him. It feels natural, easy. More, it feels emboldening, this challenge. A short drive off a long pier, off a long life. Drowning in the drink. It could be a slogan: "Take the plunge. The Buick Skylark—for those moments in life when you just have to Let Go…"

In his mind, he rises to the challenge. His body is on alert, breath shallow, concentration fierce. He's gearing up, all his thoughts and emotions shuttering around a pinpoint focus. Someone will begin the countdown. He will start his engine, shift. His foot will find the gas. Let Go.

Minutes pass this way. The motor is off. He's nestled in the woods. He notes the quiet, punctuated by rustlings outside. He allows the womb-warmth to settle him. This is what he's wanted all along. Maybe it was the plan. The drive to the woods, the last drive.

Jerry undoes his belt and the clasp and zipper of his khakis. He reaches his hand under the elastic of his boxers and touches himself. His eyes stay open. Everything is canopied, cavernous. He is at the center of it, and he is separate.

His hand moves softly at first, almost tenderly. He grows thick and hard. His soft stroking turns to tugging, his hand moving faster. It's harsh on his skin, as though he's wresting something from himself: the last good feeling keeping him here.

He's sapping his own resistance. Maybe, when he comes, he'll be depleted as well as empty. He won't need to struggle. His foot will be heavy, the weight will carry him across the threshold. Like falling off a log. Or maybe he'll sleep, a cat's nap at the end of a long day. He'll wake refreshed, ready for the bracing drive through the wall of forest that stands between him and self-removal.

Chapter 19

At Saturday breakfast, delegations from every country in the Friedkin Olympics descend on Ollie's. They carry banners made from bedsheets, hastily cut felt pennants, and facsimile national flags, painted or sewn in the dark of night.

The Olympics happen on the last weekend before the final weekend, when the shows get performed for the parents on hand to retrieve their children. The Olympics are Friedkin's eleven o'clock number, the big song and dance before the curtain comes down. They are also the one activity where the Friedkin family's utopian vision is, in practice, a kind of blindness. Determined to model peaceful cooperation and love, the family settled years ago on the Olympics. Here was the active embodiment of a one-world vision, a chance for campers to identify with people from diverse cultures and political systems. Here was a collaborative competition that rewards individual accomplishment while steering clear of the sense of One Big Prize. Everyone can be a winner. Every team can excel at something.

Of course, in the greedy, hateful hearts of children, every prize is One Big Prize, every loss is devastating, and which nation you pretend to come from is nowhere as important as which nations you beat. The 1973 Friedkin Olympics were suspended due to the hostage siege at the Munich Olympics, the real ones, in September '72. The tragedy was too fresh. But now, after a year without, the kids are ready to be unleashed. They want to crush each other. The camp is split into twelve teams of roughly twenty players each. The teams will stay together, play together and eat together for the next two days until the end of closing festivities Sunday night, splitting up only at clean-up, rest period and bedtime, when everyone returns to their cabins, a forced mingling of enemies.

Maybe it's the skipped year, maybe it's a strange dearth of real leaders among the counselors, but whatever the reason, Philip Rosen and Larry Dorfman have leapfrogged all other junior counselors and many older associate counselors and been anointed Olympic co-captains. They join the other, more senior captains in a secret naming ceremony in which the team leaders chose their countries under the censorious eye of Sylvie. The map that emerges reflects the world as it looks from the Midwest, circa 1974: the USA, Israel, the USSR, Mexico, China, West Germany, France, Sweden and Great Britain. But Sylvie shuts down smart alecks angling for the likes of North Vietnam, Cambodia and Bangladesh, places too hot, at this historical instant, to touch.

When the upstarts Philip Rosen and Larry Dorfman announce their plans to captain, "the home of the overlooked and overworked, the underdogs of the underdogs, the butt of all bad humor—the great nation of POLAND," everyone expects Sylvie to veto. They expect her to rule Poland out for the very reason

Philip and Larry are using it: that for kids growing up around Chicago in the seventies, Polack jokes are even more rampant than Helen Keller jokes, and that for a camp founded on tolerance and peace, ethnic humor is a principal no-no. This and the fact that Poland is just plain out of bounds. Obviously. Jewishly. But Philip grasps Dorfman's hand, hoists it into the air and, with his free hand, raises up a light bulb. How many seconds will it take Sylvie to unscrew their lightbulb? But quicker than she can say, "Forget it," Philip and Dorfman holler out the refrain of what will be their national cheer: "POLAND. AND THAT'S NO JOKE!"

Sylvie can only shake her head in admiration at the good-natured audacity of the two boys. She throws her arms wide with a Tevye-like "Why me?" She appeals to God above. Apparently, God blinks because Sylvie shrugs again with an "All right already". She nods her "I'm-gonna-regret-this" approval. Because Sylvie is the public powerhouse of Friedkin, because she is Lila's holy-shit-here-she-comes sister, putting one past her is a major score. If the Olympics lasted only this night, Rosen and Dorfman would have already won.

By the time Uncle Bernie announces breakfast, Ollie's has been transformed into a global cafeteria. National colors drape the poles and walls. Country names float in the air, twirl overhead. Campers crash around the dining hall, human bumper cars steering towards their new countrymen. Cheers rise up over powdered eggs and yellow pancakes.

"Brezhnev, Khrushchev, Stalin, too; we're all for one and Nyets to you. Give me a U and an S and another SR. We'll do to you what we did to the Tsar!"

"Arriba, Arriba, go, go, go! We're hot. You're not. We're Mexico!"

And the Rosen-Dorfman riff: "We're Poland. We're Poland. We love Kielbasa. / We're Poland. We're Poland. We're Poland. Que Pasa? / We're Poland. We're Poland. Go eat a pierogi. / We're Poland. We're Poland. We're Poland. No jokey."

Telephone-like, the news of Kenny Tannenbaum's drumlin Indian burial mound discovery changes as it spreads. Some believe that Kenny has found the body of a dead Indian. Others that someone tried to bury Kenny in the drumlin. Still others hear that Kenny raises turtles by the train tracks.

Only Ollie the German cook refuses to get swept up in the madness. He hates these Olympics, the mess of moving tables, the rushing this way and that. Why can't they just eat quietly in their same seats like good children? He stands in the steamy kitchen, wiping his hands on his long apron, bellowing at the kitchen staff. "Vat zlobs. Get ze hell outta my kitchen."

At the last Olympics, two years earlier, a camper asked Ollie if he would be Germany's mascot. Mascot! A month later, he watched with humiliation as his own people were accused of doing nothing to protect those Israeli athletes. Why should he feel ashamed—a man whose living demands waiting hand and foot on little Jewish children? He does his job with discipline and without complaint despite their utter lack of respect. But by this time each summer Ollie and his wife Margaret are at their wit's end. They count the hours to their ten-day camping vacation in Fond du Lac. They live for those days, their slice of heaven before classes begin at the Jesuit prep school in Milwaukee where they run the kitchen.

Kathy Klein's morning writing ritual has been interrupted by the Olympics. Breakfast is the time she writes in her journal, between slugs of sugary tea, like a baby witch scratching demon symbols into the earth with a sharp stick. Her cabinmates know to ignore her; they know better than to interrupt the author at work. *The Diary of a Young Girl* is always beside her plate, but they overlook it.

Sitting at the France table, however, she has to be friendly, has to pay attention. It's hard. She hasn't slept. Her brain is a jumble of Philip, Dion, Philip. Surreptitiously, she grabs her napkin and, pulling a pen from her pocket, scrawls something on it and barrels towards Poland.

"Anne Frankenstein!" Larry Dorfman greets her. She pointedly ignores the jerk and drops the note on Philip's plate. Philip cups the napkin in one hand and, still conducting his team's cheer, reads it: "Sorry. Stupid to say everything will be okay. Your dad's strong, though. I believe he will make it through. Love, Kathy."

"Love notes?" Dorfman asks him.

Philip, Dion, Philip. Anne Frank prides herself on looking life dead in the eye. She scrutinizes her actions as she would a stranger's—without sentiment. She's no moral paragon—such a description would be laughable—but, if pressed, she would label her personal ethics, 'fastidious verging on the ferocious'. Her philosophic rectitude and devotion to truth, she could argue, have cost her friendships—most notably her former best friend Jody's. Her honesty has lost her opportunities as well. For instance, she blew the chance to direct a play at school when she told the student-author exactly what she thought of his work.

So who is the girl skulking out of Ollie's, a full five minutes after Dion leaves? *I'm the world's biggest worm*, she thinks. *No, littlest worm—incapable of turning even a dime-sized patch of earth.*

But Dion won't be bypassed. He's behind the camouflage netting that surrounds the tennis court, waiting for her. He's trying to figure out what just happened with them, just being last night, happened being a huge and lasting kiss. He sizes her up. She's pretty, but sometimes she's got a big old cloud over her head. What his mom would call a 'muddle cloud'.

"How are you doing this morning, my friend?" he asks, popping out and falling into rhythm with her steps.

"Fine," she says, her head dipping into her shoulders. "How are you, Dion?"

"I'm doing quite well, thank you. Got to love the Olympics because everyone's true colors come out. We get to see exactly where we live."

Kathy fights the impulse to stop and engage him on this point. Truth to tell, even before it occurred to her to kiss him last night, she thought that Dion was one of the most interesting kids at camp—insightful, verbally precise, original. He's just fifteen but seems older. What did he mean, "We get to see exactly where we live?" She opts for silent affirmation over inquiry.

"I've always liked you, Kathy. You're a stand-up girl. Smart, pretty. You've always been decent with me."

"I like you, too," she offers, dread crawling up her spine. "All those things are true for you. Except maybe pretty." If she would meet his eyes, he'd catch the glint of a joke.

Dion chuckles, part real appreciation, part politician's bluff. "I don't know. Some of the girls think I'm pretty." *No, he's exactly fifteen,* she thinks.

"Let me come to the point." Dion says to the air. "We spent some serious time together last night, kissing and such." He pauses, and Kathy wishes she could be sucked through some wrinkle in the universe. "Thing is," Dion continues, "this has me a little confused. Not knowing where I stand or what to do."

They stop on a vast slab of handprints from 1967. He strokes his beardless chin. "So I thought I'd ask you, just what you're thinking. Feeling maybe. Intentions and like that."

Anne Frank's mortified. She squints at him. "When you run for president, Dion, I'm going to vote for you."

He nods, smiling, genuine. "I appreciate your vote."

She matches his smile before lowering her gaze. "You know," he says, "I'm still a stranger here. Doesn't matter how long I've been coming." Something like a moan of sympathy escapes from her. Looking up, she sees him whole: the perfect cropping of his afro, the pearl of his teeth and the startling hesitancy of his eyes. So much happens in so little time each summer. It was just yesterday she saw Jody in the infirmary, she sat with Philip on the dock, she kissed Dion at the riding rink. What was she thinking? What is he asking her? Why wasn't it Philip she was kissing?

"I'm prepared to stand by my actions." Kathy sounds like a Southern gentleman who knocked up the mayor's daughter.

Dion releases breath in a long, slow stream. "Good," he says. "Solid," he adds, with the jerk of a fist.

"I've got to go now," she says. She moves quickly forward, her lips glancing off his cheek so quickly it isn't clear whether or not they touched.

"Tha's cool," he accepts, with a shrug. "Sure. Cool."

And from that moment of romantic agreement until the end of camp, Kathy Klein will do everything in her power to avoid Dion Robinson.

* * *

Jody has gathered pills from each of her hiding places—three Quaaludes, a handful of reds, three Valium and two tabs of White Cross speed. It's an unspectacular stash, just what's left at the end of the summer. Jody throws the latch on the door to the second-floor bathroom. She arranges her holdings on the thin glass shelf under the bathroom mirror. She tries to anticipate the effect of taking them all at once. She squints at herself in the mirror, calculating the damage. There's sweat above her top lip.

She feels sick. Jody turns to the toilet and expertly sticks two fingers into the gag spot in her throat. Just the smell of her breath off the back of her hand trips the reflex. She heaves several times, but little comes up. Not surprising. It's Saturday, and she's hardly eaten anything since Thursday night. Her throat burns.

Now her whole face is sweating, and she's shivering in that way she does. She goes back to the mirror. She's ghostlier. Her legs are antsy. She recalls little of the night she 'almost died', as she thinks of it, but her body remembers—being hoisted up by Dion, bouncing sick on his shoulder as he ran, the cold sweats of her day in the infirmary, the humiliation of rasping at Katie Klein as she bent over Jody's forehead with a wet cloth.

She rinses her mouth with water and without thinking reaches for the reds, plucking one out of the plastic bag. She's about to place it on her tongue when she remembers what she's there for. She flicks the capsule into the toilet watching the little red canoe of it float in the bowl. She dumps the barbiturates, then the Quaaludes, then the speed. She pulls four joints from her pants pocket and rips them in two. Rolling the halves between finger and thumb, she sprinkles grass into the water. She drops one Valium in and slips the last two into her pocket, as if hiding the switch even from herself.

She flushes and watches the swirl. She flushes a second time and checks to see there's no backup. As the bowl empties, she thrusts her hand back into her pocket and chucks the last two Valium in, where they catch the whirlpool and drown.

Jody wishes she could wash away her fear as easily as the drugs. She thinks she can do this. But even at an old fifteen, Jody knows that promises you make to yourself get remade. Lines get redrawn. They inch forward. Here she is throwing all kinds of pills down the drain less than two years after she snubbed druggie kids at school, dismissing them as 'heads'. *Them…*

For all her rebellious magnetism, Jody wants nothing much more for her future than the life she already knows. She wants to sing. She wants to be a mother. She wants a house on the North Shore, to be active at her temple. In order to get that, she's got to clean up her act. She will be good. Starting now. When she thinks of 'good', she thinks of Philip. He is her better self, and if she can ever let herself be with him, she can be that self.

She splashes water on her face, patting it dry with a stiff towel. She checks her face and pinches color into each cheek. She sprays several shots of Binaca on her tongue, swishes the foam and spits two times like a superstitious old woman. She flushes one more time for good measure and, catching her own reflection again, reaches for the door.

Chapter 20

Philip's story happens in several places at once, some known to him and some unknown. He's connected to these places, strangely, by the telephone in Uncle Bernie's office. The phone calls keep coming, and they are, as he's said of Kathy Klein, 'never not weird'. The Joni Mitchell lyric is in his head: "Tethered to a ringing telephone. In a room full of mirrors."

"Hi sweetheart," Philip's mother says on the other end.

"Mom?"

"I have it on very good information that your father's run away."

"What?" Bernie tracked Philip down on the Olympic soccer field to take his call, and half of him is still there.

"He's pulled a Marv," Judy says.

Philip can't make sense of any of this. She's talking about their friend Marv Shepard, who one day just disappeared. "Run away where?" he asks.

"Exactly," his mom exclaims, venomous.

"Why would he do that?"

"Oh, honey. Use your head. That's your father. I'm sorry to have to say it, but when the going gets tough, he gets going. It has ever been so."

Why does she sound like this, as if she's rehearsed her lines? "How do you know? I just saw him."

"You did? When?"

"What day's this? Saturday. I saw him Thursday," Philip calculates. "He took me out to lunch." He fingers the plastic wallet full of Traveler's Cheques in his pocket. "He told me about..."

"I knew it. They were right," she says.

"Who? Who's right?"

"The Jerrys. I talked to both of them, Jer and Jerome. They figured he'd gone up to tell you and kept on driving. He was supposed to have dinner with them both Friday night, before, well you know, before he pays the price. He never showed up."

"Driving where? Where would he go?"

"Anywhere. Oh honey, this is your dad all over. He makes a mess and runs away.

"So I called Mickey," she continues, "but, of course, he won't say anything. He's his lawyer. Pretends he doesn't know. He was a bastard during the divorce. Why should I expect different now?"

"Mom" is all he can say, as if the word means stop.

He's sitting at Uncle Bernie's office desk, but he might as well be at home with his mom after they split up. After the crying jags. She would get rational and begin sentences, "I'm sorry to say it, but…It pains me to talk about your father this way, but…" Sometimes he preferred the crying.

"And now, once again, just when my life is so full, so happy, it's the Jerry show again. Jerry ruining everybody's good time, ruining my chances…"

He can hear it begin, the livid tears. Pull it together, Mom, please, he thinks. "Who's there with you? Where are you?" Someone must be nearby, the way she's trying to control it.

"Eduardo's here. And our friends. I'm in New Jersey. You knew that. We were supposed to leave from New York."

"Well, you're still going, aren't you?" Philip asks, afraid of either answer. "I mean we don't know for sure."

"How can I leave? We're scheduled to fly out day after tomorrow."

"That's the day Dad goes to court."

"Of course, it is! How perfect! Could he have chosen a more perfect day?"

"I don't think he chose it, Mom."

"He won't show up. I know him. We might as well face it. Your father's gone."

Philip is straightening and rebending a paper clip from a shallow cup on the desk. He can't take any of it in. He can't believe his father's run away. This is just Mom and her theatrics.

"I'll just have to undo everything. When's your play? I'll come see your play. Why not? I don't have anything better to do now."

His play. All his plays. The only thing his parents ever agreed on. The way they asked him about rehearsals. The way they'd hang around the parties when he played the kids roles in startup theatres downtown or in local colleges. The way they'd soak up all the praise he got as if it were their own. Even at home, each of them would talk to him about his part, about the other people in the show, what this person said about how wonderful their boy was or what that person said about his stage presence. They would shine on him and blot each other out. They never fought in front of him, though his father's biting humor was relentless, as were his mother's imploring eyes.

"Look," he says, "we don't know anything for sure. Don't do anything sudden. Let's see what happens next week. I just saw him. He's probably been home since then. He'll show up in court and they'll figure something out." And as he says it, he knows it's not true. He understands all at once that his father is gone. He's known it all along. That's what he was trying to tell Kathy last night; he just didn't know he knew it.

"You don't know your father."

What can he say to that? "Mom. I have an idea. Don't change your plans. I'm here for two more weeks—the final week of camp and the week of post-camp. Go to Mexico. At least, you'll have a vacation. If you have to come back—"

"Of course, I can always come back. And I will, you know. I'll hop on the next plane."

"I know, Mom. We have two whole weeks. By then, we'll hear something for sure." He could feel her lightening at the end of the line. This is the way it works. This is how he takes care of her.

"You're right. I've let him rain on my parade enough. I deserve a vacation, at the very least. And who knows, maybe it will work out."

"I'm sure it will, Mom. Things always work out." Without thinking, Philip has been tearing Bernie's 'While You Were Out' memos off the pad. He pinches the phone between his shoulder and ear and tries to shuffle the pages back into a neat stack, looking around for some way to reattach them.

They talk for a little while more, but about how hot it is in Jersey, about how he's been made captain in the Olympics and how his team has only lost one game. "I have to go down to the Volleyball game. Then we have to finish writing our song and cheer," he says. The words are suddenly drained of meaning and size: 'game', 'song' and 'cheer'.

"Of course you do, Captain," she says. "You'll knock 'em dead."

"Thanks, Mom." When he hangs up—"Love you too"—he keeps checking the phone to make sure it's firm on the cradle. It can't be true what she said about his father. He can't have run away. It's just his mother making a scene.

Before he can even begin to figure it out someone bangs on the door. Philip jumps. The door flies open and Ollie, dressed in his apron and kitchen whites, bullies into the office and up to the lip of Bernie's desk. He is fuming.

"Dat's it!" Ollie bellows. "I'm through! These ingrateful, horrible, spoilt children!" He spits the word, a mouthful of sour milk. Only then does he see the sixteen-year-old Philip Rosen. He unties his apron and wrestles his way out of it.

Bernie is at the door behind him. "Ollie, Ollie, please. Settle down and tell me. Please," Uncle Bernie implores him. His hands are open wide, like a Jew on a mountain in a movie, questioning God.

"Svastikas is what is happening, Mr. Levine. Svastikas nail on my door. And no, I vill not settle down! This is not for settling. This is for quitting."

"For qvitting," echoes another voice from the doorway. Ollie's wife, Margaret, bustles into the office. She hooks her husband's arm and straightens up tall. She, too, quivers with fury.

"Please, Oliver, Margaret," Uncle Bernie says, sidling out of the way, "tell me what happened. There must be something we can do."

"I have told you vat has happened," Ollie roars. "These monster children you indulge, these animals dat run vild—they have pushed us too far." He snorts down at Philip.

"Too far," Margaret repeats, sticking out her proud bosom.

"Ve have come to expect rudeness. Ve have come to expect vulgarity. Ve have come to expect hooligans and looking down noses. But this is too much, writing svastikas on our door." He shakes his apron at Bernie and slams it on the desk. "No more! Ve vish now to be paid for our vork. Ve vill leave at once."

"At once!" Margaret agrees.

Philip tries to get to the door behind them. He's a small creature, slipping around mountainous backs and promontory breasts, a wall of agitated, heaving white. Harpo Marx in a world of Margaret Dumonts, the world suddenly clown show, all buffoon gestures, bellowed threats. Ollie and Margaret notice him escaping and turn together like skating bears on a music box. They glare at him.

"Philip, please," Uncle Bernie says. "Please excuse us."

"Sure, Uncle Bernie," he says and continues out of the camp office, down the hall, and through Anatevka's vacant lobby.

Each summer for sixteen years, with Swiss clock precision, Ollie the cook has threatened to quit. Each summer for sixteen years, Uncle Bernie's diplomacy has prevailed. Until now. His calming voice fails, his empathy fails, his humor fails. Words fail.

"Show me what they did," he finally says to the couple. "Show me what they did to you."

They form a furious, if blunt, parade, the three of them. Ollie leads, steaming out the side door of Anatevka, down the porch steps and across the camp's interior road. Margaret chugs behind him. Bernie's loose gait matches their pace. They bypass the dining hall entrance and enter an unobtrusive door, overwhelmed by a tall, pointy bush. Ollie pounds up a steep flight of stairs with framed embroidery patterns on the wall.

The cook and his wife halt at their two-room suite. The hand-painted scrollwork and room numbers have been recently retouched. This is Margaret's specialty. She has adorned the halls and landing. Each door is as bright and welcoming as an Alpine lodge. Birds hover, flowers wink and flat Bavarian couples stand ready. Ollie and Margaret block Bernie's view. They cluck and huff. Tall as he is, he can't see past them or over them. When the couple finally steps aside, he has to jockey around them in the cramped space.

He recognizes the symbol immediately. His heart bumps, his breath catches. Painted with the same confident precision as Margaret's Bauernmalerei, it is sheer black. It isn't a swastika, but it may as well be.

Screwed into the front door of Ollie and Margaret's private room is a large oval plaque, on which is painted a double cross in a vertical oval, the spoof-Nazi icon from Chaplin's *The Great Dictator*.

Bernie will later say, "I didn't know whether to laugh or cry."

In the moment, however, he snaps, "Some stupid kid. A stupid stunt, disgusting and hurtful. I'm so sorry, Oliver. I'm sorry, Margaret. Please accept my apologies. I will get to the bottom of this and make sure nothing like it ever happens again."

"Ve cannot accept your apology, Mr. Levine."

They stand at awful proximity in the hallway, a panting stalemate.

"This is from a movie, you know. Charlie Chaplin. It's no joke, of course, but it was meant as one." It's all he can think to say.

"I know vat it is, and I know vat it means," Ollie says.

"A sick joke," Bernie elaborates, flailing.

"And vould it be a joke," Ollie asks, "if I vere to paint the Yellow Star of Texas on the door to Friedkin's?"

The eloquent malapropism stuns Bernie. They clock the silence for a long minute staring at the image. "You have been an important and much-appreciated part of this family for a long time. I'll write you a check," Bernie says.

Chapter 21

He can't do it. He can't drive those final yards. After decades of inventing slogans to sell people things they don't need, he can't buy his own, can't 'take the plunge' or 'let go'. He can't remove himself. Despite all his planning, despite the bank accounts and credit cards, despite the beater car and the disintegrating trail. Jerry Rosen can't make himself vanish. He's the bogus magician and the dumpy assistant both, waving the wand, chanting the words and, arms flung in a spiffy showman's reveal, opening the starry box to find himself still inside, whore's corset and puckered tights, lipstick smeared and feathers limp.

No, he can't do it. He drove north from Duluth, but the border is impermeable. This invisible threshold might as well be the Berlin Wall.

He turns back onto Route 169 and stops in Ely for gas. He finds a bar in town and orders a beer. He's vamping, killing time before it kills him. He checks his watch. Minutes pass. He checks it again.

He has a friend, Marv Shepard, who did it. He left Chicago and disappeared for years. Marv was a pussy-whipped milquetoast of a guy and the last person on earth you'd think would have the chutzpah to leave his wife and kids, drop his business. But Marv made a new identity for himself. He stayed away for six years. One day—Jerry was never sure how—he turned up again. His family took him back. He got a job as a manager at Polk Brothers. He returned to something like the life he'd had before. His secrets stayed secret.

Jerry is a helluva lot ballsier than Marv. At least, he thought so. But he thought wrong. It is time to concede. He's been planning this a long time, and all the plans just crumble before the memory of afternoon sun off of Swallow Heart Lake. The image of his son standing in that sunlight. The sound of kids' voices floating up from the beach to the road.

Philip had been leaning against the gatepost outside of camp when Jerry drove up two days before (two days that might have been a lifetime). The boy's eyes were closed, as though he were listening to music. So much concentration on his face. So much future. Jerry can feel the spot where a meshuggeneh stick of a girl calling herself Anne Frank brushed against the corner of his mouth. She toppled across the front seat of his car, a pratfall from a kid who knows no more of the world than a cricket. Such innocents, all of them.

Now, he is in a bar alone in a damp northern town. If he had kept moving, he'd be alone in this damp bar, in some version of this town, every day of his life. But it wasn't this loneliness that pulled him back from the border. He sat in the stopped Buick at the edge of a lake with his hand in his pants. He shut his eyes and mentally flipped pictures: the mouths, breasts, bedroom eyes of this girl or that, ones he'd known or fantasized, photos from the deck of nude playing cards in the drawer by his bed and from the book of Swedish porn in the same drawer—trigger images he'd often used to bring himself to climax. Nothing worked. All the skin on the planet couldn't blot out the glistening of that lake, the arresting concentration on his son's face, the graze of the girl's mouth against his cheek. There's no death yet where Philip is. The world, where he is, is still clean. *There's a difference,* Jerry thought, *between spoiling the kid's naivety*—as he'd already done—*and ruining his life*. He had pulled his useless hand out of his pants and turned the car around.

The distance between Ely, Minnesota and Chicago is a little under 600 miles. Ordinarily, the drive would be a quick one, but earlier in the year, still-President Richard Nixon signed into law the 55-mph speed limit. Distracted as he is, Jerry Rosen sticks to it. The last thing he needs is to get stopped near the Canadian border. He heads south. He's choosing prison over exile is the way he thinks of it. More, he's choosing his youngest son's shining life over his own dirty one. He'll drive, sleep a few hours in a cheap motel and drive some more. He will get home Sunday afternoon, shower and make his court date Monday morning. He will face the music.

Where did that expression come from—face the music? Probably those Cagney or Edward G. Robinson movies where the gangsters pull Tommy guns out of violin cases, before mowing down their enemies. St Valentine's Day massacre, St Paddy's Day slaughter, Columbus Day genocide—some bulldog Napoleon in a fedora, talking out of the side of his mouth, is always ready to shoot the shit out of a bunch of guys waiting around for a concert. "We can make beautiful music together" ends with a pile of bodies. It's a bleak day for Jerry Rosen as he backtracks south, but he's feeling some brave oats, too. He was running from the rat-a-tat-tat, and now he's staring it down.

Chapter 22

The sign above the dining hall door still reads, "Ollie's Place," but Max is the one manning the kitchen at dinnertime. Max is Lila's husband; he has arrived for the weekend, as he does every weekend at the end of his workweek in Chicago. Every weekend, they are complete, the sisters and their husbands: Lila and Max Sahlins, Sylvie and Bernie Levine. Max drives up to camp late Fridays and leaves at dawn on Mondays. He takes the teenagers water-skiing and scuba diving, smokes his cigars on the side porch of Anatevka, and shoots the shit as he serves up Bratwurst and burgers at the all-camp cook-out each Sunday night. He has rapport with the boys. It's the sergeant in him. Bernie, by contrast, a former Air Force captain, stationed in London from 1942-45, relies on a gentleman's persuasion, a handshake instead of a crack on the back of the skull. Both are effective, even beloved, but Bernie is here day after day, so his influence is more overarching. They are business partners, but it's clear to everyone that, even thirty years after the war, Bernie still outranks his brother-in-law.

Max always stays for the final nine days of camp, the end-of-season descent into chaos—the Friedkin Olympics; dress rehearsals; the handprint ceremony; visiting weekend; closing performances arranged so that every one of 250 kids gets part of a part, including at least one song and scene; teen prom and that blessed Sunday when every last one of them trickles off home. This time, though, Ollie is gone, and the day the family knew would come is here. Max will cook for the masses. So much for the motorboat and skis. They all know the mock-swastikas upstairs were one of Marty Ball's pranks, like the time he painted Lila's dog, Miffed, red, white and blue for the Fourth of July. Marty made a smart-ass move, and Max has traded his scuba gear for a chef's apron.

He has his 'I'm concentrating here' look on, and Lila knows better than to bother him. She can't keep away. She keeps 'just checking in'. She wants him to have his vacation—God knows he works hard enough—wants him to have his water-time, his porch sitting, his nights with her when it's quiet and the trees are stirring. That Robert Frost line about trees is a stuck record in her mind: "They are that that talks of going, but never gets away." It's Max's song: a Kerouac who never found the road, remained home in the Midwest, raised a family through the labor of staying put.

Her dear man will be rooted in the kitchen, from 5:30 in the morning until two in the afternoon, and again from four to seven or eight. He won't complain. But the set of his jaw will grow stern and the spot on his upper lip above his pencil moustache will tremble. They all work hard, but they work for love. He works to make their labor of love possible, holding up his corner of the family by managing operations at a liquor distributor. Every year they think will be his last, and it never is. Bernie is too conservative. Someday the camp will sustain them all, but not yet. So Max does his duty. The warehouse gets him, the systems and the men. Hendrickson Fine Liquors—"We Ship Everywhere"—is Friedkin's silent partner.

What is Lila doing crowding him? *Not helping* is what she's doing. She should be pestering Ziggy, their technical director and one-man scene shop. She heads back to her table to do just that. After all these years, Ziggy still thinks that as long as scenery shows up for opening, everything's fine. Rehearsal means nothing to him. Tech means time to finish building and hanging. She sits beside him and, for a moment, watches while he sword swallows fish sticks. "I've been thinking, Ziggy," she says, "it might be nice for the children to practice on the platforms and get used to the lights. Don't you think?"

And he answers the same way he has a hundred times before: "They're more spontaneous when they discover the environment for the first time."

"Ten-year-olds don't need more spontaneity," she argues. "They need to know where they're going, so they don't bump into each other."

"Everybody needs more spontaneity," he smiles.

How do you argue with daisies and peace signs and happy happy? *We couldn't do like that*, she thinks. *We had to build a world, so that these Candides could lark around in it. Oy, sometimes you wouldn't know there was a war on, you wouldn't know we've had a crook in the White House choking the life out of everything Roosevelt (a god!) and Johnson (a bastard!) built.*

Max prods the kitchen staff with affectionate sarcasm and gruff direction. Kids shuttle through with platters and bowls for refills. The sight of Max in kitchen whites sparks speculation, first at lunch and now at dinner. Ollie quit. Ollie was fired. One of the kitchen boys punched him out. Ollie left town with a woman on the Schwartzkopf's cleaning staff. Margaret went on a bender and Ollie is babysitting her in the drunk tank.

Staff prankster Marty Ball—almost certainly the guy who hung the sign on Ollie's door— meanders into the kitchen on the pretense of filling a bowl of salad. He sidles over to the walk-in. Max is there, hauling out an eight-gallon jar of bug juice. "Where's Colonel Klink?" he asks with a twinkle.

Max pauses. His arms bulge with the weight of the cherry drink. "You tell me." Marty flashes a heck-if-I-know-what-you're-talking-about grin and spreads his arms, as if he has nothing to hide. Max gives him a calm scorcher of a look and says, "Marty, stop being so full of shit."

* * *

The Olympics song and cheer competition follows dinner clean-up. Poland's song 'Stanislaw, Superstar' is a hit. On top of this first-place finish, Philip and his co-captain Larry Dorfman have hit upon an inspired, winning idea for their final team skit. In four games, they have a single loss behind them—soccer. Now, fresh from the night's singing sensation, they taste victory on their tongues. It's leaking out the corners of their mouths. For them, mere junior counselors, to win the Olympics would be historic, a coup.

After the Saturday night song competition, the co-captains head to a bar out of town in Philip's new Triumph to write their sure-to-be-winning skit. It's been two days since he drove out of the parking lot at Injun Joe's. Two days since his father, preparing him for what was to come—the car itself—tossed him the keys and said, "Take a turn. Drive me somewhere. Let's see how you handle it." Now it's foreign to him, indecipherable, possibly explosive.

He sticks the key in the ignition and turns it, half expecting detonation. The car starts like any other. He revs the motor and searches the five-speed for reverse. When he tries to back up, the car dies.

"Every car is its own beast," Dorfman says.

"Yeah."

"Just like every girl," Dorfman adds.

Please don't be an asshole all night, Philip thinks.

Dorfman is, in fact, a handsome and talented asshole. He is also Philip's biggest competitor—for roles and girls. A latecomer to Swallow Heart Lake, Larry was a grown-up fourteen when he arrived three summers ago. With his Music Man smile and muscular immigrant drive—he is one of a handful of kids at camp whose parents still speak Yiddish at home—he wowed Sylvie. Within a fortnight of his arrival, Sylvie let it be known that she was grooming him for great parts: Billy Bigelow in *Carousel*, the King in *King and I*, Tevye—roles Philip had dreamed of doing since he was eight.

Burning with jealousy, sweet Philip Rosen started badmouthing Larry before midsummer of Dorfman's first year. "He's a prick," Philip announced to his then-girlfriend Jody Gold while they were making out on the beach one night. "Melly says he pushed her into a tree when she wouldn't kiss him."

"Melly Barber has never refused to kiss anyone," Jody replied, "let alone Dorfman."

"What do you mean, let alone Dorfman?"

"Well, c'mon, you know…He's cute. He's manly."

"He looks like Dudley Do-Right."

"Maybe that's why girls like him."

"He's a pompous bastard."

"You're just jealous," Jody said sweetly. "I don't know why. Everybody loves you. All the girls want to marry you."

"Yeah, in ten years. Now they want to fuck around with assholes like Dorfman."

Does Dorfman note Philip's antagonism? Yes, and it irks him because he likes Philip, respects him, just as, truth to tell, Philip likes and respects Dorfman. For three summers as cabinmates, Dorfman has in his own way tried to befriend Philip. More than once he's burst out, "What did I ever do to you, Rosen?" This year, as first-year junior counselors, they've mostly avoided each other. Now, they are co-captains of a winning Olympics team. Philip is trying to rise about jealousy.

The car jerks backwards, but he keeps it running. At the desolate corner, he waits extra-long before turning, as though another car might come out of nowhere.

None of the local bars card anyone, but they want to get away to write in peace. They head for Woodee Bar in Pontiac Point, between Swallow Heart Lake and Sheboygan.

Dorfman muses. "I'd hate to be the poor schmuck it's named after. A guy called Woodee has gotta have something to prove."

They hit Route 57. Philip shifts into fifth and tightens his grip on the steering wheel. He has a palpable sense of his father sitting where Dorfman's sitting now. He fights the urge to look.

"What a day!" Dorfman calls. He sings the theme song from *Mister Rogers' Neighborhood*, interrupting himself only to say, "Nice car."

Dorfman's right about all of it: the day, the car. Half right. Tonight's victory was sweet, but driving through the dark country, Philip finds himself at the wrong end of the tunnel. He's flying blind.

The terrain doesn't change, but the drive feels treacherous. Philip holds his breath at each twist and turn. He can't always see what's ahead. His brights hit the centerline, but every time there's a hill or rise, the line seems to stop at the crest of the road. He's afraid that the road will end, and they will plummet into something endless and empty. Like falling into the black sky.

"Larry?" he ventures, and though he's speaking loudly to be heard over the sounds of driving, his voice is tentative. "Was your mom really in the holocaust?"

Dorfman looks at him and, after a beat, chuckles. Then, as if beating Philip to the punch-line of a joke, says, "She still is."

Philip clutches for no reason. He rides the brake. When they see illuminated signs for Old Style, Pabst and Schlitz, he swings too fast into the gravel parking lot, and the car fishtails. "You should downshift," Dorfman says.

"Yeah," Philip pulls up to the low, wide cabin that is Woodee, in between a pickup and a modest motorcycle. Another pickup with a trailer holding a racecar is parked at the far end of the lot.

Nobody looks up when they enter. Four skinny guys play Foosball. At the bar a couple of men talk while staring straight ahead. Philip cranes his neck to see the face of the girl on the other side of them. Dorfman smacks his hands together and rubs the palms. He orders two Special Export beers, fried cheese curds and a couple of brats. "One mit *zauerkraut!*" he demands. He grabs the pints and moves to a table by the front picture window, the brightest spot in the room to write the best Olympics skit in history.

Sitting at the far end of the bar, Melly Barber pays no attention to them. She smokes a filterless cigarette with macho ease. She may be a fifteen-year-old summer camp deserter, but she's got the air of a world-hardened, film noir broad. Melly is one of the few Californians at camp. She's from Malibu, a kid who gets stoned with the children of movie stars. But she might have grown up on a horse farm, the way she rides. She wears cowboy boots to the beach, and, legend has it, has been fucking, unapologetically, *unselectively*—(boys, girls, teachers, counselors, townies)—since she was twelve. Philip has known her since he was nine. She's the most intimidating friend he has, that magnetic sister who pops in after months away, tells tall, fabulous tales of places off the map and disappears, taking the family silver with her.

Philip reaches across the bar for napkins, "Hey Mel."

"Hey sweet boy. What are you doing with dickhead?"

"We're writing our skit."

"Oh right," she says. "Everybody's a champion."

"How'd you get here, Melly?"

She raises her cigarette like someone throwing a dart, "Guy over there gave me a ride on his bike."

"Where'd you meet him?"

"Hitching."

"Jesus, Melly. Be careful."

"You're such a good boy, Philip." She mashes her cigarette out, takes his hand and kisses his palm.

"Yeah, thanks. Let me give you a ride home when we're done. I have a car."

"Maybe baby."

He looks over at Dorfman who's eating a brat with one hand and writing with the other. "What team're you on?"

She raises an unenthusiastic fist. "El Salvador. Making the world safe for the revolution."

"Right, the national anthem, 'El Salvador, The Beautiful', that was pretty bogus."

"Why do you think I'm drinking?" She throws back the last of her bourbon and bumps the empty glass forward, raising one finger to the bartender.

"Let me know when you want to go or, whatever, vice versa," Philip says.

When he turns to go, she pinches his butt. "Such a good boy."

"Don't mess with that one, my man," Dorfman says as Philip sits down. "She'll eat your balls for breakfast."

Philip ignores him. "Your funeral," Dorfman says.

By 1:00 a.m., Philip and Dorfman are flying—high on creative juice, thrumming with the knowledge that they've found the vein, struck gold. The history of Friedkin is about to be rewritten. Dorfman raises the holy text up, where it shimmers blue and red in the light of the Pabst sign.

Philip finds Melly. She's smart-mouthing a couple of Plymouth boys, the type who played high school football ten years ago and still think they're on the team. She's flirting by telling them how stupid they are. Philip forklifts her out and she flips the guys off, swearing, "I'll be back!"

"We'll still be here."

"Bet you will, Tin Man." They blow kisses.

Dorfman starts right in. "You're such a slut, Barber. Didn't your mother tell you not to talk to strange men?"

"I talk to you."

"You act like a 40-year-old drunk divorcee. What are you, thirteen? Have you had your Bat Mitzvah yet?"

"I'm not Jewish, Dorkman."

"Maybe you should convert," Dorfman says.

"I like foreskin too much."

"Acchh," Dorfman gags. "What a pig."

"Guess you can't eat me then."

"I'm gonna make you guys walk." Philip guns the engine.

"Do you know what treyf is, Barber?"

"Mom! Dad!" Philip shouts over the motor.

"Does the concept of unclean mean anything to you?" Dorfman asks.

"Does the concept of look in the mirror mean anything to you?"

"Take my advice, Melissa—"

"I wouldn't take anything you have, Dorkman—"

"—I know you think it's cute to be all *slutty* and *dangerous*—"

"I know you think it's cute to be all slutty and dangerous," Melly mimics.

"—But one day you're gonna turn up naked and dead in one of these fields."

"I guess that'll be your best chance to screw me."

"Jesus Christ, you two. Fucking shut up!" Philip grips the wheel, shaking. They haven't left the parking lot.

Melly sits on the shelf in the back of the two-seater. She sulks.

Philip pushes the tape in. Paul McCartney sings 'Two of Us'. He jacks up the volume. They crawl over the gravel and turn onto the road.

Melly stretches her arms as far as they go. She drops her head back. When they pass under streetlights, Philip catches sight of her in the mirror. Her hair ripples out behind them.

"Pull over," she says.

Philip doesn't hear her.

"Philip, pull over!" They are maybe a mile from camp.

"What is it?" he asks, slowing.

She doesn't respond, but her head lolls. Philip brakes to the shoulder. She hangs out of the car.

Melly vomits. Dorfman makes disgusted noises from the front. Philip puts a hand on her back.

"Just cleaning the palette," Melly says, wiping her mouth on tail of her shirt. She climbs out. "Thanks for the ride, Philip. I'll walk from here."

Philip opens his door and follows her.

"No problem, sweet guy," she says. "I know the way from here. We're almost at the stables." She tramps away.

"Let her go," Dorfman says.

"You sure?" Philip calls to Melly. She waves without turning.

"She'll find her way," Dorfman says. "Girls like that always do."

Philip watches her hew a path along the side of the road. He drives slowly keeping Melly in his sights.

"Pick up the pace, captain," Dorfman says. "Long day tomorrow."

Philip trains an eye on the rearview.

"She'll get back," Dorfman assures him. "Trust me. Even the cows aren't stupid enough to fuck with her."

Chapter 23

"What the hell are you doing?" Jerry asks himself out loud. Canada is behind him, with its promise of escape. Minnesota is behind him, too, a black hole of memory and provenance. It's dark on Wisconsin roads at night. No cars. Stars he ignores. Dark road, dark fields. Dark night of the soul. He wishes it were somebody else's night and somebody else's soul.

For all he's been through, why is it the call to his ex-wife that makes him jumpy? This is facing the music. She will look at him and see a man as bad as the one he sees. Worse. It's one thing to be your own monster. To be someone else's, someone who once loved you—that's bottom. How could he take the boy away, too? But Philip kept on him. And this year, with early admission to college an eager year away—Philip always racing ahead of himself—Jerry had relented and offered a home away from her. Now he'll have to beg.

He tried a month earlier, and she told him to clean up his own mess. Once he committed to leaving the country, he figured, "Fuck it, fuck her. She'll have to figure it out." He hates to admit it—that he'd planned to leave the boy hanging that way.

But he can't really blame Judy—Judith, as she's now calling herself. She owes him nothing. Yes, she was a miserable, self-centered basket case, but Jerry was a bona fide bastard. He cheated from day one, schtupping anything that crossed his path. He treated her like an idiot. He sniped at her in public, belittled her over a thousand hands of bridge, sliced her with sarcasm and diced her with superior knowledge. And he wasn't just a bastard; he was a coward. He knew the minute they got married it was the wrong thing. Where was the gorgeous, independent girl he'd fallen in love with? Her get-up-and-go, as they say in the song, got-up-and-went. He knew, yet he dug in for twenty years, intent on punishing her for the betrayal.

The biggest punishment was the one he never revealed. Soon after Philip was born in '58, Jerry determined that Judy's maternal competence was in limited supply. Jerry saw her with the baby, heard her misery, month after month—she didn't know how to be a mother, she cried. Her life was being stolen from her.

He hired a live-in 'to help with the kid and house'. To the solidly middle-class Skokie neighbors, this smacked of pretension and neglect. The Rosens thought they were big shots. He hurried her back to their nightclubs, bridge and cocktail parties, anything to get her out of the house and back to the land of the living. Then he got a vasectomy. No more kids, he decided, without telling his wife. Enough with the drama.

A couple of years later, when she made noises about a sister for Philip, he said, "Sure," and they had a time of it for a year or two. "Maybe it's for the best," he comforted her when nothing happened. It may have been the one loss she ever took in stride. She *knew*, he believed. Not that he'd made himself sterile, but that she was no parent. She knew.

Halfway home, he pulled over to call her, to prostrate himself for Philip's benefit, to swallow the last gob of his pride. He had a number in Fort Lee, New Jersey, where she was staying before her pilgrimage to Mexico. Same place they'd honeymooned. Nice touch.

All he was asking was for her to look after their kid. She would rake him over the coals.

"Is Judy there?"

"Who's calling please?"

"It's Jerry. Could you tell her it's important, please?"

"Judith?" the voice said, off the phone, "Jerry for you. Says it's important."

"Hello?" she answers, as if she has no idea who is calling.

"Judy, it's me. We have to talk. Can you talk?"

"Jerry? Where are you?" Silence on his end. "Where are you, Jerry? Where are you calling from?"

"Why? What does it matter where I am?"

"I heard you'd run away. Should I say 'run away as usual'? Where are you?"

"Who told you that?" he asks. She says nothing. "Who'd you hear that from?"

"I have my sources."

"I'm in Chicago," he lies. "Where else would I be?"

"How long will you be there, Jerry? How long will you be staying in Chicago?"

"What do you mean? I live here."

"Really, Jerry? Where's here?"

"C'mon, Judy. You know very well where I live."

"I don't know any such thing," she says, "I don't know anything about you. And it's Judith."

"Oh, Jesus."

She relaxes. Maybe Jerry—despite his lying tongue—is speaking the truth. "So if you're in Chicago, I guess I can go ahead with my plans, even though I've spent the past two days rearranging everything, after you abandoned your only son."

"No," he says.

"No what, Jerry? No I haven't undone months of planning or no you haven't abandoned Philip?" What can he say? "What is it, Jerry? I'm very busy. I can't really talk."

Busy? What the hell has she ever been busy with? She hasn't done a fucking thing in her life, he thinks. He bullies on. "Look, you were right, okay? I'm a schmuck and this proves it, but I'm going to jail. Monday. It's settled, except for how long. You need to come back and take Philip."

Dramatic pause. Always dramatic, that Judy. "I thought you wanted him to live with you this year," she says, as if she hasn't heard the most essential facts.

"I did. I do." But they don't take kids where I'm going, he wants to say. "I'm not sure what you expect me to do…"

"I'm not sure what you expect me to do. I wanted Philip with me. I always want him with me. But you worked out this little scheme with him and I made other plans. Do you need me to remind you what we arranged? He'll be with me in San Miguel over Christmas and spring vacation. I'll come back early in May, so he can be with me for a month before he leaves for camp and college. That's what we worked out."

"I thought you rearranged everything."

"I just arranged it back. You being in Chicago."

"What, did you call the airlines while we were on the phone?"

"Don't get sarcastic with me. You have no right to get sarcastic with me. No one will blame me if I hang up on you."

"Okay, okay, Judy. Look. What do you want me to do? I fucked up. I'm going to be downtown. In a cell. You know this. How much do you need me to spell out? I can't make this one right. There's no right. There's just fucked. Me. Fucked."

"For a change," she says.

"Look. Nobody's asking you to do anything for me—"

"Good…because I wouldn't—"

"It's Philip. It's his last year…"

"You don't have to remind me of my responsibility to my son, Jerry. Maybe someone should remind you. You promised him this. You did whatever it is you do to make him think his mom is a nut job and he should live with you—"

"I never—"

"And so he planned on it. Like Christmas. A year with Dad like Christmas all year. You made a promise, Jerry. Not that that ever meant anything to you."

"What do you want me to do? What can I do?"

"How about screwing yourself, Jerry. You screwed everyone else."

He knew she would find a way to hang up on him. And he knew that when he called her back, the phone would just keep ringing. He couldn't blame her.

He can only hope that when it comes to their son, she will step up and step in. He's done what he can.

Chapter 24

Jody Gold is drooling from the side of her mouth, burrowed in her pillow like she means to stay for winter. Philip has a hard time waking her. He taps her shoulder then shakes it. He whispers her name closer and closer to her ear. He tugs at her pillow; she tugs back. He's about to give up when her eyes open, and she sits up.

She's disoriented. The illuminated dial on the dresser reads 1:40, but it feels like five a.m., like she's been popping reds and crashed. She hasn't. She went to bed early and clean, nothing in her body but the day.

What's Philip doing here, she wonders. Then she thinks, *That can't be Philip.* Philip is her old boyfriend, was her old...oh, it's too confusing. What summer is this? She's dreaming a sweet dream reward for going to bed sober. She promised herself to be good, and now goodness itself has come to her bedside in the shape of Philip Rosen. She drops back onto the pillow.

Philip shakes her again. A light from Tobacco Road sets her adorable face aglow. He wants to kiss it.

"Jodyyyyy," he calls from the spirit world.

She's up again, on one elbow. She covers her dragon-breath mouth with her free hand. She flips her hair to loosen it. "Hi, Philly."

"What are you doing here?" Philip prompts.

"What are you doing here?" Jody echoes.

"Right. What?"

Jody's heart races. She wonders if he can hear it.

"Can you come out and play?" Philip asks.

"Are you drunk, Philly?"

"Hell, no," he says, stage-slurring like a sloshed guy. He smiles, straight again. "Just a couple beers for courage."

It's quiet. Other girls might be listening. Lisa Climan rolls over in her bunk.

"Wait out the back," she whispers. "Gimme a minute."

He starts to go, stops. "You're coming? For real?"

"Te adoro, Anton," Jody says, in her demure, Maria voice. As Tony and Maria, they play a love scene in *West Side Story*. Their duet seems to have rekindled another scene they've played on and off over the past three summers, when one or the other of them decides it's time to get together again, which they inevitably do, until it's not time anymore or Jody remembers the reasons she'd rather be with a different, more experienced, less *nice* boy. Jody is, as her former-best-friend Katie Klein says, "The girl who cries *for wolf*."

Philip exits backwards, not bothering to check the hall for counselors. His heart flies after him.

There's a movie in his mind: Jody clutching her pillow, Melly crossing a field, Dorfman singing in the wind. "Stanislaw Superstar, where did you find such a fancy car?"

At night, the quietest spot at Friedkin may be the place where two fences meet below Philip's cabin, Paint Your Wagon. Coved by trees, it's protected from camp traffic and sheltered from the sky. Philip and Jody gravitate there, as Philip recaps the feud between Melly and Dorfman. He wants to talk to her, and he wants to touch her. He wants to kiss her, and he wants to ask her about something. He wants to ask her about damage.

He wants to tell her about the Ho-Chunk Indians that Kenny Tannenbaum thinks are buried under the drumlin in the field. How Philip now thinks we're dancing on bones. He wants to ask Jody about this thing she told him the last time they were together.

"You know when my Bubbe died, Zayde went into his room and never came out," Jody confessed.

"But that was two years ago," Philip remembered.

"I know how long it is. And my dad acts like nothing's wrong."

Philip doesn't know how to believe her. Jody will say whatever she needs to say to draw sympathy. But he can see this is true. "But your mom would never let that happen…"

Jody hesitates, "My mom brings him his meals and newspapers and cigars. He won't let her take anything away."

"What do you mean," he asked.

"The man got out of Dachau, but he's afraid to come out of his room."

He had no idea how to make sense of what she was telling him then. Now, he thinks he needs to understand.

"I'm so glad you came for me, Philly. I think I was dreaming of you," Jody says.

"Me, too," he says, chest expanding.

Philip sits on a stump against the fence, Jody on his knees. Jody has that look in her eyes. Does she practice it? It slays him.

"I've been thinking," she says. "Why aren't we together?"

"I don't know," he says.

"We should be."

"I know."

"I want to be," Jody tells him.

"Me too."

"And not just for now."

It's Philip's turn to think he must be dreaming. Or maybe they're rehearsing some grand love story. He kisses her. She kisses back. They fit like a puzzle. Click. He remembers everything about the way she kisses.

"What about Jack?" He has the presence of mind to ask about Jody's current boyfriend when they come up for air.

"Old news. We broke up last week."

"Why? Why'd you break up?"

"Well, for one thing, he told me he'd fucked Melly."

"And you were surprised?"

"I know. I shouldn't be surprised about anything with that guy. Anyway, I'm on the straight and narrow." She kisses his ear. "I've always loved you, Philly."

It registers with Philip that he is 'the straight' choice, that he's just been called 'narrow'. But his skin is so alive, and Jody's breath is warm and perfect. He kisses her again. His hand, under her blouse, runs up and down the satin of her back.

Something moves over Jody's shoulder, a shadow weaving through the trees. Someone is bobbing up and down outside Philip's cabin window. Someone is looking for Philip. They both see her.

"K!" Jody calls in a hoarse whisper. "Klein!"

Kathy doesn't hear. "K!" Jody hops off of Philip.

"Klein!" Jody brims with delight. This is too much. In one night, she has the chance to get together with Philip and to make up with her best-ever friend. "Klein!"

Philip loves the way Jody sprints, the light tennis step, the pendulum swing of her hips.

"What are you doing here?" Kathy asks, stricken.

"I'm so happy to see you. Philip and I are so happy to see you."

When Philip appears at Jody's shoulder, Kathy winces the way you would at a fist flying towards your nose. She's been all over camp, combing the camp for an hour, after seeing that Philip's car was back. Worried about Philip. Worried sick. "Philip and I," Jody said. *When did they become Philip and I?*

"No," she says. "I was looking for—" She's staring at Philip.

"Hey babe, what are you looking for?" Jody asks, quoting a song they both like.

Jody is teasing her as if they were friends, best friends. But that was years ago, three years ago, when they were twelve and their cabin was Alice in Wonderland; Jody Gold and then-Katie had been inseparable. They'd shared their first cigarette. They'd written letters for each other to friends back home. And they were compelling. Younger girls emulated them; younger boys lined up to brush their hair, pining for them in exquisite presexual ways. Older guys swaggered and flirted in their presence. Even the full-blown teenage girls felt the attraction. Like precocious, beautiful baby sisters, the pair inspired pride and fear. They infected the universal dream life of Friedkin. The twelve-year-old power couple of Jody and Katie became known as The Alices.

The next summer Jody threw Philip over for a state senator's druggie son named Elliot. She broke Philip's heart and, as always, left Kathy to play nursemaid to the boy she loved best. To their cigarette stash, Jody added Quaaludes, reds and White Cross speed. She added a 20-year-old counselor named Cutler to her collection of boy trophies, and Kathy, who had grown serious, decided her best friend was, in fact, the devil. They went from telling each other everything to barely speaking. Now it's happening again: Jody's wrapping gullible Philip around her witchy fingers.

"I was worried because—"

Kathy trickles off and crashes into the woods.

Jody and Philip hear the crack of branches. They hear her grunt, "Fuck! Fuck!" when she gets jabbed, when she trips on a root. Kathy doesn't know where she's going or even why she ran away from Jody and Philip. She couldn't stomach Jody's happy face or Philip's love-drunk eyes.

They let her disappear, take each other's hands, and walk back the way they came.

Kathy plunges deeper into the woods, ducking under limbs of trees, holding her arms in front of her eyes.

* * *

There is singing in the woods. It's coming from somewhere in front of her. Kathy recognizes the voice. She knows the song. She moves towards it.

She slows, brushing leaves off her face. There's a clearing around the Butcher's House, hidden in the thick summer foliage, a jagged circle of tree stumps. The nearly full moon has found the opening and given it luster. She glimpses something like dancing. The singing is deep and confident, a listen-if-you-will voice, rehearsing, getting it right. Beside the Butcher's House, where no one goes, at two-something in the morning, Larry Dorfman is practicing 'If I Were a Rich Man'.

He moves as though directing himself. He repeats the 'didle, didle, didles' several times. He dances around a tree stump, arms overhead, hands and fingers like so many snakes, cavorting in the air. He capers back the other way, alone under God's droll gaze.

When he finishes the song, Larry yawns, kicks a stump with the toe of his sneaker. Kathy steps out of the trees. "You make a good Tevye," she says. If he's surprised, he doesn't show it. He just says, "Thank you." He looks like he's about to say something else, but he doesn't. He just arches an eyebrow histrionically.

If Kathy Klein had a top ten most despicable list, Larry Dorfman would take first place. He's puffed up and superior, a poseur, an unfailing misogynist. He's also a thrilling singer, she has to admit, and a magnetic presence onstage. He's the type of jackass her mother dates.

Kathy crosses to Dorfman and kisses him on the mouth. He doesn't kiss her back. "I thought you had a boyfriend. Isn't Philip your *boyfriend?*" The word oozes out.

"Philip is not my anything," she says without feeling. She goes for Dorfman's mouth again, as if to wreck herself against it.

He lets her kiss him. Pushes his tongue against hers, before breaking off. "I thought you loathed me."

"I do," she says and means it. She kisses him to avoid looking at him. But Dorfman steps back.

"Why should I kiss you, Frankenstein, if you hate me so much?"

"Because I'll let you."

She lurches for his face. There's something pathetic about Kathy playing the slut to Dorfman, and he feels it. He shoves her away, hard, but she flies at him again, pressing not just her mouth against his, but her whole scraping body. His fingers dig at the back of her rib cage. Again, he pushes her off him.

Again, she steps at him, head up, almost defiantly.

Dorfman hits her. Smacks her across the cheek and jawline with the flat of his hand. The slap stuns her. She can't move. She is a very young girl.

He raises his hand again, taunting. "Hey," is all she manages. Dorfman pulls Kathy to him, crams both of his hands into her shirt and squeezes her breasts. "You're so flat," he says, in a tone that says 'how very odd.'

Kathy freezes. Through their clothes she feels his penis against her hip bone. He forces her to the ground. Her knees buckle. "No, Larry, stop."

She can't tell if he hears, can't even tell if she's said the words out loud. He keeps pressing her down until she's lying on a bed of sticks and leaves. Dorfman kisses her, if it can be called that, this mashing at her mouth. He pins her shoulder with his left hand. His free hand wrestles with his belt and button and zipper. He yanks his shorts down, but he isn't all the way out of his pants. His erection knuckles into the muscle of her thigh.

He grabs at her zipper. She screams no, no, no, but the sound doesn't get past her throat. From above, she looks like a girl who fell to earth and lies where she fell, paralyzed and suddenly awake.

He doesn't strip her, but tugs away enough of her underpants to shove two fingers inside. He jams his fingers in and out, while he humps her leg through his shorts. The cutting pain brings her back to herself. The way she pictures it, as if she's standing over herself, it looks as though he's stabbing her.

Still grinding against her thigh, Larry groans like something strangled. He stops. He adjusts his pants, his belt. He shakes his left wrist, the one he'd used to pin her. He kneels over her, as though he were about to kiss her. His face is friendly—no malevolence. "I'm glad you found me tonight," he says. "We should do this again sometime." He opens his two hands to the sky and shrugs genially, as if to say, 'what can you do?' He gives her a thumbs-up and says, "L'Chaim," disappearing in the direction of La Mancha.

Chapter 25

The Butcher's House, legend has it, was built to store wood when the campground was still a resort for German Americans. The dilapidated shack has all the requisite rusted nails, jagged glass, gnarled ivy and mossy lumber, quavering with insect life. The image of a mad Bavarian slaughter man, wielding knife and axe, has been, for nearly twenty years, enough to keep most children out of the woods. No one knows the legend's derivation, probably as simple as a counselor ad-libbing on a nature walk: "That's the Butcher's House." And so it came to be. The dangling shelf by the door, the hook in the beam, the pile of leaves in a corner, the broken glass of a side window—all give evidence of struggle, hanging and burial. Enough to scare the hell out of any kid.

Kathy Klein is beyond such nonsense, has been since she was small. As she fumbles with her shirt, things rustle and chirr in and around the shack. The breeze is cold. It rattles the vines crawling up the Butcher's House. She feels the building's evil, iconic presence.

She rolls to her side and pulls her knees in, hoping to stop shivering. She feels hollowed out. Someone has carved her from inside, scraped until there's neither wood nor green. Just pulp.

It's hard to say how long she remains like that. There are many voices in her head. She has a vague notion, probably from TV, that emergency workers talk loudly to accident victims to keep them conscious, as though falling asleep is the path to death. She hears a voice like that. Increasingly loud. Calling her name in reverb.

She has a dream, or maybe fantasy. A man comes to her from deep in the woods, as though he's been watching. He wants to tell her something. He wants her to stay awake. He touches her tenderly, first her face, then her hand. He says, "Hey... You have to move." Is it the Butcher? No, it's someone she knows.

What are you doing here? she thinks.

"You'll be okay, you really will, but you have to move." It's the damnedest thing because she's so far away, because everything's swimming. Philip's father, Jerry Rosen, comes to her from out of the woods. He says, "Kathy. You have to move. You'll be okay."

Mr. Rosen, you've come for me, she thinks.

Jerry Rosen shakes her shoulder, ever so carefully, and says, "Move."

He looks as though he would take her in his arms. She pictures it that way, him lifting her up, cradling her in his arms, carrying her out of the woods, across the field. In this dream, this fantasy, she imagines a whole scenario of comfort and care, as Philip's father rescues her from the terrors of the trees. She is, this dreamer, the real Anne Frank, but this time, she gets saved.

"Move" is all he says. "Please."

She stirs, begins the painful push-up that will get her to her feet. Elbows. Hands. Straighten to sit. Turn towards the man. Lift a hand to him to raise her up. But he's gone.

By the time Kathy finds her way out of the woods and onto Tobacco Road, camp is eerie-quiet, as though deserted. Across the dark expanse of Green Fields, porch lights and streetlamps halo like distant stars. She gravitates towards the rows of evergreens that border Green Fields. She walks, in fits and starts, along the edge of the spruce thicket, as though looking for a place to lie down again.

Someone comes up behind her, making *notice me* noises. She hopes it's Tex-Mecks, someone of strength and authority. It's Dion.

"Hi. I was hoping that was you."

"Dion." Kathy whispers, the fact of his name the most she can manage. She is heavy-tired, ungodly tired, dead-tired. She's so tired that she would brush right past Dion, if she weren't too tired to move at all. She could fall backwards, a trust exercise with the trees. She could sleep.

"Not that I've been searching for you or anything," he says, laughing off any such desperation.

"No," she says, having trouble standing.

"I was helping Ziggy out in the shop."

"Ziggy."

"Painting platforms."

"Sure."

"He kept bringing more of them outside."

What is he talking about? Is it a language she knows?

"There must have been a hundred of them, all shapes and sizes."

"Dion, please…"

"I'm not sure how Ziggy could have done them all by himself. He's always getting distracted, going off and doing other things, or doing three things at once."

"Not now," she speaks almost too softly to be heard. She won't meet his eyes.

"He's like a too-many-things-at-once machine."

Kathy tries to go away without moving.

"I don't know why I thought maybe you'd show up at the scene shop to help us out."

"How?"

"Right. How could you even have known I was there?"

Is this the boy she kissed last night? Does he always smile like that to be charming?

"I'm glad I've found you now," he says.

Was that last night? "Dion, I—"

"Maybe we could go for a walk. I'm covered in paint, though. I hope you don't mind."

She puts out her hand, as though to stop him from talking. He follows her hand and looks down at his chest.

"I look like one of Ziggy's platforms, splattered with every color paint."

There is a third voice all of a sudden—a wry voice, way too loud: "Top of the evenin', Mrs. Robinson."

It's weirdo Brian Kotlicky smoking a cigarette. "I do declare, Miss Anne Frank, you look like you're about to lie down in those trees." Brian stands too close to them, an alien from a planet where lunacy loves company.

Kathy wants to disappear into the brush. Dion can't stop himself from being polite, "Hi Brian. How you doin'?"

Kotlicky stays there, as though waiting for someone to offer him a chair and, when no one does, says, "Nice night tonight, if you like that sort of thing."

"Yes, it's nice," Dion says.

Kathy thinks she feels like weeping. She thinks she feels.

"Yeah," Kotlicky agrees. "As for me, I enjoy an evening constitutional before lying awake all night."

Ordinarily, Kathy would tell Kotlicky to go away, but she wants him here. If she can't be alone, she doesn't want to be alone with Dion.

But Dion has other ideas and, uncharacteristically brusque, says. "Brian, we were about to go for a walk..."

"I love to walk," Brian chirps.

"Just the two of us. We were going to walk just the two of us."

Brian peers at Dion over his glasses, as though disbelieving that this inhospitable fellow could be the real President Dion Robinson. "Sure, sure. No problemo. Just thought I'd wander over and say some really irrelevant things. Abysinnia!" He strolls back the way he came, blowing smoke rings as he goes. He flips the cigarette butt into the road and spends an extra-long minute stamping it out, a mini-performance for anyone who might be watching.

Someone turns up the volume on the crickets.

Last summer, the northern lights made a spectacular show in the sky over camp. Dion remembers everything about it. All the older kids gathered in the middle of Green Fields. They laid down on their backs, on beach towels and factory-made Indian blankets, and stared up. The sky swirled like a kaleidoscope, a color show that seemed like a dream, colors turning inside out, shimmering. The sky even flapped, like God was waving silk of every color in the world, glory come down.

"Do you remember the Northern Lights last year? Wasn't that something? The Aurora Borealis."

"Dion" is all she can say.

"I wish we could have seen it together," he says it in a way that squeezes the sentiment out, as though saying, "We need groceries."

"No," she says.

"I wish we could see it together right now."

"Oh, you idiot," she says the words to herself, but there's no way Dion could know this.

"You disgusting idiot!" she almost shouts it, condemning herself for all the wrongs of the past twenty-four hours, which are the wrongs of a lifetime.

Dion freezes. He only hears the words, with no sense that he's not their target. Lights go out in him. He stops seeing her, the way she rocks on her feet, the way she crosses her arms across her chest, as if to press herself more deeply into herself.

Kathy Klein moves, in fits and starts, across Green Fields, leaving Dion where he stands, turned to stone. She passes behind Gershwin and around De Mille under the infirmary stairs. She crosses the empty, mostly darkened lobby, reaches over the door of the music library for the key there. She steals into the room without closing the door. She gropes behind the *Bye Bye Birdie* score for a nearly finished pack of cigarettes, a pack of matches. She's out the door again, banging it shut behind her, key still in the lock. She's sobbing, moving jerkily, as though pushed from behind.

Anyone can get in the costume shop. The back door doesn't quite meet the jamb, so even when it's locked, you can wedge a stick or a script in and pry the latch forward. It's an old trick. Kathy uses a long splinter of wood she picks off the ground. It's too dark to see the space, though so she pokes at it again and again. Finally, she shoves her way in.

She heads for the costume shop's far corner, under the long petticoats of Anna Leonowens, tutor to the children of the King of Siam. She burrows under these skirts the way the smallest Siamese child burrows under Mrs. Anna's hoops in *The King and I*. Her face is burning wet. She swipes at her nose with her arm.

Legs crossed Indian style, bent forward, she's hunched beneath walls and walls of clothes—sailor suits and suede fringe cowboy chaps. She lights a cigarette from the pack. She breathes the smoke in, holds it as long as she can. It stills her. She inhales again.

Kathy lies sideways on the floor, tucked into herself. She takes another drag and lets it out. She rests the hand with the cigarette on her hip, the tip pointing behind her. She falls asleep.

Chapter 26

Brian Kotlicky takes fairly radical steps to keep his habits of thinking separate from the herd. He stays awake when they sleep and sleeps when they're awake. He works at opposites and contraries, cultivates randomness in his behavior. He listens to Schoenberg and that furious nerd music erupting from London and New York, none of this sugar-tit (Joni Mitchell) or pap-rock (Styx), a radiation cloud of bad taste hanging over the suburbs. He mails himself letters from Patty Hearst—signed: "Luv, Tania"—which he shows the other kids. He contends that Nixon's an American hero, a man who loves his dog. Last year, a bookstore clerk turned him on to Alfred Jarry, the French guy who wrote *Ubu Roi*. Anything that starts with 'merde' and stays with it is all right by him.

On the night of the fire, Kathy passes Kotlicky twice, though she sees him neither time. Brian's got a front row seat on her comings and goings, which is just fine with him. He's always liked that brainy girl with her oddball intensity, Anne Frank-obsessed—his kind of sexy. It's a stupid time to be fifteen, actually. Everyone's talking about following different drummers and being freaks or nonconformists, but it's a crock. There are maybe three people at camp with an original thought in their heads. This Kathy Klein chick might be one of them. Somehow, she's got half the camp calling her 'Anne Frank'. Brilliant.

He watches while, in the shadows, Kathy works at the costume shop door. He catches the last glimpse of her, as she disappears inside. It occurs to him that she might play dress up in there after dark, a very pleasant thought indeed. He mulls it over. Probably she's just pilfering a costume before Sunday's Olympics—*Oh-lame-pics*—song and skit. Maybe he should help her try it on.

Kotlicky smells the smoke before he sees it. Then he's like an enchanted person in a cartoon, hypnotically lured by an unseen power. He's no hero. He's fascinated and afraid. But when he pushes the door open to find clothes burning in one corner and Kathy frozen with panic in another, he acts without thinking. He dashes in and grabs her by the wrist and yanks her out after him.

He doesn't notice the details, the way the crinolines curl before they catch, the way the smoke drifts in patches. He doesn't notice that flames really do lick upward, and he doesn't hear how loud the fire is, how many sounds—hissing, seething, popping, roaring—it contains. He just flings her out the back. The way you do in Crack the Whip. Kathy keeps going, not looking back. Kotlicky can't tell what registered, if she even knows who pulled her out.

Once he, too, is clear of the burning building, he succumbs to fascination, like a kid before a tank of neon fish, tilting his head this way and that. A steel-trap hand seizes his upper arm. Tex-Mecks barks at him, "Anyone in there?"

"No," Kotlicky answers calmly.

Tex-Mecks kicks open the back door anyway, just to make sure. He drags Kotlicky back to the edge of the gravel drive, jabs a finger at his face as if to nail him in place. Kotlicky stays. Good dog. Tex-Mecks bolts into Anatevka.

For Kotlicky, the next five minutes seem to last forever. The fire is brilliant. The staff bursts out of Anatevka two or three at a time and scatters, shouting improvised orders to each other. They carry their shirts and sandals, dressing as they run.

Big Bird, the camp's 6'5" tennis pro, sprints into Friedkin's. Lights flash on in the windows over Ollie's. More people rush up. Cars brake on the gravel beside De Mille, and volunteer firemen pile out and confer. They cordon off a wide ring around the burning building, clearing a path for fire trucks. Two arrive, unlatch, unravel and extend. Water smashes into the cracking structure. Tex-Mecks and Max, in his kitchen whites, join the effort.

Of all the buildings at Friedkin, the costume shop is the most isolated, a solitary bonfire. What the scene lacks in danger, it makes up for in spectacle and excitement. A flaming board tumbles two stories and the crowd gasps. A wall crashes, and they all jump back. For the rangy, adrenaline-pumped volunteer firemen—guys from town, teachers, farmers, mechanics, bartenders, water-skiing instructors—it's mostly show. The burn is easily contained and doused at relative leisure, but they perform for a captive audience of college-girl counselors and kids who think they're heroes. The firefighters butch it up. They shout orders over the roar of water and fire. They dash when they could walk. Their muscles flex and strain as they aim the hoses. Risk, daring and precision. Later, among themselves, they will talk about how straightforward it all was. "Textbook," they'll call it. No big deal to them. To the fans: The Justice League of America.

Forty or fifty people surround the conflagration. Some of them weep. The staff tries to console the worst. Jody is among them, and Philip holds her. They stand at the back corner of De Mille, having followed the scent of burning from the edge of camp. Philip's eyes are on the blaze, but Jody, pressed to his body, is more real. He feels the heat radiating off her face, smells salt and metal in her tears. Jody slips down a corridor inside herself, a dark place in this glaring night. Every time something good happens to her, catastrophe hits.

The last wall topples inward. The storage loft collapses into the center of the fire. No one can look away. Rooms full of clothes burn before their eyes: cotton and wool, rayon and suede, Scotch plaids and Emerald City greens, glass and ruby slippers, fedoras, sailor caps, top hats, gun belts, feather boas, Harpo wigs and Harlequin pants, boxes of costume jewelry. A dress parade from *South Pacific, Plain and Fancy, West Side Story, Wonderful Town*. Every garment has a story. All are consumed.

Gradually, Kotlicky takes it in. People are staring. Whispering. Uncle Bernie is talking with Officer Dill, the town's only cop. And they're looking right at him. They think he did this. Irrelevant thoughts pass through his mind: he hasn't heard a loudspeaker announcement. They've kept the little kids away.

"Know how this happened?" Officer Dill asks Kotlicky.

"Smoking," Kotlicky says. "Musta fallen asleep."

The cop nods his head like he's seen it all. "You're a lucky kid," he says. "Stupid but lucky."

"Dumber than lint," Kotlicky agrees.

Dorfman bumps into him, almost knocking him over, "Nice work, Kotlicky." His tone says, 'Piece of shit.'

Next thing he knows, Bernie's standing there. Sylvie's a step behind, and they're holding hands. "We're going to call your parents," Bernie says, "and tell them that we plan to prosecute you to the full extent of the law for endangering our children." Kotlicky sees the pulse when Bernie squeezes Sylvie's hand. "Look at me," Bernie commands. Kotlicky does. "Someone will supervise you while you pack your bags. I hope to never see your face again." Bernie runs his eyes over Kotlicky noting evidence of smoke and ash. Sylvie searches for evidence of remorse.

Sylvie says something Kotlicky doesn't understand. Another language, German or Polish maybe. Bernie pulls her away.

Lila stands immobile on the walkway from Ollie's with Miffed in her arms. Estelle Nye, the camp's long-time costumer, and the junior counselor advisor, Marla Bensinger, are on either side of her, Marla reaching for the dog. Lila knows every stitch in the building, every eyelet and hem. There are costumes she's altered twenty times in twenty years. Every year she amazes the children with the old method actor's pantomime—sewing with invisible needle and thread. But there's nothing imaginary about the years of needles and thread she used here, about the calluses and blood on her fingertips.

After a while, there's nothing left to burn. Max, gray with soot, puts his strong, ashy arm around Lila. It's hard to tell whether she's drawing strength from him or merely imitating his stoic mask. With his free hand, he takes her elbow and turns her from the sight, a partner in a courtly dance.

As the wreckage smolders, the volunteers grab shovels and throw sand on the embers.

Chapter 27

The day after the fire, six kids leave camp: two eight-year-olds, one girl and one boy, the eleven-year-old Boetcher twins from Colorado and Gary Eckerling, a fifteen-year-old in Bali Hai, whose mom freaks and yanks him out. "Her aunt died in a fire," Gary tells anyone who'll listen, "so she's like sensitive or something." The last to leave is Brian Kotlicky.

Bernie, Sylvie and Lila make the calls themselves. By noon, Sunday, they have reached the parents of 264 campers and junior counselors. They call parents by their first names and say, "I wanted you to hear this from me directly." They recite a few basic facts, stressing that the children were at no time in danger. The building was nowhere near the cabins themselves. In fact, following the advice of the country fire chief, they let most of the children sleep through the fire, as Bernie tells the parents, "to not frighten them unduly."

"The firefighters got everything under control within minutes. It was a simple matter," they say. "No one was hurt in any way. Not even smoke. I just wanted to make sure you knew the details." When asked, which they inevitably are, they explain, "A teenager with a cigarette. He's on his way home."

Most of the conversations end in gratitude, a promise that "The show must go on" and "I'll see you next weekend." A few are knottier, negotiations with anxiety and blame.

There is only one set of parents the Friedkin family can't reach. Bernie pages Philip Rosen to his office and the boy runs.

"We haven't been able to contact your parents," Bernie tells him. "No one is answering anywhere."

"That's okay," Philip says. "You don't need to talk to them." He tries to catch his breath.

"Actually, we do," Bernie says.

"They won't mind," Philip insists. "As long as everything's okay. Everything's okay, isn't it?" There's dread in his voice.

"Of course it is," Bernie says. It's been a miserable ten hours, a pressure-cooker ten hours, and he's feeling the strain. Even so it's impossible to miss the tension in the boy's eyes, the stress he's been under. Philip stayed behind to help with cleanup; he wishes he hadn't. Bernie softens. He steps out from behind his desk. Philip is still in the doorway. Bernie rests a warm hand on his shoulder. "Here. You take the big seat." He ushers Philip into the desk chair.

"Why don't you try your mom? Maybe you'll have better luck." Philip doesn't budge. "Philip? It's all right. Just try." No response. "You can always try again later." Bernie tries to quell his frustration.

"I don't know how," Philip says, finally, to the desk blotter. Bernie grimaces with incomprehension. "I mean I don't have her number."

"Where is she?" Bernie asks.

"She's with friends until she leaves for Mexico. Monday. I don't have their number."

"She's going on vacation?"

"She's moving. I think she's moving there."

Bernie swallows, stymied. "Well, how about your dad. Can you call him?" Philip tenses.

"No."

"Nowhere you can think he might be this time of day?"

"No."

"No one who might know?"

"No."

Bernie has heard rumors about Jerry Rosen's legal troubles, including a mention of prison, but it didn't compute. Until now. The spate of phone calls, the request to take Philip out of camp for lunch, the kid showing up with the car. The boy's in a panic. It doesn't take a genius to see he's making things worse. Philip doesn't move a muscle, but he's racing inside. He's staring at the phone, petrified. "It's okay," Bernie says. "It's okay." He cradles the back of the boy's neck with his large hand.

Bernie could kick himself. Why did I have to press the boy? The father's trouble is his trouble. He reaches for the cup of cold coffee on his desk.

"My aunt. My dad's sister might know. Aunt Phyllis."

"Good. Good. Maybe I'll give her a call then." He fishes a BIC pen out of a mug on his desk and hands it to Philip, "Just leave her number." Bernie points to a notepad on the desk, covered with curlicue doodles he's made during his morning calls.

* * *

Before the calls begin, Tex-Mecks rounds up the senior counselors and staff. The theatre teachers, nocturnal as the bats in the attic of Anatevka, blink at him in disbelief. It's 7:15 in the morning. Last night never ended. He lays out plans for the suspension of the Olympics and a day of diversion. The idea is to get the kids off site while the grounds are cleaned up.

"We had a fire last night, but that was last night. Today is just another day. So keep spirits high, answer questions briefly and without alarm. A lot is riding on today, including whether parents let their kids come back next year. Nineteen years of fun and sun. The twentieth is up to you." He waits for the import of his statement to sink in.

"Remember three rules of thumb: distraction, distraction, distraction. And please—something you've never heard around here—check the drama at the door."

By 11:00, Tex-Mecks has lined up buses to take the Blue, Silver and Gold divisions to Milwaukee's Melody Tent theatre for a matinee of *Cabaret*, starring Tommy Tune and Imogene Coca. The red and white divisions have been booked at the Sheboygan roller rink, with its bratwurst stand and disco ball. The Junior counselors have been organized into clean-up crews, with go-karting and dinner at the A & W as reward.

The theatre staff rallies to save the shows. Costumer Estelle Nye lines up a tent—used mostly for weddings—to function as a temporary costume shop. Markie the choreographer and accompanist Neil Roven call every college, high school and community theatre between Kenosha and Madison, borrowing clothes for next week's performances—a fire sale in reverse. They are good thespians with a bone-deep love of crisis. They strike like Red Cross fundraisers after a natural disaster.

When Kotlicky's parents arrive, the camp is all but empty. Kotlicky sits alone on the front steps with a duffel bag and a footlocker. He angles his knees to the side, the way they tell you to do in camp photos. *They should make this the 1974 all-camp picture,* he thinks, *one kid with luggage.*

His parents drive a yellow Impala. Bernie marches out of Anatevka, past Brian, and over to the driver's side. He bends into the window and speaks in low, forbidding tones, Brian waiting dutifully on the bottom step. When Bernie walks away, Brian steps forward. His father hands the keys through the window without comment. Brian unlocks the trunk, wrestles his footlocker in and heaves the duffel on top of it. He slams the trunk, returns the keys to his dad, and slinks into the back seat, instantly small.

On the porch, Bernie stands guard, as if to make sure they'll leave. "Bar the gate," he mutters. Bernie prides himself on never giving up on a child. He's seen the slouching delinquents of the fifties, the burnouts and hyper, self-anointed radicals of the sixties, but this one is something new. This boy's utter lack of concern feels like violence, his weird irony an assault, a rudeness deeper than anyone has a right to. For years, Bernie has made his 'eight charred bodies' speech during pre-camp, recounting the nightmarish fire that took place at another camp. And here's this boy, remorseless, sociopathic. "Good riddance to bad rubbish," he says. As the car disappears, he turns his back to the gate, the final shunning. He heads to the office to finish his calls.

Kathy Klein steals forth from the edge of the big building. She's been watching the scene through square holes of the low cinder-block wall. She stole out of the infirmary, after convincing the counselors she was too sick to take the bus ride to the show in Milwaukee; she's been ghosting Kotlicky all morning. He ate alone at a table in the staff dining room, was escorted back and forth to Bali Hai by his counselor. He lugged his footlocker up the stairs—still under guard—and returned for the duffel bag.

What was she looking for? What did she hope to hear? Recantation? Accusation? "I didn't do it! That girl did!" Or was she preparing to confess, to throw herself at Kotlicky's feet and beg forgiveness? Is she the heroine of her own 19th Century novel, one of those ethics queens on the precipice of her fall to earth, dreaming of absolution?

Will she stalk him this way for years to come, wondering why he took the rap for her? Has she set in motion some lifelong spiral that will leave him homeless and destitute? Or has she just, in some way she will never understand, set him free? He's been trying to 'run away from camp' for years, by his own admission. Is it in her hands to bless his freedom by staying out of the way until he makes it through the gates?

The more she watches, the more depraved she feels, or worse: evil. She doesn't understand her motives now, and she won't when she looks back years later. This much is clear: she lets Kotlicky take the fall. She never speaks to him again. She tells no one. Bury it. Let time do the dirty work.

Chapter 28

By Monday, the fire has begun its fade to memory, myth and dream. They raise a temporary costume tent just after noon. The preparations have a circus feel, as the rental company's roadies' pound stakes every couple of feet, run ropes, shoulder support beams, fold and unfold canvas and, finally, move in unison away from each other to hoist the canopy up. With its eight corners and soaring poles, the effect is wondrous. The vast, round tent has a hub-like appearance, and the rest of camp seems to have been laid out around it on a great revolve. Kids dart and roll under the loose flaps. It's cool inside, the light pink.

A squad of Lila's costume assistants—all true blondes from Wisconsin state schools—and townie kitchen boys unpack, organize, wash and press station wagons full of borrowed costumes. Lila walks among them, holding up a shirt, handing off a robe, mixing an apricot flared skirt with a pale blue top, giving orders in a voice that is both fierce and gentle. Ziggy paints a sign for the new costume shop, a picture of a walrus, a fox, an orange-haired boy puppet and a girl with a broad-brimmed hat peering over the word, 'Carnival'.

Bernie plans to welcome the parents in the tent on Saturday morning. It's a coup de théâtre. Now you see rubble, now you don't. Together they can celebrate the survival, ingenuity and spirit—the carnival—that is Friedkin. He deputizes Kenny Tannenbaum to arrange the welcome, including renting 350 folding chairs. Maybe it will occupy the kid, so he stops jabbering on about the Indian Burial Mound he thinks he's found in the field.

Once again, Philip hears his name over the PA. He races to the office. "Philip, I reached your mother," Bernie tells the barely breathing boy. "Her number is on my desk. I told her you'd call right away." Bernie taps the corner of his desk, as if to say, 'Make yourself at home.'

Philip's mom is effervescent. "How amazing that Bernie called. I was just about to phone you. Well, I guess we're going ahead with plan B. Eduardo and I are leaving in a couple hours. Then if you need me to come back, I will. But I doubt we'll have to. Isn't it exciting?"

Her ebullience confuses him. Last time he'd spoken to her, she'd called his dad 'a runaway'.

"But did you talk to Dad?"

"Yes, I talked to your *father*..." She says the word as though his paternity is in question. "I've heard all about his troubles, and I have no reason to believe everything won't work out. You are not to worry, sweetie. Your dad will work something out with the judge. He always does. And you have your key to the house, if you need it. Don't worry about a thing."

"But you said he'd run away."

"Oh no, that was just one of his little games. He called me and said he was home. 'Tell it to the judge,' I should have said."

She sounds giddy, and Philip doesn't want to burst her bubble, but he suspects that, as they're talking—as she's talking—his father is being carted off to prison. "Have you talked to him today?"

"I don't need to speak with him about all this again. Ever. I'm sure you'll hear from him once he's cut some kind of deal."

Philip swallows.

"Everything will work out. This is such a happy time. Finally, happiness!"

"I'm glad, Mom."

"I'm not really moving there. It's a trial relocation."

He hears 'trial'.

"I'll always be there if you need me," she insists. "You know that, right?"

"I know," Philip says.

"Okay, then. I have to run now. Our friends are picking us up for the airport."

"Okay. Have a good trip, Mom."

"Terrible thing about the costume shop burning down," she adds happily. "Bernie told me everything. I'm so glad to hear everyone's all right."

"Thanks, Mom."

"I love you so much. I'll see you before you know it."

"I love you, too. Bye, Mom."

"Hasta la vista, sweetie!"

It's no exaggeration to say he's never felt more alone, his father—somewhere—facing sentencing, his mother off to a new adventure, his home uncertain. What connects him? Jody? In a few days, she'll go home and become that other Jody, the fickle, push-me pull-you one, caught up with the wide, enticing world of not-him. A play? Everything here is a play. They play at suffering. They play at life and death. They know nothing.

* * *

A lifetime has passed for Kathy. She's suspended in a numb afterlife. People pass. She hears their voices. She notes their urgencies. But she's not part of it. She was part of something else, in a time and place she can barely recall.

Kathy tries to remember the last time she ate anything. She forked salad around her plate at lunch. She served herself mashed potatoes at dinner, passed on the mystery meat. But she can't recall her last actual bite. Her stomach churns at the thought of food. Her counselor Colleen Kramer is working Canteen, manning the shelves of candy and the freezer full of Dixie cups. She calls to Kathy. But Kathy just says, "Nothing."

She sits in the shadows of the cabin porch, curled on a green wicker sofa. It's dark and the late August foliage shrouds the screens. Who can she tell her story to? Who could follow its jagged course? Who would believe her?

And what would be the point? To accuse Dorfman? Of what? He didn't throw himself at her alone in the woods at night. She'd done that. Mere days after she'd thrown herself at Dion. Oh God, what must Dion be thinking? Would the point be to exonerate Kotlicky? What for? He's already home where he wants to be.

And even if she did confess, how convoluted would that be? She wants to, but, more than anything, this girl who has caused so much trouble is paralyzed by the complications she's wrought, the undoing of which could hardly be more twisted.

Can she confess to the fire without bringing Dorfman into it? Can she explain being alone in the woods without describing her jealous panic at seeing Jody and Philip together? And how can she explain—if she knows—exactly what she's trying to accomplish by carrying the *Diary* with her everywhere? Is she trying to ape a dead girl? Is she suggesting her suffering has meaning, that by playing at being like that famous girl, she can become her, like one of those sad sack wannabe poets who thinks a suicide attempt makes her Sylvia Plath? She let other kids call her Anne Frank, reveled in it. If she loves the *Diary* so much, why has she dirtied it up with such shameful pretend? This literary stalking now seems to her obviously insane.

Kathy is weighed down. She is dense with trouble, coal pressed under the tonnage of earth, hoping to become diamond but waking to find herself filthy and impacted. She has to tell someone. That's the only way out from under. There are no friends she can tell. Her mother would blow everything out of proportion. Her father has no interest in her 'dramas'. With three kids under age seven, his hands are full. The only person she can tell, the only one who would understand, is the last person she can tell. Telling Philip means giving everything away, revealing that he's with her at the center of the story.

Back in her room, she retrieves her journal. Everyone else is sleeping. She returns to the porch sofa, sits on the edge, book on her knees. She opens her journal without looking at it and fingers the pages until she comes to the one marked by a ribbon running up the book's spine. She dates the top left corner by feel. She writes the way a blind woman might, touching the edges of the paper, intuiting the lines, fixed on the dead space in front of her. "Dear Philip. Everyone's asleep but me. Where are you? I know it's not the time to tell you everything I have to say, but maybe if I write it all down, I can give it to you when the time comes. When will the time come? Please let it be soon."

She fills this page and another. She covers page after page. There is one thing she can't write, that despite her long-held determination to write all truth and only truth, she can't even remember: the time with Dorfman on the ground. She kissed him and kissed him again. He slapped her. Hit her? Slapped her? That's all she remembers and even that isn't certain. She knows she's forgetting something important.

She writes faster. She can't read her scrawl in the near dark. Could anyone read this? If it is legible, though, with its undifferentiated crests and swirls, the blotting and x's, the double and triple horizontal lines—if someone can read this, he will be reading her.

When she finally stops, she notices how cold she is. She's about to cap her pen, when a phrase comes to her, a fragment of a poem. She prints it out in block letters, in couplet form at the end of her letter:

All I am and all I do.

Is all I want to say to you.

She tears these pages from the binding. She folds them over and over in a desperate origami, middle, corner, side, until the diamond of paper resembles a cootie catcher or finger fortune teller—lift the flap for the answer to your question: Philip. Other flap: Philip.

She walks inside and opens her trunk. She locks her journal away, but she won't let go of this folded thing.

She slips out of her clogs and onto her lumpy bed. She cups the letter and holds it at her mouth. She breathes into it.

Chapter 29

Philip is distraught. The morning ends, lunch comes and goes, and still no word from his father. He pockets all the change he can muster and heads to town. There is a pay phone on the back porch of The Depot, sentry to deserted train tracks. He takes out the yellow legal paper his father gave him along with the safe deposit box key and reads the number for Mickey Brodkey, Jerry's old friend and lawyer. He feeds coins into the slot.

"I've been meaning to call, Philip, but frankly, I didn't know what to tell you," Mickey says when they connect. "I guess you need to know," he muses, as if to himself.

"What?" Philip asks, not wanting to hear the answer.

"He never showed up in court this morning. Jerry. Your dad."

"Why? Where is he? Is he all right?"

"I don't know, Philip. I don't know."

"My mom talked to him. Yesterday, I think. She said he was in Chicago."

"Well, that's nice to hear, but he wasn't in the part of Chicago he was supposed to be in this morning." Philip doesn't breathe. "I'm sorry, Philip. That came out harsher than I meant. You father has his reasons for doing things. I'm sure he thinks he knows what he's doing. I'm sure we'll hear from him soon."

Philip fingers the paper he's holding. He remembers his father's words as he rifled the plastic wallet of money, "Consider it allowance." He doesn't know what to say or do.

"Look, Philip. It'll be all right. Everything will work out, you'll see. Your dad's a survivor. Don't worry." He wants off the phone. "I'll let you know when I hear something. When," he says again for emphasis, "I'm sure it'll be soon. Where can I reach you?"

Philip tells him the name of the camp. "Swallow Heart Lake, Wisconsin," he adds.

"It's gonna be all right," Mickey says. "You got that?"

"Sure, sure. It'll be all right."

"Okay. Good. Look, I gotta go."

"Thanks, Mickey."

"Nothing to thank me for. You keep your chin up. I'll call."

"Okay."

"Gotta go."

It's all too much to take in. The details are murky. What does any of it mean? Who can he tell? What could they possibly say to help? He walks back to camp as rest period ends, thinking about everything but what Mickey just told him. He fixates on the Olympics. The final events were cancelled after the fire, so he and Dorfman never got to present their skit. They came so close to winning and now nothing.

No one sees their masterpiece, the script for the Olympics skit that Philip Rosen and Larry Dorfman never got to stage. In the years to come, it grows legendary, like a missing symphony or a breakthrough album that never got released. Their creation, *A Polish Family*, was a cinéma-verité-style take on the PBS series, *An American Family*. Like its model, which captures seven months in the lives of the Louds, a middle-class American family from California, the Rosen-Dorfman production would have captured not just a family but a place, an era. It was to have been played straight, voice-over narrated, with Dorfman and Philip questioning the characters over the Gershwin PA system. Real characters, real situations from Communist Eastern Europe, real life, post-Holocaust life.

Based on the gay, Andy Warhol-worshipping drag queen Lance Loud, Lech, the oldest brother in a big Catholic family, leaves for Warsaw to play in a subversive, Western-style rock band. Once there he works for the pro-democracy underground. Lech's activism imperils his adoring family. A Polish Family was to have revealed that family's struggles. It was to have departed from all the Friedkin clichés, trading in show tunes for a garage-band soundtrack. It was to have delivered something previously unseen at camp: realism, real realism.

"Was to have"—the tense of regret, of never happened, of what might have been. The future perfect rewritten as imperfect past.

"It was the best thing I've ever written. We really had something," he tells Jody in rehearsal. He's had so much bad news, but this is the piece he's latched onto. "It was one of those times where you know you have something right in the vein, and you've got to get it out. People have to see it."

"It's a skit, Philly. A *camp* skit. Stop obsessing." Her eyes sweep the dance studio. "Have you seen Klein?"

"It isn't a skit. That's what I'm saying. It's actually art. It would have changed everything."

"I haven't seen her since last night. She looked like hell," Jody adds.

"They have no ambition. Let's do everything the same, year after year—same musicals, same dances, same moves."

"I hope she's not too sick to do the show," she says.

"Who cares about the stupid show?" he half shouts.

"Philip Rosen and Jody Gold," Markie calls out, cutting short a pirouette. "We're dancing here."

Markie always yells at someone, always makes a scene. This time, though, he's not just a choreographer having a hissy fit. To Philip, he's *everything wrong in the world*.

Philip explodes, "Oh keep your fucking skirt on, princess."

The room goes quiet. Markie's mouth drops open. Everyone's mouth drops open. Philip Rosen has been possessed by Linda Blair from *The Exorcist*. They're waiting for him to hurl.

Philip knows he's lost control. Something ugly has entered his body.

Here's what would normally happen: Markie would throw a tantrum and storm out. When he returned a few minutes later, Philip would apologize, and they'd all get back to work. It happens once a week, at least. Only this time, it doesn't go that way. Markie stays still. His face overheats, starting at his cheeks and ending at temples. He doesn't blow, though. He says, "You're out of the dance, Philip. Now get out of my class."

There must be a moment when everything can go in reverse. Philip has been at Friedkin for nine summers. He's never been kicked out of anything. He's been the goody-goody star of everything. Can Markie take his dance away, a part of his part? Can he fire Philip from the 'Somewhere Ballet'? Can anyone fire Philip Rosen from anything? All he needs to do is apologize. Leave for a few minutes, pull Markie aside and apologize.

Philip looks to Jody. Jody Gold prides herself on being un-shockable—guys have been saying heinous things to her forever, and she doesn't flinch. Philip spooked her, though. Like a stranger, gone psycho on the street. She won't meet his eyes. He reaches a hand towards her, and, in front of everybody, Jody steps away.

"Krup you," he growls at Markie, guttural enough that no one can be sure what he said. And he's gone, the screen door smacking the frame behind him.

Ricky Gross, the lesser Tony, replaces Philip in the ballet. The cast retreats to the mirrored walls of De Mille, while Markie walks Ricky through 'his' pas de deux with the dancing Maria, Sheila Aspillaga. An actual Latina from Chile, Sheila and her parents moved to Milwaukee a couple of years before. Her parents spend half of each summer on the Friedkin tennis courts and work, incidentally, as the camp doctor and nurse. A wispy fifteen-year-old with green eyes and crowded freckles, Sheila moves airily about with the stilted grace of someone who's studied a little too much ballet a little too diligently. Her slip of a body makes the lifts and catches a breeze. Just not for Ricky.

When Kathy arrives late, Jody stops her. "He kicked Philip out," she whispers, "of the dance."

The stiff, disinterested Gross marks the steps with the lithe Sheila, honey hair coiled on top of her head in a dancer's bun. Ricky's been at Friedkin almost as long as Philip has, but while Philip has spent years dreaming of doing West Side Story—of playing this role—Ricky's spent his days riding or talking about Lyle, the horse he boards at the stables on route 57. It's Philip's dance, has been since he was their Tony-in-waiting, age ten. And now, just six days from the performance of his dreams, Philip just walks?!? It doesn't make sense.

Sheila puts her hands on Ricky's shoulders and jumps as he lifts, her left leg prettily trailing her right. He is supposed to slide her down his body. But Gross looks like he just farted. Markie says, "Float her down, Ricky."

"The Nowhere Ballet," Kathy says out loud.

By drama class everyone knows, including Lila. Philip's back in the room, but he acts like he's got blinders on. Ricky Gross tells him, "I don't want the ballet. Can't you do something?"

"It's yours," Philip says.

Rehearsal passes slowly. Philip does what he's asked. He and Kathy run through their scene. It takes place on the last night of Tony's life when he climbs through Maria's window to find her praying. She rages at him for killing her brother Bernardo, "Killer! Killer!" Then she melts into his arms. (Dion plays Bernardo, so he's dead, watching from the audience.)

Lila looks on from the wings. This is one scene she can always count on to ignite; these two throw themselves into it every time. This afternoon, though, they are automata. Kathy Klein looks like a stunned stick drawing animated, slightly, to life. Philip has a dark, sullen aspect Lila's seen a million times, just never on this boy. She's heard about his outburst in dance, and she will deal with it. But she reads him well: he's suffering and in trouble.

Maria (Kathy) kneels, presses her palms together. "Pray to get your brother back," Lila urges. "To bring him back to life." Kathy doesn't need to imagine her own little brother's death. She just has to look at Philip and she knows who to pray for. But she can't pray. How do people pray anyway? What do they pray to?

All Lila sees is a black hole onstage. The light has collapsed, and Kathy isn't even pretending to pretend. She's just kneeling there, hands steepled. Lila says nothing to Philip, but when his cue comes to repeat the scene, she pushes him onto the stage. Hard. He stumbles, his hand coming down on Kathy's shoulder, to regain balance. Propelled by forces outside of himself, he is—Philip and Tony both—startled to find himself there. Kathy throws his hand off, stands up, steps back. Her eyes flood with fear.

Subtext doesn't rank high on the list of acting values at Friedkin, but today Tony and Maria, startled into being by Philip's sudden propulsion into the scene, break into a conversation under the lines that is dense and impenetrable, even to them. They question each other; their answers fail. Love is offered, deflected and withdrawn. They don't know what's happening, but they are lost in it.

Kathy doesn't want the scene to end, at least not the scene they were playing under the scene. Lila has no notes. "After class" is all she says to Philip. Philip seats himself behind Jody; Kathy takes the bench across the aisle. Something even more dangerous is happening onstage now. Soon they are all glued to it.

Melly Barber, as Anita, enters Doc's drugstore in search of Tony. Anita is the Shark firecracker, the sexy, smart-mouthed lover of the dead Bernardo, gang-leader and brother to Maria. She's there as a friend, carrying a message from Maria, but the Jets treat her like the enemy.

Larry Dorfman, playing Arab, leads the charge. He mocks her when she speaks. He blocks her when she moves. He shoves her. Another boy shoves her back. They're passing her around like it's a game of keep-away, and she's the ball. Melly (Anita) is pushed from boy to boy, table to table. She wrests and spins, tries to slip out of their hands, but they close in, grabbing her tighter, pulling her harder. She pleads with them. This powerhouse Puerto Rican woman is helpless against the godless surge of American boys. Doc rushes in, cutting short the gang rape, but the die is cast. She spits out the lie that will seal the star-crossed lovers' fate: Maria is dead.

It's just Melly Barber up there, and she's fighting off Dorfman, Michael Dupler and Howie Weiss, but Tony's inevitable death will belong to them all.

Tony will die, and they'll all want out of this sick, violent world. They'll all want to run away—'Somewhere' with its peace and open air.

Transcendence is a word these kids know. It's a coin of the times. They don't find it through meditation or hallucinogens or Hare Krishna whirling. They find it in moments of group longing, flights of story and song fashioned out of rag and bone by peddlers, now mostly dead, from the alleys of Broadway. They find it in the diasporic parade out of Anatevka in *Fiddler*, in the heavenly chorus at the end of *Carousel*, in the convergence of loss in a gangland as far from their lives as the mountains of Nepal. For an instant, though, they transcend this makeshift theatre with its bad sightlines and coffee-can lights.

Then the scene is over, and they break for General Swim.

Lila spots Philip. She gathers her papers, unhoops Miffed's leash from the back of a bench and lets the dog lead her to the boy. "Follow," she says.

Chapter 30

After nine years, few corners of Friedkin are foreign to Philip. The apartment above the dining hall, from which Ollie and Margaret recently fled, is one such corner, exotic and otherworldly. Entering it feels the way a dream feels, when you open a door and a hidden room appears beyond your room, a house within your house. For an instant, he thinks they've taken a secret passageway to Schwartzkopf's, with its kitschy German fraüleins and milking cows painted on the doors.

There are men in lederhosen, intricate floral borders, baskets of apples and pears. Bouquets dense with country flowers in rust and ocher. Alpine touches that make him think of the von Trapp family singers in *Sound of Music*. He looks for a cuckoo-clock on the wall. There is none, only a round electric clock with green glow-in-the-dark arms on an ornate mantel made of a molded plastic the color of an old man's teeth.

They are in a sitting room. Miffed circles a small chocolate rug and settles snugly in its longhaired fake fur. There is a worn gold couch and a comfy chair with a white slipcover. Lila gestures to the couch, and Philip sits, perched on the edge.

She scrutinizes him. Philip has that too-familiar sensation that Lila is trying to read his mind, that she can read his mind. He tries to dump his brain of thoughts, his face of feelings. He wears an empty mask. She sees everything, he knows.

Ordinarily, he gives her what she's looking for—quick attention, depth, seriousness. But he's fed up. Lila and Sylvie butt in on the privacy of every kid here. He never asked her to crawl up in his brain and play conscience. Suddenly, the entire enterprise seems a grand intrusion, one big incestuous mind-fuck, a musical theatre Manson family.

Lila reads the defiance, sidesteps it. She lets out an end-of-a-long-day sigh. "I want you to see something," she says.

He doesn't want to 'see something', doesn't want to stand up and plod over to her. He wants to make his stand by sitting. "Here," she says, simply, lifting a picture off the mantel. "This was Gramma. Seventeen years old. Hard to believe, no?" She pauses, drinking in the browned studio portrait. It's in a stiff, dark tri-fold envelope that stands when opened.

"Huh," Philip says.

"As often as I look, I still can't see it, how she got from this to where she was…later." The picture makes Philip nauseous. It's old, and he's just discovered that old things repulse him. Gramma Della was an old lady when he knew her, and the photo shows the rigid pose of an old-world girl. Sepia is old. Lila, too.

"Sure," she goes on, "I can see her eyes and the crinkle right there. Her mouth and her nose, all of that. I can see her features, but I can't see the woman she became."

Is Lila trying to bore him into submission?

"She was ferocious. You probably didn't know that."

"No."

"People didn't see it because she was quiet and sweet in the end—maybe more like the girl here. But the things she knew…" Another sigh.

Philip can't tell if she's going to hand him the picture. She's just mooning over it. He gnaws a cuticle. It's hot in the room, and Lila, photograph still in hand, twists the knob on a window fan. It whirrs, stirring the soup of August air. Reaching the picture back to the mantel, she asks, "Where are your grandparents from?"

"I don't know," Philip says to his thumb.

"I don't know," she repeats with a nod, as if recognizing the familiar refrain of history. "Kiev, Vilnius, Kishinev, who knows? One big blur. Anatevka." she half-smiles, an eyebrow raised. He counts the green stripes on his Adidas.

"They were all from here," he says.

She chews on this, still eyeing him. "Yes, everybody's from here. All the Jews were Algonquian Indians first."

What the hell is she getting at? Water torture.

"You are not mean," she says.

"What?"

"I know you, Philip Rosen. You are not mean."

"Maybe I am."

"Maybe, maybe not. But that was a mean thing you said to Markie. And I know you said it, which is why I haven't asked for your side of the story."

"Whatever he said I said, I said."

"Did you try to be hurtful? Did you aim to humiliate him in front of his students?"

"If you say so."

"What do you say?"

"What do you want me to say?"

"We have nothing to eat here," Lila says suddenly. "I have to go down to the dining hall just to get a glass of tea. I'm sorry I have nothing to give you. No Kugel, no noodle pudding, no nothing."

"I'm not hungry anyway," Philip mumbles. But he is hungry. He's starving, like he could eat the place, tear it to pieces and grind the bone. He can't remember a hungrier hunger.

"You realize I'm not going to let you out of here until you talk with me." Philip refuses to stir or lift his eyes. "We've known each other too long and, I think I can say, we've loved each other too much for that."

He wants to eat, and he wants to retch. She seems so old. Her skin is decay. Her breath stinks. She is not of his world. She can't know. *This is not yours,* he thinks to himself, *and I have nothing to say to you.*

"Okay, then *I'll* talk. When we started this camp, Sylvie, Bernie, Max and I, we had lots of ideas about what we'd do. We'd been teaching for years, running our studio in Chicago. We thought camp would be like that, only with more classes, more activities. Little did we know.

"Little do we ever know, yes?" She waits for agreement, a grunt, something. Philip shifts his weight.

"We don't know anything, though we think we do. This time, it will all turn out just the way I imagined it. And we're wrong. Wrong as cheese on a pig, my father used to say."

Philip doesn't know what the hell she's talking about.

"Who knew that we weren't teaching classes? Who knew we were making lives? Who knew Mama would die here, that boys would go off to war, that some juvenile delinquent, some putz, would burn down that beautiful building—" She falters. "We didn't know. It didn't even occur to us."

She draws breath, holds it. When she exhales, the world drains from her face. Philip, still glowering, sees it: boys fighting, mothers dying, a house of clothes leaping in flames. And he sees himself, slouched on her couch, a boy with a life.

The room slows. He knows how she works. The guilt of the world.

"I feel guilty enough," he says.

She's on him in a second, "You should feel guilty. It was wrong. You were wrong. You are humane and your actions were not."

"You don't know."

"I don't know." A restatement of someone else's fact.

He says nothing. Loudly.

"I have no mind, I'm the village idiot," she says, quoting *West Side*. "Tell me what I don't know."

"Markie's psycho. He throws a fit every five minutes. You surround us with these weirdos who think they have something to teach us. Nobody cares who Markie sleeps with—or who he wishes he could sleep with. We care that he's crazy. And then we all pretend we're one big happy family. We lie all the time."

"How do we lie all the time?"

"This whole place is a lie. 'You'll never walk alone.' Really? 'We're all connected.' Really? All of us? What about Kotlicky? Ollie? The kid in La Mancha who sends me love letters signed Missy Lonelyhearts? They're freaks. It's a freak show. No freak is an island. Jesus."

Lila wants to punch him, and she wants to throw her arms around him, he's suffering so.

"So we're freaks. What else is new?" she asks. "The Jews are freaks, the blacks are freaks, the homosexuals are freaks, actors are freaks, everybody over thirty is a freak, old ladies who run summer camps are freaks, presidents are freaks.

"You make a world from freaks. You make a world from freaks who do kindness to each other, who show a little respect because they have that, at least, in common. You know this. If you don't know it in your head, you know it in your kishkes." Her fist presses into her gut as she says it.

Philip closes his eyes and thinks about Jody. The way they kissed against the fence the night of the fire, the way he pressed her to him. It's all so fresh on him that he can feel her. Like he doesn't have the strength to pull her close enough.

He's never seen her fully naked, but that night with her shirt unbuttoned the shadows striped the outer curve of her breasts like jacket lapels. The sight was almost unbearable. He'd traced the ring of her nipple with his finger.

He inhales. He doesn't need this shit. He doesn't need anything but her.

"Nu?"

He opens his eyes. Jody is gone.

"So what do you have to say for yourself?" Lila asks.

"I don't know. Sorry, I guess."

"You guess?"

"Sorry."

"And you'll tell this to your dance teacher?"

"All right."

"All right, then. You understand that you won't be dancing the ballet?"

"Yes."

"You also understand that, sorry or not, your actions have consequences?"

Silence. "I understand."

"Okay," Lila looks again at the photo of her mother in her hand. She's been unable to put it down. Philip expects her to speak to it. She lets out a loud sigh and, without taking her eyes off her mother's face, says, "A year ago today."

"Yeah."

"One year," she says it as if the year was the first of a hundred concrete blocks she has to carry up a hundred steps. Lila rocks to her feet. What happens next happens fast. As she replaces the picture on the mantel, she lets go of it. It slides between the mantel facade and the wall.

Lila cries out, a piercing sound. Her fingers stab at the edge of the fireplace, she pokes at the crack behind the mantel shelf with the sewing scissors on a cord around her neck, she pounds the facade with the heel of her hand. She moves so quickly. She calls, "Mama! Mama!"

Philip is riveted. She's crazed, screeching for her dead mother, digging at the sides of the mantelpiece, the fissure where the caulking was long ago stripped away. He heaves himself out of the couch. Lila steps back, signaling for help, making zombie sounds like a mute. He crouches down. The façade is hollowed out, molded in such a way that the picture has fallen forward into the cavity, impossible to fish out.

"Mama! Mama!" she pitches herself at the hearth, wailing and scratching.

Philip has never witnessed anything like this. His mom cried a lot after the divorce, but she would cry and then schedule a facial or have dinner with girlfriends. Or she'd fly off to Europe with some guy, happy as a parakeet. This is grotesque; this is opera. He doesn't recognize the music. It hurts his ears. Lila plays a woman shouting for help in a storm. The storm tears at his clothes, too. He thinks he might be crying.

She's on her knees, clutching at him. "Don't tell Max, please! Don't tell Max you saw me like this! Promise me!"

"I promise." He wants her off him. He wants to run out and keep running.

"Promise," she begs.

"I promise." Now he is crying.

Lila slaps the fireplace with open hands. She's on her knees, slapping, davening, banging. She rubs her face, as though smearing it with ashes from the fireplace. But there are no ashes.

"I'm sorry," he says, "I'm sorry."

As he closes the door, he hears her call her mother's name. Della.

Chapter 31

Jerry shows up at the courthouse Monday around lunchtime and asks to see the judge. His lawyer Mickey Brodkey left an hour ago after Jerry failed to show. For some reason, the judge agrees to meet him in his chambers. He has a bailiff present. The judge calls him Mr. Rosen with pity in his tone, tells him he'll be out before too long and not to lose hope. Does he intuit how hungover Jerry is, how little he registers? "Family," he says, "that's what matters."

But despite the Hallmark wisdom and the merciful pass for a runaway half-day, Jerry Rosen doesn't contact his family. Not his son, his sister or either ex-wife. Not a single cousin. His lawyer doesn't find out for three days. How do you check yourself into prison? Jerry Rosen manages.

When Mickey finds him in jail, Jerry makes him swear not to tell anyone. "I have the right to decide, Mickey. Lawyer-client confidentiality."

"I'm not going to argue with you, Jerry. I've known you since we were five; I know it wouldn't do any good. I just want you to consider. Your kid," he adds.

"All right, I'll consider. Now go home."

Jerry doesn't consider. He convinces himself that Philip will be okay, that Judy will come back and take him in. It's only a year, and he's itching to grow up and get out anyway, he tells himself. This man who can sell anybody anything sells himself one big idea: his son will always be his son, will always love him.

For now, he'd rather everyone believe he's vamoosed, an outlaw. Rather they picture him living some other kind of life—cowboy rocking on a porch in Billings or high roller in Tahoe—any romance but the minimum-security cell, the jumpsuit, the cafeteria trays and black cons with what sounds like 'mudfucker' every couple words, on their halfway between Joliet and Cabrini Green. Rather die here than be seen here. So for eighteen months, he'll tough it out, unwitnessed. The last place anyone'll look.

And when he returns, he can say anything, make up some wild story—how he bought his way out of the verdict, how he'd done a guy a favor, how he's returned with nothing to fear. Or with no one on his trail, he can disappear again.

Jerry spends hours on his prison bed smoking Camels, trying to imagine how Philip will react to his disappearance. He tries to imagine, and he tries not to. *It's better that he thinks I'm gone.* He wishes Philip was five or six years older to deal with this bullshit. What does he recall about the last twenty-four hours he spent in Wisconsin? Not much, thankfully. His eyes drift towards the upper corner of the wall, where it meets the ceiling. A lot of time passes this way, time not thinking, not being, just stepping to the side of himself, numb to everything but the bite of smoke.

He knows I love him, he thinks. *I told him. I sent him the car.*

Jerry is alone in a room with a door and a window with crosshatched metal. It's more industrial broom closet than prison cell. He has a stack of paperbacks from the prison library, Nazi thrillers. His tastes aren't schmantzy, so this crap will do. He devours them, can't slow his reading but that hardly matters. He can't remember them either, so he never knows if he's read them before.

When he moves off the bed, his body is stiff and achy. He's not the only guy here looking at fifty, not the only white, white-collar, small-time hump. He makes friends with Bruce who transported stolen abstract paintings across the Iowa border, and with a Naperville underwriter named Porter, who says he 'fell into arrears' on his ex-wife's alimony, but who drinks methadone out of Dixie cups in the prison's rehab program. Jerry works in the kitchen with a Mick alderman who's fallen out of favor with Mayor Daley's machine. Like a bad Cagney impersonator, the Mick tells the same story over and over: "I'm nobody's stooge, and I weren't born yesterday, but whaddaya know they give me the bum's rush all because I backed a colored guy from the neighborhood."

Jerry has this life in his muscles from the alleys around Roosevelt High, from the army and the car lot, this man's life. He knows it, knows to blinker himself, keep his jaw tight and his talk coarse. Join the poker game, crack wise—but not at anybody. Stay impersonal. Don't take, don't give. Terror isn't an option, even for an old man nobody gives a shit what he does. But Jerry, who was a scrappy kid not above taunts and fists when he was playing sidewalk ball or scheming with other soon-to-be soldiers about how to get rich or get pussy, hasn't used more than sarcasm to defend himself in thirty years.

In the service, he hated KP but always got stuck with it for shooting off his smarter-than-thou mouth at the drop of a helmet. In here, he knows the kitchen is the best place for him. A fastidious cleaner—empties ashtrays before you flick your cigarette—he can get lost in mops and buckets, the generic cans of shit you wouldn't serve your ex. *Give me a couple thousand potatoes to peel,* he thinks, *and I'll peel them till the end of time.* But even white-collar criminals in minimum security don't rate paring knives.

What did I do? How did I get here? He can't understand and replays the sequence of events to find the moment when everything could have gone another way, where 'if only' might be a key to this cage. He knows better. He can't shut his planning mind off, but this time, he's planning the past, a party he wasn't invited to.

There are two moments, two 'what if' moments he picks at like a maniac. The first phone call from Milt the bigshot, the 'send me money' call. Jerry knew it was wrong; he saw the hole gaping in front of him. What should he have said? "You know I can't do that, Milt?" Or he could have laughed, as though it was the funniest joke from the biggest kidder on the block. "I know guys do this all the time, but I'm a fucking pansy, Milt, you know that. I can't come up with that kind of gelt, Milt." Gelt, Milt. Melt, Guilt. He could never have said that. He could never have said no.

Why not? Is this easier than no? Is this better than losing Milt's account and the business going down the toilet? What's worse than lying on a flat, stained mattress in a downtown, high-rise prison, rationing cigarettes and reading shitty books, when everyone thinks I'm dead?

He thinks about telling his son only—when was it?—a week ago. It feels like fourteen winters. He thinks about never seeing him again. Someone might as well rip his ribs apart with their bare hands. He tries to unthink it, but he keeps picturing Philip, keeps trying to read his mind from this box he's in. You wipe a kid's ass and hold his hand to cross a street where cars never come. Then you deal him this and run away—your shit not his. You are the car, barreling down on him. *Will he ever forgive me?*

Jerry's own father summers year-round in the California desert, where the *alte kakers* go to dry and die. He still doesn't know. *And I'm never gonna tell him,* Jerry thinks. *What made me think I was so fucking superior to Dad? What did he ever do, other than put up with Mom's endless, grasping caw, clean up after her for five years while she died, and then try to find himself a little piece of peace with a couple of women who knew a good, unimpressive man to wear the pants for when they saw one?*

"You put $10,000 in cash in a briefcase and gave it to a guy from the IRS!?" his lawyer Mickey had blurted it out.

He was right. How can he rationalize this B-movie blunder? But what should he have said: "I can't do that, Milt?" *Think for once in your life, schmuck.*

"You put $10,000 in a fucking briefcase!? What were you smoking?"

That's moment number two. If only. *What was I smoking?*

How much time passes this way? He has no idea. You do time, they say. But Jerry knows better (he always knows better). Time does you. You bend over and time does you.

Chapter 32

As soon as Wednesday breakfast ends, preparations for Friday's handprint ceremony begin. The camp caretaker, Wim Zell, has his pickup parked under the pines maybe fifty yards from the front of Brigadoon. The truck bed gate is down with a mound of gravel overflowing it. The great, noisy cement drum grinds on, churning together sand, gravel and concrete mix, a green hose trickling water into the chewed grass around its base.

Tex-Mecks works at Wim's side, smoothing wet cement into the orderly rows marked out by two-by-fours and sawn pegs hammered into the earth. Twenty-eight such rows are designated for the fourteen cabins, and another three rows are laid out for staff and family, including the square that will contain Miffed's perennial paw prints. They begin with the rows closest to the fence. Tex-Mecks spends the day squatting, etching names into the fresh cement with a pointed stick.

It's thrilling. The squish of wet cement between your fingers and toes, the permanence of your name (or nickname) in concrete, the eternal proximity to your cabinmates, boyfriend or girlfriend, and the chance—where else do you get it?—to make a mark in the present that will live without alteration into the future, to wave your hand or wiggle your toes to the person you will one day be. Kilroy was here, and here Kilroy will stay.

Great latitude is allowed for names. Pet names show up in quotation marks, as with Marcia 'Cookie' Cohen. Sometimes a catch phrase occupies that spot, like Billy 'Be Free' Hechtman. Diminutives are ubiquitous, as are nicknames that emphasize the diminutive, like 'Tink' and 'Twerp'. And sometimes you get the person's handle, no quotes: Doctor Dave Mosher, Ziggy Stardust Zimmerman, Big Bird. Others opt for the formal: Tex-Mecks lists himself as Sgt David Mecklenberg. There's room for everyone to self-create.

Over the years, Kathy Klein has left behind a litany of selves: Katie, Kate, Kathy. Now she is empty. She wants to tell Tex-Mecks to leave her block blank. No name. Nothing. "How do you want it?" he asks.

"Just K," she says.

Tex-Mecks seems confused. "Just the letter?"

"If that," she replies, cryptically.

Before she sticks her hand in the smooth wet cement, Tex-Mecks has already begun to write, "K. Klein." Capital letter. Period. The 'K' is kicking a small stone into the rest of her. She lifts the hose and rinses the crumbly muck off her right foot and left hand, the combination that denotes nine years.

Just before dinner, Tex-Mecks cuts thick plastic sheets from a long roll. He spreads the plastic over the drying handprints, pinning it at the corners with large rocks. This way, the prints can set undisturbed.

* * *

Time is Philip's enemy. The week is flying, and the curfew Bernie imposed after the fire is keeping him from the one thing, the one person, he still cares about. He would happily close the door on camp, if it weren't for Jody. Jody and the glaring fact that he has no place to go. His mother has begun her Mexican pilgrimage, and his father has lit out for no one knows where. Philip has been cut loose. He used to have two homes, three if you count Friedkin (he would have). Now he has none.

What he has is $2000 worth of Traveler's Cheques in his pocket. "Consider it allowance," his dad said, which, under the circumstances, might translate as 'See ya. Wouldn't want to be ya.'

He's got the plastic wallet in the pocket of his jeans, folded in a lump. It protrudes like a second erection, and it makes him self-conscious. He doesn't know where else to stash so much money. It's what he's got. That and one beautiful thing: Jody. She's the last string that keeps him tethered to this place, to anything at all. But time is slipping away. She is slipping away.

"We make a world from freaks." Lila admitted it. Right before she went nuts, wailing like a lunatic, proving her own point. Freaks and liars, hypocrites and tyrants, from the president on down. A lifetime has come and gone in no time. A curtain has lifted on this freak show of a world. He wishes he'd been as crazy as Kotlicky, that he'd had the balls to light a match to the house of dress-up. He doesn't, so he performs the one small act of protest he can think of to show them to themselves.

* * *

The Abe Burrows Theatre sits on Swallow Heart Lake's Main Street; it's named for a Broadway luminary who visited camp in 1959, while on vacation at Schwartzkopf's. As *West Side's* night rehearsal ends in Burrows, Uncle Bernie and Tex-Mecks are coming up the front steps. They march down the aisle in tandem, looking dour, and approach Sylvie. Bernie holds her arm above the elbow, gently, and speaks low in her ear. The room quiets. Sylvie's face goes stern. "I'll go with you," Sylvie says.

She hands a sheaf of rehearsal notes to Neil Roven at the piano and proceeds with Bernie up the aisle. Tex-Mecks, falling in behind, pauses when he reaches Kathy, he opens one palm towards the door, saying only, "Please."

The girl trails him, expressionless.

At the edge of camp, Tex-Mecks clicks on a large lantern-style flashlight whose bright throw points their way. Sylvie and her husband, Bernie, walk arm in arm, the girl behind.

Children pass and greet them, but nothing detours them. They skirt the main building, cross the drive on which they can feel the bumps and pits of handprints from the camp's early years under their feet. They continue through the trees in the direction of the fence. Bernie and Sylvie stop. Tex-Mecks blocks the girl with his arm. He approaches Sylvie and Bernie and shines the light down at their feet. Two planks span the width of the new cement, propped on the two-by-four edges of the plot, a bridge of boards. Tex-Mecks ushers Bernie onto one of the planks. Bernie extends his hand to Sylvie.

Tex-Mecks peels back the plastic drop. The girl hears Sylvie snarl. She has been trained to project her emotions across an expanse, and she does. She projects revulsion. The girl steps out of the shadow over to the adults. Even Kathy is shocked to see the name.

"I didn't do this," she says. "You know I would never do that." Kathy musters all her strength to face Sylvie. "Tex-Mecks wrote it. He'll remember: 'K. Klein'."

There is no malice in Sylvie's voice, but there's no compassion either. "What do you think you're playing?"

Sylvie, Bernie and Tex-Mecks become statues. Their silence says, 'look at yourself.' Kathy had nothing to do with the name before them, but she feels the guilt anyway. She has done so much wrong. Shame rises off of her, wave after wave. What does she think she's playing? She carried the *Diary* into camp, clutched it to her everywhere. She didn't only *allow* other kids to call her Anne Frank; she reveled in it. She made the century's horror a drama of her puny self. She was jealous of Jody, so she threw herself at Dorfman and wound up burning down the costume shop. She let Kotlicky take the blame, let him be exiled in her shame. What does she think she's playing? The question cuts through the summer. It pierces her self-incriminating heart.

Philip searches for Jody. By the time he passes the place where the new handprints harden, everyone is gone but Tex-Mecks, working by flashlight, on his hands and knees, wielding a chisel and mallet. Philip stops long enough to see the former Green Beret smash a block of hardening concrete to pieces, as if the name of a girl who died thirty years ago might kill.

Chapter 33

It's hard to drink yourself to death. Your throat doesn't want you to do it. Your throat, whose every evolutionary instinct is to keep anything that might kill you from getting down, fights you for your own life. You see those suicidal sons of bitches in movies slug it down the hatch before the hatch closes. They're fighting to stop their own gag reflexes from saving their lives. Jerry Rosen drank. He vomited. He poured it back. He vomited. Finally, he poured it back until he stopped vomiting. He tricked the trip wire of his throat.

He had led a tough little alley life and read the dailies and watched the newsreels. He'd watched his mother take her sweet time dying. He had arrived in Europe as a medic, prepared to see it all. And he had. He'd seen men blown apart, limbs torn from their joints, intestines hanging outside their bodies. His CO had been carried past him, face gone. Jerry had spent four months in the European theatre, but none of what he was walking into was covered in basic, or in the weeks of medical technician training. He was walking into something that had never happened before.

Jerry is a kid. If he drinks himself to death and lives through it, which he won't really, his eyes will chill like ice. He'll grow a thick, jowly five-o'clock shadow—think Nixon in bad light on TV. Now, though, his beard is wisp and dirt. He's got a dimple in his chin. He's a kid for Christ's sake, and he's walking into Buchenwald with a rucksack of medical supplies and a cigarette hanging out of his mouth.

Bud Moll is next to him, a little behind. Hank Greer next to Bud. A couple of the other guys are footsteps further back. You'd think they'd stop at the gate. Go silent and slack-jawed staring because there's nothing else they can do unless it's to lie down in a ball and sleep. Or turn around and run. But the ground here is mucky. It isn't long before they figure out they're walking in human excrement and piss. Soon their boots are caked with it. Even Patton went behind a building and puked the first time he entered one of the camps. Patton, Eisenhower and Bradley were only days ahead of Jerry, Bud and Henry. No one is prepared, however thoroughly he's been briefed.

But they are American GIs, medics, so at 19, 20, 21, they keep walking. The heroes got here a couple of days earlier, and if there was any fanfare, it happened then. The American Flag was flown. A few guys got hoisted into the air by the inmates still strong enough to lift them. One of the German guards, trying to pass himself off as a prisoner, was beaten to death in his striped uniform while the soldiers stood back. Civilians from town were being rounded up and led through the barracks and crematorium. Now, they're digging a mass grave and carrying body after body on makeshift stretchers. This processional, with its endless supply of dead will last for days. Another will follow. Then another.

Jerry and the boys are stragglers after the parade, taking it in, though, of course, that's impossible. They will join the burial brigade and continue to lay bodies in the earth after the townspeople have been led away. They will jab their shovels in the barely thawed earth. Sometimes, they will lay the bodies down and, sometimes, they will toss them or simply tip the stretchers or wooden wheelbarrows and watch the rigid corpses roll clumsily off. Somebody who should know estimates that, all told, they bury 10,000 corpses. They will clean out the dysentery barracks. They will try to feed the starving. Jerry will hand a man a chocolate bar and watch him choke to death on it.

Most of the boys won't eat much. They'll give their food away and feed themselves in a partial, distracted way. There are a few, like Whitey Morrison, who eat like pigs, stuffing their faces quickly and compulsively, grabbing uneaten portions off their mess mates' tins. There are more, like Jerry, who drink and tell macabre jokes in voices that are too loud, who spend long minutes following, with lazy eyes, the drift of their own cigarette smoke.

They will try to tackle disease one case at a time. They will have to remind themselves that the creatures they encounter once had families and hometowns and professions. At first, they will ask these creatures their names. Then they won't. They will try to avoid their eyes, and they will be unable to look away. Soon, they'll master the look that wipes the field of visions even as it scans, the look that doesn't see fuck-all. They will hike from camp to camp, and they will never leave.

A couple of years later, when, as an ex-GI, Jerry tries his hand at acting, he will be a supernumerary in an abridged *Henry V* at the Pasadena Playhouse with Shelley Berman as King Henry and Geraldine Page as the French queen-to-be, Katherine. He will seize on the Chorus' line: "From camp to camp through the foul womb of night…" That's how, from then on, Jerry will describe it to himself. *The foul womb of night.* That's how he will boil the whole thing down, reduce it, pressing it in a dusty book of Shakespeare histories until, brown and brittle, it can be shelved and forgotten.

Given the image, given the smell of *foul* and his associations with *womb*, it's surprising he can ever fuck again. But he does, he will, even after he drinks himself to death. That's where he's more like Whitey, fucking whoever he's got on his plate and whoever he can grab off someone else's. Stuffing his face with fucking. Fucking like there is no tomorrow.

Everything smells like shit in a war, including your own body. Your feet and other feet. Your mouth and other mouths. In war, it's the dark ages, before plumbing, before sewers, people throwing personal sludge from buckets out the window into the street. You get used to a lot—what you see and what you smell.

Jerry's dad used to roll up the windows of the car when they drove past the factories of Gary, Indiana, but the smoke and stench would still get in. His father isn't here. No one is driving this car. This smell is tidal, sudden and suffocating, more a condition of the world than a sensory experience. His skin and eyes smell it. His organs taste it. Even if you could hold your breath you couldn't keep it out. It is the most pervasive, most horrible thing he's ever experienced, even more than what he sees. The afterdeath, Bud starts calling it.

They will keep walking for three months, following the path of liberation from here to Mathausen and Gusen. It is here, though, in these first days, that Jerry Rosen died. The kid, at least, died. The kid died, and the seething man lived to not tell the tale. The boy drank till he died and, after one night or two, a day or several days—he would never know—he woke in a German bunk in what had been the guard barracks and was now the Allied military hospital. He was sick or crazy or both, it didn't matter because he was dead. And from that you never recover. You don't get to tell the story of your own death. That's one of the rules.

He told so many stories—just not about this. This is the one that floods his prison cell and that keeps him awake. It's the one that plays in the background of the Nazi thrillers he reads and the kitchen clean-up he does so well. This is the one story he told only to himself, never stopping to check the facts. Checking facts would entail looking back, something you don't do. Look back and you turn to stone—or ash or a pillar of salt. So he never checked, and, when her story came out, he told himself (and only himself) that he'd buried a young girl, the one from the diary, the one who became known to everyone: Anne Frank.

He elaborated the story, remembering (imagining?) an afternoon when he was strangely alone among the dead. He saw a small stiff slightly apart from the others, as though it had fallen from a wheelbarrow and been left there. He walked to the skeleton and lifted it in his arms. He had a mask on and thick gloves, but still this you didn't do. You didn't cradle bones. You kept contact minimal, if you made contact at all. You hoisted a body by the radiocarpal joint and your partner grabbed the tibia bone above the ankle. But that afternoon something compelled him, and he carried the small remains like a lover. He placed her in the ground. He secreted that story in his cold heart until the day in August of 1974 when he told his son, "I buried her."

He believed it. Without knowing he was doing so, he held this belief sacred, fed it. Not that the camp burials were careful or dignified or kind, but they were final. Maybe there had been deliverance in the act, offering that smart young girl with her lofty dreams a final place to rest. She was a few years younger than he was, a few years older than his sister. Jerry Rosen might play the big shot, he might be wiseass fun at a party, but he never did a noble thing in his life. If you asked him, he'd tell you. He drank his way through the war. He fucked his way through Pigalle after. He was mean and sarcastic. He was too smart for his own good. He never loved his wives, hardly loved anyone. A minor shitheel in a major shithole world. But one day, in his twentieth year, his little life had crossed paths with history, and he'd done right by it. He had buried Anne Frank.

He never went back to map the trip. If he had, the truth would have been obvious: Anne Frank died in Bergen-Belsen. He never set foot there. Some Brits interred her, if the Nazis didn't. He didn't bury her or save her, didn't even save himself. If anyone had put two and two together and told him, he might have responded, "Okay, some other girl then; it doesn't matter. There were lots of young people there. Maybe one of them was another like her."

But no one ever set him straight because no one knew what he carried and believed. Even Philip. He heard what his father said, but it mostly went past him. His dad didn't mean it literally. He meant he *might* have buried her, may as well have. Just as he'd failed to read his father's pain on that trip to Yad Vashem in Israel, among holocaust photos, he lost, in the emotional blur of their lunch at Injun Joe's, his father's secret. Jerry believed, as though it were fact, that he'd lain that girl in her grave.

Chapter 34

Crisis is the normal of the theatre, and so the frenzy of these last days doesn't faze the veterans. The costume tent has become a fixture. Estelle Nye and a corps of helpers man the tent around the clock to gather, sort, alter, appliqué, repair, press, drape and jury-rig several hundred outfits, from hats to boots, even as children stream through for fittings. The wry, unflappable Estelle doesn't drop a stitch, an ash (though she smokes nonstop) or a joke. Lila joins in between rehearsals and picks up whatever is at hand, as though she never left.

Ziggy, too, works at night, alongside a band of assistants. They swarm the stages of Burrows and Gershwin, the two camp theatres, painting flats and platforms, and hanging, focusing and gelling lights. No one knows how Ziggy manages to be in both spaces at once. "I astrally project," he claims when asked. "It's the only sensible way."

Counselors drill lines, accompanists pound out harmonies, dance teachers shout steps over the choral croaking of dozens of kids whose vocal cords are shot from too much use with too little diaphragm support. The children do what children do: squirm in their costumes, stare off into the wings and audience, mouth each other's lines. They prompt each other to move or speak. They smile—breaking character completely—when anybody laughs or applauds. In other words, they prepare to be great.

And then, as happens every year at this time, a miracle occurs. Every year at this time, 250 kids, most of whom have less than a passing interest in acting, singing and dancing, crack open the shells of their young selves and emerge transformed—and just a little magnificent. When the tailor Motel Kamzoil sings, "Wonder of wonders, miracle of miracles," he might be describing this.

But before the miracle, *dreck.*

And then it's over. There will be no more classes, no more rehearsals, no more blocking changes or 'take it from the top'. Everyone will go to bed. The next morning, Saturday, after breakfast, the ultimate clean-up will begin before the mad parental dash, before one show after another takes each stage, before Sunday, when the last of them goes home.

The end. They hear it coming, the low rumble and engine roar, a weekend of too many events and too many goodbyes.

For Philip, the end is a cliff. And he's falling the way you do in those Road Runner dreams where you're the Wily Coyote and, instead of hitting earth with a *Poof* of dust, you keep falling, falling.

It's like that David Crosby song, "Where will I be when I go back home?" "Nowhere!" is Philip's answer. There is no home. Mom can't even get herself to visiting day. Dad will miss more than *West Side Story*. He'll miss everything.

* * *

Like a badly written play by a dramatist addicted to serial theatrical event, camp has several false endings. The past weekend was meant to be one of them: closing ceremonies for the Olympics, an ending preempted by the fire. Friday night's handprint ceremony is the ritual ending of all-camp activities. Saturday's parental stampede ends the homesick part of summer, but the production schedule spills into Sunday. By Sunday at 4:00, the last campers will be gone. Before that, on Saturday night—mid-parents' weekend—the teens get carted away for yet another celebration of summer's end: Prom. But first, handprints.

They come from all corners of camp. They home in on the handprints and surround them. The red glow of flares bordering the handprints illuminates their expectant faces. A rosy haze rises above the new cement and filters through the overhanging branches and into the dark night sky, a mournful mist.

Lila waits at the far end of the new cement, Miffed at her feet. She patiently directs the children into place.

Nervous giggling and the shushing of counselors. Of course, the kids are nervous. Lila is about to unleash the demons of sadness and longing. The tear-fest is about to begin.

It's a spooky memorial. They circle the handprints like people at the edge of their own graves. They are burying the summer. The air smells of sulfur and metal.

Lila raises her arm, the signal for quiet. The hand goes up; the mouth goes shut. Three hundred hands rise up. The human world is silent. The natural world drones and clicks around them.

Lila lowers one arm around little Suzie Shinder; the other enwraps Marla Bensinger, the junior counselor advisor. As if choreographed, hundreds of arms hover and descend this way, until they are all linked, like dancers or protesters, woven together, one big braid, looping endlessly into itself. Will the circle be unbroken? Never. This will be Lila's theme. It is always Lila's theme.

"I can't believe how quickly the summer has passed," Lila says. "I can't believe how much you have all grown. We press our hands and feet into the cement, so that we will always remember who we were when we arrived, and who we were when we parted. We press them into the cement, so that we will always be together. Here. In this place.

"And we will always be together no matter how far we travel. We have this bond, this connection, and it lasts forever."

Philip has one arm around his co-junior counselor Doctor Dave and the other around Jody, linking him, also, to Kathy Klein and, by extension, to her counselor Colleen Kramer and to Sheila Aspillaga. Jody is warm against his ribs and sweating slightly. The scent of Charlie perfume is on her skin, Gee Your Hair Smells Terrific shampoo in her hair. The little boys from his cabin are in front of him, with their tawny, athletic counselor, Terry Heisman, towering over. Philip has a smoky view of Dorfman across the way, Jack close behind, Jody's now-ex, Jack.

Philip traces the plait of arms, the human lanyard of people he used to call family. He has had camp brothers and sisters, close friends, best friends, rivals, an enemy or two. Girls he has kissed and girls he's wanted to kiss. He has been a junior counselor and a camper with counselors of his own, some, like Marty Ball, still around the circle. Why is Marty still here? What kind of empty lives do these people live that they keep coming back year after year?

He has called Lila his 'other mother' and sat at her feet, soaking up wisdom about acting and life. Sylvie and Bernie have been his 'aunt' and 'uncle'. Lila rolls out the big "we are all connected" waterworks at the end of every summer to seal the deal. Seeing them now in this hellish light, he knows it's all a sham, one big sales pitch.

Philip tightens his arm around Jody. He looks for the square holding Klein's hand and foot. It was his one rebellion in all these years. He'd grabbed a paint mixer from backstage at Gershwin and dragged it back and forth across the drying cement, like a window squeegee. Then he'd used the edge to cut in the name: Anne Frank. Why should it matter? Nothing they do here means anything in the world beyond. Why is one name more dangerous than another? Why was he afraid? He wishes he'd wiped out all the other names, left only the dead girl's.

But there it is: "K. Klein," left hand, right foot, just like all the others, as if nothing happened.

"Camp." Michael Kitzke, the guy who brought his dad's car, had laughed when he said the word. He was right to laugh. Friedkin is a joke, a self-serious joke.

Lila invokes Gramma Della, "How proud she would be to see us all here together, to see how we lived side by side this summer, how well we loved one another..."

The sound of weeping punctuates her words. Sniffles become sobs, gasps for breath. Little kids bawl. Thirteen-year-old boys stare at their feet and shift back and forth, swiping their eyes with their elbows. Even Big Bird, the unnaturally tall tennis pro, who has proclaimed the Handprint Ceremony 'the sexiest moment of the summer' has wet red streaks on his cheeks.

Now, they're all squeezing the hell out of each other, the lacing of arms tightening into a universal embrace. Jody begins to tremble. Philip kisses her tears and hair. He draws her in, and Kathy, still under Jody's arm, gets pulled in with her. She's knotted up in them, smushed against Jody's shoulder and Philip's ear. Their breath heats her cheek. She smells Philip's sweat as he kisses Jody's face.

Lila paraphrases John Donne's meditation, "No man is an island, entire of itself; every man is a piece of the continent, a part of the main. Like the land and the lake and the sky," she says, "we are all part of one another. We always will be." This, as everyone knows, is the cue for the camp anthem, the heart of everything: "You'll Never Walk Alone."

They sing and cry and sway and cry. Before the night is over, Larry Dorfman will stroll into the field with Lisa Climan, who will let him French kiss her, and then politely ask him to escort her back to Brigadoon. He will bow ever so slightly, offer his elbow, and walk her home. Jack will find his way down to the archery pit with a couple cabinmates, where they will get high and remain remarkably quiet. Melly Barber will trek out to the stables on route 57 with a pint of Jack Daniels. She will break in and sing a raucous version of Melanie's 'Beautiful People' to the horses. She will leave the mostly empty bottle on the stall wall and stumble back to Friedkin.

Before the night is over, Philip will lead Jody to the back of Showboat, raging about 'hypocritical bullshit' and 'group hypnosis'. "It's a fucking cemetery," he says of the handprints. Jody will kiss him quiet. When he slips his hand into her bra, she will shudder, not with pleasure, but with aversion. She won't understand her own reaction but will know it's real. She will let him pet her, but she'll disappear. From far away, she will reach into his pants and stroke him until he ejaculates. "I have to get back," she will say and, as she hurries towards her cabin, "Bye, Philly."

Before the night is over, Marla Bensinger, the junior counselor advisor, will steal into the dining hall with Kathy Klein and make her sip apple juice through a straw. She will feed her crackers and a piece of dry toast. Fix her a cup of tea. When Max comes down to find out why the noise, he will scramble two eggs for the girl, which Marla will feed her, one fork at a time, the way you'd feed your baby sister. Later, Marla will walk the girl to her bunk and tuck her into bed, as though she knows everything but chooses to comfort her anyway.

But first, everyone sings the song that links them to this linked world, glancing around their family circle through dying flare light and sulfur haze. They hold close, very close, one final time. The song ends as, on cue, the last flare sputters out. Darkness fills the circle. They lose sight of their handprints and their names.

Chapter 35

Tex-Mecks lifts the heavy two-by-four barricading the front gate and swings it open. Parents storm the campgrounds in a Maenadic fury, with hungry arms and rapacious eyes. Within minutes, the camp population nearly triples. Chaos reigns. The air is rent with shrieks, names shouted. The hordes embrace and moan, shoving past each other's children to devour their own.

Bernie, Max and Sylvie, adorned in dress whites, wave from the front porch of Anatevka like royalty. Kids drag parents to meet counselors. Praise flies. Teenagers roll their eyes and submit to obligatory hugs with amiable condescension. The theatre staff pries the youngest campers away from their moms and dads and herds them towards their morning shows. "You'll see Daddy in a little while. It's time to get into your costume."

With warm smiles and hearty handshakes, the jovial staff corrals parents into the costume tent for the kick-off. "Come one, come all," calls Uncle Bernie, the barker's barker. "Step right up to the wonderful world of Carnival."

"Take a seat," Kenny Tannenbaum crows from his post at the tent entrance. "Plenty of chairs for everyone!" It takes every ounce of inner strength for Kenny to refrain from telling these adults about the Indian Burial Mound he's sure he's found, even more so because Bernie, after a week of hearing Kenny talk about nothing else, has forbidden him to mention it.

Most campers hang back, as ordered, letting their folks take the seats. Some giddy with the reunion, nestle onto their parents' laps or crowd the aisles, still clutching their mothers' hands. Parents "oo" and "aah" with astonishment, as they wander into the tent. This could be a wedding, a Bar Mitzvah, a lawn party on a lakefront estate. "Is this where the costume shop was?" people ask. A dad shouts to Bernie, "Mr. Magoo, you've done it again!" Bernie beams and points at the heckler, like a presidential candidate after a boffo speech.

Show business begins with show, and show at Friedkin begins with Sylvie, who appears at the front of the tent and, unexpectedly, begins to sing, accompanied by Neil Roven on a spinet that has been, by some miracle, transported there. The song is "Welcome Home," Harold Rome's lush hymn of return from *Fanny*. "Welcome home, says the street," Sylvie croons with a fervent smile, "as you hurry on your way…" The street, the lamp, the clock, the whole inanimate world stands ready to welcome the assembled families of Friedkin.

Look at her sing. She is planted center stage, her large, dark eyes moist and expressive, her hands strong. Sylvie's voice has been troubled by nodes in recent years, but the slight chafing in her upper octave, which necessitates a periodic shift into a foggy falsetto, has done nothing to temper her attack. She is the very image of power on stage, of "I am woman, hear me roar." She is so replete, so absolutely Sylvie. She embodies the very message she teaches: "Be yourself. There is no one like you. Give being you your all." Look at her. If she lives to be ninety-five—and she will—she will always be this woman.

The song ends, and the circus canvas shakes with applause. Community has been restored; fire forgotten. Let the games begin.

Lila, meanwhile, busies herself around Gershwin, where the first *Wizard of Oz* cast dresses. The players wiggle and squirm. She pins a Dorothy frock, dabs freckles on a pair of Scarecrows, and strokes the fur of a Cowardly Lion, with a roaring case of stage fright. *We will get through this*, she thinks.

Kathy Klein's mom arrives late, having decided to drive up from Evanston that morning, instead of spending the night in Swallow Heart Lake. "I couldn't remember whether it took two or two-and-a-half hours to get here. I guess it takes three," she tells her daughter, loitering outside Carnival.

"Let me look at you," she says. She twirls Kathy around the way you would in a big Broadway musical.

"Can Philip go to lunch with us?" Kathy asks.

"Absolutely!"

"He has no one visiting."

"Double absolutely," says her mom.

Kathy finds Philip at his cabin, Paint Your Wagon. He's throwing clothes into a duffel bag. He can't go to lunch. Has too much to do—see his campers in Oklahoma, go over his own lines.

"You work too hard," she tells him. "You can take an hour for lunch. Besides, my mom adores you and I have absolutely nothing to say to her. Pleeeez?"

"Sorry. Can't. Thanks anyway."

Kathy hesitates. This may be her last time alone with him, maybe for a long while. They're talking through the screen door. "How'd it go with Jody last night?" She almost chokes on the question.

"Great," he says loudly. "It's great." She can tell he's agitated, and he is. He can't stop thinking about last night. Can't sort it out, the feeling that he was touching Jody and she didn't want him to, kissing her and she wished he wasn't. Then she put her hand in his pants, which she'd never done. But it was like she didn't give a shit. He felt sick after she left. She didn't love him. He repulsed her is how it felt.

"That's great," she says at the same time. "I want it to be great for you. You deserve great."

"Thanks."

"I want Jody to be good to you," she adds.

"She is good to me," he says.

Oh, Philip, come out of there. She would scream if she wasn't afraid he'd slam the door. Philip signals the desire to go deeper into his cabin, but she can't let him. "That was an amazing idea for an Olympics skit—*A Polish Family*. It would have been excellent, instead of a joke, like the rest of them. What a travesty, cancelling the Olympics before we could see it."

"It would have been a joke, too. Like everything here."

146

He's really scaring her. She's never seen him like this, so blasé. She wants to shake him back into being Philip.

"It's not like they even understand quality," she says, trying to agree with what he's just said.

He's flicking paint chips off the doorframe.

"Marla kidnapped me last night," Kathy says. Philip shows no interest in this oddball accusation. "She actually dragged me to Ollie's and fed me like a baby. You know, 'airplane going in...'"

"That's pretty pathetic." She can barely hear him.

"I know. I mean I'm not an infant. I know how to hold a fork."

"No, it's pathetic she had to do it. What do you expect if you starve yourself? You want George Harrison to hold a concert for you?"

This she hears. Suddenly, he's talking, loud and angry, and she's glad there's a door between them. All that makes it through is 'fucking handprints'.

"Philip," she says. Her fingers touch the screen. He stops talking. Her mind is running through things she could say. She wants to ask if he was the one who changed her handprint, wrote 'Anne Frank'. She thinks he was. She has never seen violence in him, and now it's everywhere, seething through the door. She wants to ask him why. *Please Philip, say something. Philip the vandal, confess.* She still has that indecipherable letter she wrote to him in her pocket, folded like a cootie catcher. She wants to hand it over and run away.

"You sure about lunch?" she asks, finally.

"Yeah. Thanks anyway."

"Okay, well, see you at prom."

"Yeah, prom." Again, under his breath.

She spins around, 360 degrees. He's still there. She spins again, a ballerina. She remembers this same spin, a moment like this – 1972. Out of the blue, Philip had asked her to go steady. He'd given her his ID bracelet, an etched silver rectangle with beveled sides. He kissed her left cheek to seal the exchange and watched her trace 'Philip' with her finger, as the bracelet cuffed the back of her hand. It was Wednesday. They went steady until Saturday, visiting day, when his mother made him take his ID back. Kate, as she was known that year, squeezed the latch and lowered it link by link into Philip's palm. She started to leave, pirouetted, gave him a kiss, just brushing the corner of his mouth, and said a rueful, "Goodbye, Philip." This time when she spins full circle, he's vanished into the dark cabin.

* * *

Saturday night, the last official night of camp, is yet another ending. Many of the campers have gone home, and only two Sunday morning shows remain. It is prom night. Prom is a party for the oldest cabins and junior counselors: pizza, dessert and a free jukebox for dancing on the top floor of one of Sheboygan's tallest buildings, none of which reach more than seven stories. While parents cool their heels at town resorts, over gin and tonics or fanciful summer drinks, prom keeps the teens out of Swallow Heart Lake. Out of trouble. By the time the buses bring them back from prom, everyone is whupped.

Whatever goes down in the pre-dawn hours is an afterthought. They eke out what sleep they can before performing their final shows.

Friedkin prom is the opposite of high school prom, which is an exercise in independence, a closing blowout on the town. Friedkin prom offers no independence, no room for blowouts, and no town. The kids are stuck in a large, non-descript room—like a stripped hotel restaurant up on cinder blocks—without beer or privacy, with yesterday's pizza and a selection of music that would feel dated to their parents. Nobody dances.

Larry Dorfman is soaking it up. He's scored big as Tevye in *Fiddler on the Roof*—Sylvie told him he 'out-Tevyed Marty Ball'—and is reliving the triumph. Michael Dupler estimates that the applause after 'If I Were a Rich Man' lasted a solid two minutes. "I thought you should take a bow right then," he says. Dorfman replies with an enigmatic, "Old World!"

Their parents wept the way parents aren't supposed to weep, as the cast tore itself away from 'tumble-down, work-a-day' Anatevka. "I didn't even know my dad *could cry*," a girl says.

Jody Gold occupies the center of another large claque, clustered on padded restaurant chairs angled in a dozen directions. The boys tip their chairs back or straddle them, the girls, shoeless, sit cross-legged. Philip stands just outside the circle. Jody's talking a mile a minute and looking everywhere but at him.

"I mean he saw me walking out of the woods, but he asked me where I was coming from. I said, 'C'mon, Tex-Mecks, you can never know where another person is coming from!'" A laugh goes up from her court. Philip shifts and groans, a mast on a churning sea. Does she even know he's there?

"Then I looked at him really seriously," she lowers her voice to a whisper, her sexy overbite catching her bottom lip. "I mean, I was doing reds and totally calm—and I said, 'Where are you coming from, Dave?'"

"What did he say?" Lisa Climan asks.

"Nothing at first. Shit, he's so eerie calm sometimes, I think he does downers. He just stared at me, you know, like he does, like he's some cowboy deciding whether to kill you or buy you a drink. He just stares. But no way I'm giving him the satisfaction of showing him I'm FREAKIN' OUT. So I just eyeball him. Then he says, 'But I know where you're going.'

"And he points to the cabin. So I give him a little wave and say, sweet as I can, 'Night, hon.'"

They laugh, appreciative of Jody's subtlety. But Jody lets it pass. Subtlety is not daring, daring is not danger. "When I got to the back porch," she says almost casually, "I lifted my shirt and flashed him."

"NO!"

"Jody!"

"You didn't!"

"No!"

Jody smiles with one corner of her mouth, knowing what she knows. Jack takes a contented drag on his cigarette. He's smoking and none of the adults seem to notice or care.

Philip can't figure out if Jody's high. She flushed her stash, she said. She was through with Jack, she also said, but here she is putting on this show for him.

And she said she loved Philip, which he believed until last night got weird. Until he touched her, and she shuddered. Revolted. Yes, that's what it was.

Jody unfolds her bare legs and plops her feet in Jack's lap.

Philip takes off. There's a door at the back of the room, and he heads for it. As he passes Dorfman and his sycophants, Dorfman hails him, "Stanislaw!"

Kathy finds him on the back stairs six flights down, doubled over himself on one of the lowest steps. The stairwell is industrial gray. On the door at the bottom, a red sign reads 'Emergency Exit'. She crouches a few steps above.

"Philip," she says, softly.

"They all just go their merry way," he says.

"That's what people do. That's what makes them such sorry specimens." She sits sideways a few stairs above him, feet up on the vertical rails. She can feel the bulge of the letter she wrote to Philip in the dark.

"If I opened that door, would an alarm go off?" he asks.

"Only if it's an emergency. Is it an emergency?"

"I don't know."

"Do you want the alarm to go off?"

"I don't know."

"Yeah," she says, not sure what she's agreeing to.

"I keep wanting to go through that door," he says.

"To set off the alarm or to get out?"

"I don't know." It's a question. He wants an answer.

"Philip," she says, the only answer she knows.

"I thought she wanted what I wanted."

She says nothing.

"I believed."

Nothing again.

He straightens up, his body acknowledging her for the first time. "Why did you two stop talking? You were fucking Siamese twins and then, suddenly, you don't even speak for almost two years."

"You have to ask Jody."

"I did."

"What did she say?"

"She said it was girl stuff."

Kathy sneers.

"Was it about me?" he asks.

She takes a second. They're talking about years ago, but it's still fresh. Jody with her leash, leading on a boy she didn't desire. Because she could. Some sick power. This boy. "She said something to me. I couldn't trust her anymore. That's all."

"Said something about me?" His hope makes him stupid.

"Oh Philip, leave it alone. We had a fight."

Philip stands. He's in the space between the bottom of the stairs and the door. The stairwell is airless. She's pinching the letter as though it's part of her leg, and she needs the pain to stay present. "Look at me," she says.

He does. It chills her.

"My father says he buried Anne Frank," Philip says.

"What?"

"He buried her. He thinks he did. And her sister. He went into whatever camp it was and dug a hole and dumped them all into it. Like cordwood, he said."

"Oh my God."

"She was probably there."

"That's horrible."

"And you waltz around with your book like you're playing a part in some high school play."

"No, Philip. That's not it—"

"You act it out, like there's a Joni Mitchell soundtrack, and your life is such a burden."

"You don't want to do this."

"Like all the pain is great fun."

"Don't be mad at me. Please."

"I mean, Jesus, Klein, what the hell have you ever had to live through? What the hell have you ever suffered?"

"Please, Philip, I'm your friend—"

"Mommy and Daddy got divorced. Guess I'll go starve myself now."

"This is me—"

"And who is that? Anne Frank?"

"Dorfman hit me."

"Great, so now you have some real-life experience."

"He did more than that."

"Do you write this stuff as you go along?"

"And Kotlicky—"

"Did Kotlicky laugh at you?"

"I'm sorry about Jody, Philip. I'm sorry that she cringed like that last night..."

"Cringed? Cringed? Did she tell you that? What did she say?"

"She didn't tell me anything, doesn't tell me anything. I just heard her talking."

"She told people that?"

"I'm sorry. I shouldn't have said anything."

"Tell me."

"No, Philip. There's nothing to tell. Nothing. Jody's nothing. She feels nothing."

"She loves me." It's a plea.

"She doesn't."

"You're a fucking nightmare, Klein."

She holds the letter out to him...

He pushes through the door. No sound.

"I'm sorry," she says, still holding it.

* * *

Prom ends around 2:00, and the teenagers straggle onto the bus. Philip is already there when the others arrive. He's sitting near the rear leaning against a window, feigning sleep. Kathy spots him as soon as she boards. She watches

150

him but does not approach. She has set herself a task, and she has to carry it through.

Kathy sits down next to Dion, determined. Dion nods his head, a wary combo of "this is good" and "uh-oh". As the bus pulls out, Kathy spins a monologue, starting with the fateful phrase, "I really like you, Dion..." Then for a period of time that seems to Dion to last the entire ride back to camp, she explicates the "but" that follows. "A kiss is just a kiss" is the gist of what she says. To apologize is her underlying action. And in the way of teen confessions, which are really entreaties for comfort from the angst of growing a self, her apology for leading him on culminates with her crying while he holds her in his arms, loosely, as though to protect himself from too much warm proximity. His attention drifts to the window, from which he can see, in the unlit Wisconsin night, mostly nothing.

When the bus gets to Swallow Heart just shy of an hour later, Kathy thanks Dion for understanding and gives him the smallest 'friends only but with a past' kiss on the cheek. She lets him exit before her. Kathy slips back into the seat. She hangs out there until Philip passes down the aisle. She follows him off the bus, a few people behind.

Prom night is over. Some diehards take to the fields, out of a sense of duty. It is the last night of camp; they're supposed to stay out all night. The others are happy to crawl into bed and sleep as long as possible. Eight hours till curtain.

Having 'resolved her issues' with Dion, Kathy Klein doesn't notice anyone but Philip. She's afraid for him, maybe afraid of him. She tracks him from a distance, sticking to the shadows, hiding behind trees like a kid who's supposed to count to ten but peeks. She trails him this way for fifteen or twenty minutes, as he walks with no clear goal. Many of the cabins are empty, the kids already home. It might be off-season, she and Philip intruders, prowling the empty grounds in winter.

Philip stops at The Shed where the camp handyman, Wim Zell, keeps his tools. There's a padlock hanging there, but the hasp is open. Philip goes in. He comes out carrying a shovel.

Now his movements are sure. By the time Kathy reaches the riding rink, she can see Philip's silhouette against the sky, digging, stomping the shovelhead with his heel, throwing dirt around him. He pries stones out with the point of the shovel. He swings the metal like a pickaxe against the ground.

Philip works with a vengeance. When he digs as deeply as he can, he gets on his knees and uses his hands. He's looking for something. He doesn't find it. He stalks to another part of the drumlin and digs again.

This is crazy, she thinks. *He's going to hurt himself.* Kathy squats against the bottom plank of the corral fence. Her fingers paw the ground, testing for softness. She wants to know what he's up against, how hard the soil is. She can't believe he's still going at it—three holes, four holes, one of them deep enough to stand in, halfway up his calves. The sky behind him begins to show pink, but he doesn't notice.

"You waltz around like it's some part in a high school play," he said to her in the stairwell. "What the hell have you ever suffered?"

He was right. But Philip isn't playing. She feels the difference, the distance between herself—an imposter—and him. In the weeks and months that follow, she will blame herself for not going to him, to calm and comfort him. She will blame herself for everything, as if she had held the magic to change the course of his life.

She stays where she is. Fury drives him, some hurt she can't touch. He is trying to break up the crust of the earth. He is looking for *something*, she knows, digging for something. He is digging for bone.

Chapter 36

West Side Story tells the simple story of a boy and girl from warring New York City gangs who fall in love but are destroyed by hate. On this August Sunday morning, the lives of the people who play it are woven invisibly into the fabric of the drama. For an artist like Lila, personal intensity is the grail, the thing you seek. But this summer, with so much loss, so much event, she'd be happy for a solid production, where the kids don't trip over the furniture or break on the high notes.

What she gets is almost too real. Boys so pressurized that even their cool feels crazy. Tony—her Philip as Tony—is tied in knots. He sings 'Something's Coming' with a hope that borders on the desperate. He's beautiful in his scenes with different Marias. You sense that their love is the last thread tying him to anything.

The girls, awkward and provocative, act too old for their age. This, too, is right. Lila has been anxious about Melly Barber all summer, and seeing her play Anita, passed again from hand to hand on stage, bucking back against the threat of rape, she tries to intuit not the girl's past—that's almost evident—but her future. Every Maria is complicated in her own way. Jody Gold, the bridal Maria, plays the scene on tiptoe, as though striving to leave her skin. She views her lover with a mixture of eagerness—to drink in his goodness before he goes—and a skeptical foreknowledge that he will bring about the very opposite of what she longs for. The last Maria—Kathy Klein—is raw with emotion. She moves as though driven by profound questions—how can she love someone who has brought such pain into her life?

The final scene is more than Lila bargained for. Tony enters thinking that his lover, his almost-bride, has been killed. He shouts for her killer, Chino, to kill him, too. But Philip has left the wings to avoid watching Ricky Gross dance his dance, the dance Markie the choreographer banished him from. When the time comes for his death scene, Philip doesn't return.

The stage is empty. Lila waits, listening for Tony's (Philip's) shout of arrival, watching the stairs for a sign of him. She thinks, *He couldn't stand to watch them dance without him.* Philip doesn't appear. She thinks, *He's lost track of how long it takes.* He doesn't appear. She thinks, *He's staging a protest, a walk-out.* "You can do this," she whispers to embolden Ricky Gross, before nudging him back on stage and into the scene that should be Philip's.

All of a sudden, Philip races up the stairs, freezing at the moment he is about to step onstage. He spots Ricky Gross center, turning frantically in every direction. Ricky has seen the show umpteen times. He's sat through a summer of rehearsals. Still he can't remember a single line of the scene, except "Come and get me too, Chino". He keeps repeating it.

Lila is in the wings on the other side, clenching her prompt book, as though willing the words towards him. Philip just stands there, on the brink of the stage, watching his lesser double maul his lines. "Come, too, and get me Chino, too."

Chino shoots Tony. Tony (Ricky) falls. When Lila looks to Philip, he is gone.

As the other actors enter, they are truly confused, a confusion that pushes them past their usual clichés. The audience, unaware that Philip missed his entrance, catches none of this. They are moved by the fallen boy and by the shock on the faces of the gangs as they wander in. They see one story while another, the under-story, is played out, making it more alive: Where is Philip?

Kathy Klein returns as Maria. She gestures towards Chino and demands the gun. Gun in hand, Maria (Kathy) is stricken, as if seeing the unintentional Tony in her arms deepens her awareness of what she is missing. It is a painful, naked performance, and one that Lila wishes she had never witnessed.

Kathy knows right away—even onstage as Maria—that something has gone inexorably wrong. She has witnessed the events leading up to Philip's flight and intuited the depth of his distress. She knows him well enough—or thinks she does—to doubt that he would actually run away. No matter how confused or sad Philip gets, his whole personality, his whole character, is predicated on showing up for other people. Philip Rosen doesn't just flee the theatre like that. He doesn't just leave everybody in the lurch.

But he has. And most of all—and, yes, it is horrendously self-centered to think this way, even in these first moments of his disappearance—he has left her.

Chapter 37

The girl sits the way she always sits, legs crossed in a pipe-cleaner tangle, head bent, elbow out, writing. Furtive little pricks of the pen. That dark inward look, the terminal frown. Ink everywhere. Other girls dot their i's with circles or hearts. She makes slashes and stabs. Whatever she's writing isn't working. She keeps scratching it out.

She's on the steps behind Brigadoon. Almost everyone else gone, her mom is in Anatevka, biding time. She does one thing—this non-writing writing—and obsesses about another: Philip. She has somehow pushed him to it. He reached out to her—the night Nixon resigned, on the pier, in the stairwell at prom—and she failed him utterly. She crowded him, and he fled. Give him space, she advises herself. He will go home to his mother's (no one thinks, otherwise, at first) and get away from here. Kathy doesn't know that Philip believes his father is gone for good; she hopes they'll let him visit Jerry. Then life can regain footing. He'll get back to school, start rehearsals for some lead role in whatever they're doing at Niles North. Only then will she call him. She'll meet him downtown for brunch. Meanwhile, she'll obsess.

She knows that, in time, she'll be able to talk to him about everything—Dorfman, Dion, the fire, maybe even Jody. She can name the place his father might have buried Anne Frank and her sister Margot: Bergen-Belsen. She has the letter she wrote on the porch of Brigadoon in the pocket of her shorts. Maybe she'll rewrite it. Or take the plunge, stick it in the mail.

She has to talk to him. And she has to wait. But this rawness she feels can't wait. She's full and empty all at once. *It's only been a few hours,* she thinks. *Give him couple of days to figure things out. I can live through a couple of days.*

She flips to the front of her journal where she's copied out the famous passage from Anne Frank's diary:

I see the world gradually being turned into a wilderness, I hear the ever-approaching thunder, which will destroy us too, I can feel the sufferings of millions and yet, if I look up into the heavens, I think that it will all come right, that this cruelty too will end, and that peace and tranquility will return again.

In the meantime, I must uphold my ideals, for perhaps the time will come when I shall be able to carry them out.

"Will it?" she asks aloud and makes an 'X' through the whole passage.

"Will it what?" a man's voice asks.

She notices the deck shoes first at the bottom of the steps, then the pasty legs in white shorts, shiny black belt, white knit shirt with navy ribbing, familiar face, large dimpled nose. Uncle Bernie smiles at her. "Good to see you're sticking to your writing."

"Yeah," she says, "more like it's sticking to me."

Uncle Bernie chuckles. "You should write about camp," he suggests. "We have the whole world here."

She doesn't tell him that this is the stupidest thing anyone has ever said to her. She doesn't tell him about her theory that people are so desperate to feel necessary—in light of total existential pointlessness—that they consistently inflate their tiny little lives. They believe their experience will be of interest to everyone. *I'm universal. Write about me! Write about me*! They cry. *Never! Never!* That's her answer.

She just says, "Maybe."

"Think about it," he fights the urge to muss her hair. "The whole world is here."

"I hope you have a good year," she says. "And thanks." She makes a sweeping motion with her arm, as if to say, 'for this place.'

"Thank you, too." He climbs up to her and kisses the top of the head. "See you back." It's an offer.

The girl watches him walk away. She tries to describe his walk, first in her mind, then in the margins of the black sketchbook she uses for a journal. More crossing out. She leaves this: "And you, Scarecrow, I think I'll miss you most of all."

Kathy has another theory she's been toying with. Our human affinities, this theory goes, are chemical. Our bodies and spirits—maybe our biological selves—know how we feel about other people in precise, preconscious ways. Those affinities, those chemistries, are ever and always at work. This means that, separate from personal history—the things that happen in a relationship, the events that occur between us—we are attracted to and repelled by people in the same measure, the same combination, throughout our lives. The people you love, you always love; the people who creep you out, always creep you out. Mixed responses stay mixed.

In the privacy of her own desire, Kathy has sought water, those realms where we swim together, flow in and out of one another, become engulfed. That's why she's always disappointed. She resents the rocky borders of people she loves. But maybe she's missed the point. Maybe people are water and land both, flow and resistance. We fit around, not inside, each other. The fit is how we know who our people are, our tribe. Maybe how we know ourselves.

She flips to a new page, smooths it, chews her pen. She writes three words.

She tears out the page and folds it, once, twice and then from each end. On the front she prints, 'Sylvie. Lila.'

She caps the pen, snaps the journal closed. Before she leaves with her mom, she will hand one of them the note. She will kiss the paper of Sylvie's cheek, or Lila's, and say goodbye. The note—which they will not fully understand—says 'I am sorry.'

Kathy scans the white cabins, screened shanties with forest green shutters, posted along the periphery of Tobacco Road. Their symbolic power is, she believes, a matter of perspective. On visiting days, there are parents who recall

156

the quaint seaside cottages of earlier resorts where they gathered annually with the cousins after the war. Some think the whole mess looks like a Hooverville, gussied up with a shabby coat of paint. To the little kids, it can appear, especially on foggy days, like a magical ring of ancient monoliths.

The girl holds all three images at once. She takes in the field of burnt grass at the center of the circle. 'Green Fields' it's called, after a Yiddish play no one remembers. I've never seen it green, she thinks.

She slings her knapsack onto her shoulder and hefts the duffel bag from the stoop. Her lips are smudged with ink. Her heart, she feels, has been cut open and crudely stitched back together. The scar hurts, a knot behind her ribs. Her chest swells. Her eyes fill. She is so full of love for this silly, deluded little village.

Chapter 38

Philip doesn't show up for school. September comes, and none of his friends have seen him. The phone lines connecting one Friedkin camper to another go haywire. It's like one of those movies from the thirties where a piece of news gets passed through an ever-multiplying gaggle of phone operators, until the screen fractures into dozens of tiny screens. Except those old movies are funny, and this is not. Like Kathy Klein, some experience Philip's disappearance as a personal abandonment. Some have nightmares. The Friedkin kids tell their school friends about the boy who's gone missing. "He was like my best friend," they inevitably say. Lila replays the scene of losing her mother's photo behind the mantel. She recalls the horrified look on Philip's face as he watched her spectacle of mourning. She is worried sick, as though Philip were her own son.

No one answers the phone at his mom's or his dad's. No one has answers. Parents call the Friedkins. They become the center of information, though, in truth, they have none. No one has ever disappeared from Friedkin. They have had their share of sad stories, including suicides by former campers. But these troubled children were not Philip. This is unimaginable.

More troops are coming home from Vietnam. It's a turbid moment. Yellow ribbons, MIA flags, a foul return. Although Philip's missingness is unrelated in every particular, it has this cast to it, the dark misery of something altogether wrong, reaching its tainted, indeterminate end.

In the lore of Friedkin Camp, Philip Rosen ran down the outer stairs and through the pocket playground alongside the Burrows theatre. Only one person saw him go. Jody Gold's other on-again-off-again boyfriend Jack was killing time before the curtain call. Jack played Riff to Philip's Tony and, after being stabbed to death, was spending Act Two swinging on the swings, smoking Luckys and watching from the back of the house. He was finishing a last smoke, perched on the edge of a playground slide. Seeing him, Philip stopped.

Jack remembers saying something like, "Rosen, man, you're the best actor in this place. That was beautiful, man." Philip thanked him and left the yard. Only then did Jack realize that Philip was supposed to be onstage, getting shot.

From there, Philip went straight to his car, parked outside of camp. The car was already packed—a point that has provoked much speculation. He started the car and, before the cast of *West Side Story* finished its final bows, drove out of Swallow Heart Lake. It is believed that he turned north towards Green Bay in search of his father.

No one knows this, of course. Such is the nature of legend. It cannot be verified. Such is the nature of disappearance. It leaves space that only stories can fill.

There are so many stories. What is known is that on August 18th, 1974, sometime around one in the afternoon, Philip vanished.

There were no road incidents that day or that month in Wisconsin, Iowa, Minnesota, or Illinois involving a boy fitting Philip's description or a pimento red Triumph Spitfire. No one who was there that day received a call from him. No cards or letters. Thin air.

At first, Philip's disappearance is mainly puzzling, like a knotty brainteaser in Sunday's paper whose solution will be published the following week. For many, his outburst at Markie was the turning point. They should have seen it coming. The longer he's gone, the more the puzzle becomes a mystery, the more psychological the mystery grows—who was Philip? What was he hiding? What was driving him that no one could see? The mystery becomes a ghost story, then folklore: a junior counselor from camp disappeared one day and haunts the woods. Philip becomes a legend by not being.

It isn't the ghost story that haunts the kids who know him, though. They are haunted by the precipitous loss of their friend. For Kathy Klein, there are too many moments she could have handled differently. In the suspended months after camp, there are too many moments when there's nothing she can do. She will never return to Swallow Heart Lake, neither as K. Klein, the name she assumes for the remainder of high school, nor as Katherine, the name that sticks. She stows her copy of *The Diary of a Young Girl* in a box in a basement closet.

Ricky Gross freaks out. Restless with guilt, he is certain that if he had refused to dance the 'Somewhere Ballet', everything would have worked out. Philip wouldn't have run off the way he did. He pesters Bernie and Lila to check on Philip, which they both do without success. At post-camp, Ricky can talk about nothing else. Philip was supposed to stay for this week of breaking down bunk beds, cleaning and storing sporting goods and musical instruments. Post-campers, made up of junior counselors, counselors and staff, stage a spoof musical, a satire of the summer. Philip wanted to be part of that, Ricky is sure. Ricky's anxiety is extreme and persistent. When, in the fall, word spreads that Philip is, in fact, gone, Ricky, back home in Arizona, blames himself.

He dreams about Philip for years. Specifically, he dreams that Lila pushes him onstage, where he trips over Philip's cold body. In the recurring dream, it takes him several long moments to notice that he and Philip are wearing the same letter jacket and white t-shirt, the same blue jeans. When Philip won't open his eyes, no matter how much dream-Ricky shakes him, dream-Ricky screams and, from that scream, wakes up. The intensity wanes as time passes, but a small part of him never relaxes. It is the first thing Ricky asks whenever he speaks with someone from 'the day': "Any new news on Philip?" At an informal reunion several years later, the eternally preoccupied Kenny Tannenbaum bursts out at him: "Look, Ricky, you didn't make him run away. You didn't take his dance or his scene or his girl. You've got to let it go."

"But I saw him about to step onstage. I could have backed off into the wings."

"That," Kenny explains, "would have been the biggest joke in Friedkin history: the day two Tonys came onstage to die."

Jody Gold was eager to clear out of Friedkin without running into Philip, who confused her by loving her, just as she confused herself by trying to love him back when she didn't, at least, not 'in that way'. When Jody tells the story of Philip, however, she says her 'boyfriend' vanished. She fears it was her fault. For much of sophomore year, Jody stays away from boys at all, thinking herself poisonous, cursed.

The next summer, 1975, is sadder and spookier for the kids who knew Philip, especially for the previous year's Brigadoon girls, now junior counselors, many of whom return, including Jody. Among the boys, there's a generational shift, and so natural absences are added to Philip's untimely one. Larry Dorfman and Doctor Dave, both a year older than Philip, stay home and work before leaving for freshman year in college. Dion Robinson spends his first summer in Chicago since 1964, though he will reappear as a counselor the following year, thus earning the distinction of being Friedkin's first black camper *and* twelve years later—proving the arc of progress long indeed—its second black counselor. Ricky Gross can't bring himself to go back.

Over the years, the tribe of Friedkin floats many theories—a nervous breakdown, a broken heart, suicide. Rumors circulate: Philip joined a commune. He moved to LA, changed his name, writes movies. He died of AIDS in San Francisco in '83. He lives in Canada. He never left Wisconsin. With the passage of time, the story of Philip Rosen becomes an anthology of conjecture. *West Side Story* isn't performed again at Friedkin until 1981.

Chapter 39

In 1985, Katherine Klein musters the gumption to call Jerry Rosen. She is a new mother on leave from graduate school. Her baby is down for a nap in their Brooklyn apartment, and her own sleep deprivation has eroded her defenses. She dials the number she's carried for years, since copying it out of the *Chicago White Pages* on a visit to her mom's. She has tried to imagine Jerry, to understand what it might have been like for him to miss his missing son. She'd written a story about it in school:

I don't know if this happened, but I picture Jerry Rosen on his bed, dreaming back through moments from Philip's life. They are overlain with his own memories, the way you can watch a busy street through sheer curtains and never lose the surface of the fabric itself, the lights that shine off it, the shadow. Jerry Rosen travels back through his own life, he visits his son's, he goes nowhere.

The story never satisfies her. She knows why Philip ran away. He was battered by loss and confusion, the petty betrayals of adolescence. He was pushed too hard, felt he had nowhere to turn, and he ran away.

What she doesn't understand is why he stayed away. It's been eleven years. It's one thing to run out the door. He'd done it that night at the prom. But when the time had come to board the bus, there he was, head against a window near the back, pretending to sleep. Why would he stay lost? Staying away, refusing return, is the work of a lifetime.

And how did he have to remake himself to do it? When he got into his dad's car, he was still a kid. Unless he died or went crazy (she wishes she knew!), he became a man in exile, away from everything familiar. He loved Swallow Heart Lake, she's sure. And the places we love call us to them. "We are drawn to our corners of the known world by past generations and lost civilizations, hidden immensities," she wrote in that same attempt to get the story down.

Philip wouldn't have wrecked his life for Jody. He would have gotten over her within weeks. For a missed entrance, a ballet he couldn't perform? A skit? So what if he lost faith in the Friedkin family, came to think it was smaller, less ideal than he'd imagined? So what if its rituals of connection were also part of the sell? None of these complaints would have outlasted the money in his pocket. No, the reasons to stay away must have been incubating in his blood all along. They were mysteries.

The story she wrote in grad school never satisfied her because in imagining Jerry Rosen dreaming through the life of his vanished son, she missed the emotional crux. She didn't really know the boy's (the man's) father. She didn't need to imagine him. She was the dreamer. In her heart, Philip left her. She was the lost one.

Jerry answers the phone after two rings. He says what sounds like, "Yello." They speak for a long time.

Of course, he remembers her. Of course, he doesn't mind her calling. No, he doesn't know where Philip is, but he spoke with him years before.

"Will you tell me?" she asks. He does.

He tells Katherine about going to prison, about trying to disappear. He hadn't let his son know where he was. "I was just ashamed. I wanted him to think I was smarter than everybody, that I'd found a way to escape. I was the opposite of smart," he says. He sounds eager to talk about Philip, to talk to someone who knew Philip.

"I never knew that you'd tried to leave," she says. "Philip didn't tell me that part. I always thought you'd gone right to prison."

"No. I had this little fantasy plan. I was going to save face. I was going to get away. If he'd known I was in already, none of this would have happened. He went to find me."

There is a silence. Jerry says, "I didn't hear from him for a long time. The whole time I'm 'downtown', I think Philip's gone. My lawyer called the camp—against my wishes—but they said he'd run away. So I think he's gone; he thinks the same about me.

"Maybe it was too much, a jailbird father, his mother off to Mexico. What would he come home to?" Jerry's pauses are growing longer.

"After a while, Mickey convinced me to let people know where I was. I still don't know what I was thinking, keeping everybody in the dark. But by the time Mickey reached Philip, he already knew. He wouldn't call me. He was in touch with my sister, Phyllis, but he made her promise not to talk to me about him, and Phyllis is good that way. 'You know I can't,' she'd tell me, hard as it was for her. Probably called his mother, too. I wouldn't know."

"But you said you talked to him."

"Much later. He called. I had been out a long time already. I was only in for sixteen months total. He was crying on the phone, whole time, wouldn't tell me where he was, just kept crying, saying, 'Three years, three years.' That's how long had passed. I asked him to come home, please.

"I tried to keep him on the phone, but he kept saying, 'I have to go now, I can't talk anymore, I have to go.' Always crying. I tried everything I could think of, naming people who'd asked about him, telling him news about home. Anything to connect. I asked him about the car. I got a letter from the Iowa police. It had been totaled in an accident outside of Des Moines early on. You can imagine why I was so relieved to hear from him.

"He said, 'I sold it to a Polack in Green Bay.' Just like that. Just like me, he sounded. Like he was 'doing' me."

"I don't know what you mean," she says.

"He was saying, 'This is you, you did this to me.'"

"What did you say?"

"What could I say? He was right. I taught him how to never come back."

"But you did. You did come back," she says.

He laughs, "Yeah," a bitter negation.

She hears him suck down air, or maybe he's smoking. "Then he hung up."

Katherine tries not to let Jerry Rosen hear the sounds she's making. She covers the mouthpiece with her palm. She tries to listen as she sobs, wanting to remember everything he's saying. His exact words. "You still there?" Mr. Rosen asks.

"Yes," she says. "Did he ever call again?"

"I think so. He never talked, never said anything, but I always knew it was him." He pauses for several seconds, "But not in a long time."

She has to ask and, as she does, she hears how young she sounds. "Why?"

Again, the caustic "Yeah."

She wants to tell him something she's been telling herself for eleven years. She marshals the will. "I wrote him a letter," she says, "a few days before he left. I keep thinking that if I'd given it to him—I almost did, but—I keep thinking that if I'd given it to him, he might have stayed. If he'd read it, he would have known—" her breath stutters in her chest, "—that there were people thinking about him, worrying about him…"

Jerry doesn't laugh this time, but what he says cuts her as if he had. "Listen, hon, we all wrote letters we didn't give him. We all thought that this word or that kiss would have saved him. He didn't want to be saved. That's what happened."

She wants to protest, to explain why her letter was different, but she's out of air.

Jerry softens. "I'm convinced he's living somewhere with a wife and two kids, determined to be the perfect father. You know, avoid repeating the mistakes—that kind of thing. And I'll bet he is. I'll bet he is."

"Yes," she says. "Maybe he's happy wherever he is." She bites her ludicrous tongue.

Jerry pauses, and when he speaks, his tone is gentle. "Yeah, maybe," he answers, no comfort at all. Quiet again.

He thanks her for calling. "You good?" he asks, an afterthought.

"I have a baby," she blurts. In punishment for her desperate non sequitur, she smacks her forehead with her free hand. Hard.

"Mazel Tov," he says, as if by rote, 'Be well.' He hangs up.

Philip is alive. Katherine believes it now. Alive and gone. Death is more thorough. *You can't mourn the living,* she thinks.

"He didn't want to be saved," Jerry had said. "That's what happened."

* * *

He hangs up from Kathy and tries to do what he's done a hundred times before: stifle hope. The boy has cut Jerry out of his life, and for good reason. It's nearly a decade since he left what he always refers to as 'the slammer'. He's been through another failed marriage and suffered two heart attacks. Looking a sorry ten years older than his sixty, Jerry's got no illusions about the long years ahead. Maybe the girl will reach Philip. Maybe she will lead him back. But as his lawyer Mickey Brodkey likes to say, "A big I doubt it."

He sets out to distract himself, fixes a too-large drink way too early, turns on the tube—loud—goddamn Phil Donahue show. Talk and more talk. He hates it, but it's what he needs. He keeps returning, though, to something he hasn't thought about for forever. That horrible weekend drive from the border of Canada to Chicago before he turned himself in to the judge. He'd tried to flee and failed. He'd contemplated driving into the water of Tofte Lake and chickened out. He'd been drawn, almost magnetically, back to Friedkin. He wanted to see his son one more time.

For once, he didn't have a plan. He arrived after 2:00 a.m. Philip would be sleeping. He parked and entered the grounds from town, but through the woods. He was like some stalker killer in one of those creepy teen movies, coming upon children from among the pines. He followed what sounded like struggle but turned out to be a couple of kids having sex on the ground. The boy then got up, said some conciliatory words, and took off. The girl, looking stunned, stayed on the ground. It was Philip's friend Kathy Klein, the same one who just called all these years later. Maybe things had gone too far for her, or maybe she was on drugs and falling asleep. He didn't know. It didn't feel safe, her lying alone in the woods like that.

He came out of the trees and helped her to her feet. "You have to move," he said. "You'll be okay," he said. What he said was uncharacteristic. Who was he to tell the girl she'd be okay? He didn't believe anything would be okay. He didn't buy comfort, even the coldest. But he said it. He was, for a moment, fatherly. She looked at him in disbelief. What was he doing there? Who was he to tell her anything? And he saw himself in her disbelief—a fifty-year-old man on his way to prison, prowling the woods of a summer camp in the middle of the night, madly hoping to catch a glimpse of his son. He turned tail and stole off the way he came. He *decamped.*

He wound up at The Shed, a bar out by Route 17, a part of town he'd never seen. He drank. He hit on a woman named Carol, or maybe Cheryl. He failed to register when the conversation around him turned to the fire over at Friedkin. He failed to notice that the loud young guys who took over the bar and wouldn't let it close smelled of smoke and sweat. He didn't hear them piece their tales of separate heroism into a collective whopper of saving the day in front of a gaggle of college girls and rich kids. Jerry was plastered, and he was pawing Carol or Cheryl under the table and then in a room at the Motel 17.

The sun was already up when they faded. They slept till afternoon when they drank and screwed some more. At some point, Carol or Cheryl went home, leaving Jerry amid carryout chicken bags and ashtrays full of Camel butts and the lipstick-stained filters of Virginia Slims. By then, he'd lost his sense of time. He woke with a proverbial start around seven Monday morning, two hours before his scheduled sentencing.

He drove first and planned his plea later taking time only to splash water on his face, rinse his mouth out with the orange juice Carol/Cheryl had been mixing in her vodka. He slapped down a bill for three cups of black coffee that he carried in a tower out of a truck stop across the highway from the motel. He showered at home and, confronted by his immaculate apartment, in which he tried to leave no trace of panic, against the moment Philip would enter it. Fuck it, he thought, throwing his towel on the bedroom floor. He dressed and gathered up all the cash he had—maybe he could use it. He pulled his violin case from the floor of the closet, opened it on the bed. He left it that way with the vague thought that his son might want it. On the way to the door, he hesitated, returned to his room, picked up the wet towel and hung it on the bathroom rack. He left the Skylark parked in his space at the building and took a cab to the courthouse.

Chapter 40

I could find Philip Rosen if he were a snowball in a blizzard. Katherine believes it. But for all the emotional energy she has expended on the subject of him over the past decade, she's done nothing to prove it. She's never tried to locate him.

She wrote (and trashed) a novella about him. She spent months on a short story called 'The Legend of Swallow Heart Lake', in which she transposed her desperate pursuit of Philip into a Native American legend—replete with a noble trickster character (!) and 'authentic' Indian names like 'Chief Stands Looking Back', 'Rose with Thorn' and the suicidal hero 'Dark Wolf', who drowned in the arms of the author's surrogate, 'Silent Dawn'. It was, obviously, a travesty of appropriation and execution. Because the tale was based, loosely, on a verse history she'd read years before in a book she'd bought in Wisconsin at Gessler's Depot—*The Story of Swallow Heart Lake (And the Legend)*—she convinced herself it had the power of myth. She has told Philip's actual story to every close friend she ever made. She's prayed for him, despite believing in absolutely no kind of god and never praying for anything else, with the exception of the health and happiness of her infant son, Henry. And she faced down every devil in her to keep Philip's name off the list of possible names for that same son. Almost no literal day goes by without a thought of him, even if that thought is, "I haven't thought about Philip today."

When she hangs up with Jerry Rosen, having learned that Philip is alive and somewhere, she has to acknowledge fact: she never wanted him real. She never wanted to shrink memory or make him mundane. She has wanted—wants—the story of Philip, the mystery. The legend of Philip. She prizes this particular hole in her heart. She has spent eleven years nursing her own untrue truth: Philip disappeared forever. He's the boy who will never have to grow up. That is the way she wants it.

But she has to grow up. She has been sitting curled over herself, making herself small, pretending to be young Wendy Moira Angela Darling and not the big, ugly lady cowering in the corner of the nursery each time Peter Pan flies back in through the window after his unbearably long disappearances. "Take me with you, Peter," she pleads. He just laughs that pearly, heartless laugh.

Of course, Katherine has known the whole time what she is holding on to. It isn't Philip or camp or some childhood idyll. She is holding onto herself.

"Just grow up, Klein!" she says out loud, as Henry cries himself awake in the next room.

That's it. She's been acting like a grown-up since she was six, just the way her teenage self had acted at being Colette or Anne Frank or Dorfman's slut. But she was a babe in the woods then, and she's a babe in the woods now. A wry, intelligent babe in the woods, maybe, but nonetheless. *If I wait any longer, Henry will be the age I was then. I'm already ruining him, smothering him*, she thinks, lifting her baby out of the co-sleeper.

She doesn't wait. Like an over-caffeinated Harriet the Spy, she begins her hunt. She stalks the Brooklyn Public Library with Henry strapped to her in a BabyBjörn. She thumbs through phone books and makes lists of Philip Rosens but soon gives it up. There are too many P Rosens, too many states. Her Kaypro computer has a floppy disk drive, and she's heard it's possible to search some directories with the right technology, but the idea boggles her pen-and-ink brain.

She will have to track him down one phone call at a time. She must talk to everyone she can, everyone who might lead her to Philip, but she must not let on what she's doing. She knows she's diving down the rabbit hole; she knows it will come to nothing but idiocy and obsession, but she has to try.

Her first call is the most treacherous. She has spoken to Jody Gold with a kind of regular infrequency since that summer. First, they worried together, then they cried together. They theorized together and together, in time, they dropped the subject. Katherine doesn't know where Philip sits in Jody's life these days, and she would never ask, preferring, still and always, to keep him to herself, especially where Jody is concerned. Jody can't know what she's doing, but she can't do it without Jody. Jody is a hub of information. She has 'the skinny' on everyone, and she loves to let you know what she knows:

She eagerly reports that Lisa Climan's fiancé is as gorgeous as she is, and "dumb as a box of hair." She dishes on Jack, who still lives in Chicago. "He has two kids and another on the way! Do you believe it? Like a Catholic. He started dating his wife senior year in high school. I mean we were going out in high school!" Jody ran into Dave Mosher, who's in town for his residency. "Dr Dave is an actual doctor! He's going into cardiology." Brian Kotlicky, who'd been falsely accused of burning down the costume shop (the truth of which Katherine has never revealed) turns out to have become some kind of baby technology mogul. "He's our age and rich as Midas," she marvels. "Setting the world on fire, one computer at a time." Katherine winces.

"I saw your old boyfriend..."

"I hate to ask..."

"Dion. He's still in Chicago. Big community guy; may be an assemblyman or something."

"I'm so not surprised."

"You coulda been First Lady."

"We went out for less than a day. We were fifteen."

"He asked about you."

"Shut up."

Jody pivots: "Larry Dorfman is in Florida. Sarasota. Marriage on the rocks. Pretty messy situation, I hear." She interrupts herself. "I've always wanted to ask," she says with a wink in her voice, "did you and Dorfman ever—? I mean, I always suspected you'd gotten together at some point."

"God, no," Katherine says. It's been a while since she thought about Dorfman, though for years that night had haunted her—the Butcher's House,

167

the fire. Dorfman most of all. She used to dream that Dorfman picked her up in his car. He was very old, and she was very young, a teenager. She didn't know where they were driving and, in the dream, was afraid she'd never find her way back home.

"And you," Jody exclaims, "a mom!"

"Yeah," Katherine admits, uncertain as hell.

"I always thought that I'd be the one with the kids," Jody goes on.

Katherine's question goes unspoken.

"I can barely remember to walk the dogs." Jody laughs at the circus that is her life. "So much damage, so little time."

"I always said we were miscast," Jody continues. "I should have played Peter Pan." Katherine can picture Jody's adorable smile, all the way from Brooklyn. "I mean who's Wendy now?"

"Yeah," Katherine says, "I still expect Henry to fly away in the dead of the night. I live in terror."

Before they hang up, Katherine tells Jody she hasn't written a word since before Henry was born, how 'itchy-bored' she gets at home, how maybe she should call more old friends during his long naps. Jody flips through her address book, and Katherine starts writing. Call after call follows, day after day—the girls from her cabin, a few boys—now men—her age, including Dr Dave and Jody's Jack, her old counselors and junior counselors. She even reaches out to some of the staff—Marty Ball, who teaches improv at Second City in Chicago, accompanied by Neil Roven, the camp piano player. She calls Markie the choreographer and the tennis pro Big Bird. "I got your number from Jody," she tells them all. "I'm just happy to be back in touch."

She's about to give up when Neil Roven, who misunderstanding her whereabouts and thinking she's in San Francisco, says, "Hey, you should talk to Ziggy. He lives right there." Morbidly bemused by her own obsession and without a shred of hope, she dials the 415 number Neil gave her, leading surreally to Ziggy Stardust, former camp tech director, now living somewhere in Marin County. Ziggy remembers her, though, she's not sure if he's just saying that. "I was doing a lot of drugs back then," he explains, "and I can't remember what I remember!" He sounds delighted to realize it. "You know who I did see," he says, "I think she was in your group. Melly Barber."

"Melly's still alive?" Katherine says, startled by her own joy at the news.

"She's amazing. Quite a life, apparently, but she's doing incredible stuff in Berkeley, I think." He spends what feels like a lifetime searching for where he put Melly's number, riffing on memories of camp the whole time.

Melly Barber's fate has been nearly as mysterious as Philip's, and when, after several weeks of trying—Melly has no answering machine—Katherine reaches her, she understands why. Her old friend tells jovial stories of a lost decade, years of drinking and drugs and criminality, a devastation Katherine can hardly imagine. "Twenty-seven months sober and a bull-load of gratitude to spread around," she says.

Melly describes the profound satisfaction of her work, staffing a network of Bay Area women's shelters—for battered women and homeless ones, ex-addicts, parolees, the whole havoc of it. "You're a saint," Katherine says.

"Oh God," Melly laughs, "I'm the exact opposite of a saint." She laughs again. "Didn't think you'd find me alive again, did you?"

"Hope springs eternal," Katherine says. She's glad Melly can't see her, smiling like a crazy woman with tears running down her face.

Neither of them speaks. The moment is unfathomable.

"Hey," Melly says suddenly, "have you spoken to Philip lately?"

There's an awkward pause when Katherine realizes that Melly has missed the whole thing, that she never heard or registered the story of his disappearance. It makes sense. Life sped her away, same as it did him. When you live as dramatically as she has, you don't do a lot of gossiping about people you knew at summer camp.

She doesn't know what to say, where to begin. Melly picks up the slack. "I have his number right here," she says.

Katherine has no idea what Melly just said. She's confused, the way she gets dozing over a book she's reading to Henry, when she knows she's stopped saying actual words. She wakes to the sound of Melly reading numbers. Katherine asks her to repeat them. She asks again. She mutters something, more indecipherable dozing words.

Melly picks up on her muddle, "...yeah, wild huh? I ran into him just a few months ago, out of nowhere, and not even in the city. It was San Jose or somewhere. Even weirder, huh?"

All Katherine can say—and she says it ever so quietly—is "Wow".

"Oh," Melly says, "I can't believe you called out of the blue like this. I think of you all so often. I swear I think of those ladies every day of my life. You know I think they saved my life, as truly as if Lila threw me one of those floating rings that hung outside of the boathouse.

"There was this day. Man, I've never forgotten, though I can't remember the specific thing that was messing me up. I know I was struggling with something. It was so long ago. So much of life has happened, and I wasn't half-there for a lot of it. But I was a frickin' mess, and Lila knew it. The way she knew so much about us, so much we didn't even know ourselves.

"She pulled me to her, her arm around my neck. Sort of yanked me to her, godfather-like. And she said to me, not sweetly at all, but sternly, even harshly..." Melly stops talking for a second. Katherine hears her throat catch, hears her take air. "I mean this was her lesson to me and she wanted to make sure I heard, through whatever purple haze I was in. She said, 'You are a miracle. We want you here.'" Melly's voice breaks, "I mean, she said this to me, a total, unrepentant fuck-up."

"We were all so worried about you," Katherine says. She is outright weeping now but doesn't want her old friend to hear. Between Melly and the ten-digit number she holds in her clenched palm, she feels that she can exhale for maybe the first time since 1974.

They are out of words.

"I love you," Katherine says, across the years and across the continent.

"I love you, too," Melly replies. "It really helps my heart that you thought to call. Let's not lose touch again."

"No," Katherine promises.

When they hang up, Katherine uncrumples the paper she's been clutching. She stares at it, picks up the baby monitor to make sure it's on, even though she doesn't need it anymore, given the wailing Henry makes when he wakes. She hears his soft breathing through the plastic speaker. She looks for something in her desk drawer, finds it, sits up straight and dials.

The man at the other end of the phone answers, "Yello."

"Mr. Rosen," she says, "it's Katherine Klein. From Friedkin? Remember we talked about a year ago?"

"Sure, sure," he says. "Hello. Again."

"Do you have a pen handy? I have Philip's number," she says.

Chapter 41

Philip's disappearance from Friedkin wasn't a total disappearance. He was, in a literal sense, always present to himself, even if he was lost to the people who'd known him.

He fled camp without knowing where he was headed. He'd never intended to run away, living on streets or panhandling for money for food and bus tickets to the next town. He was a boy with few options. He was a boy. He'd grown up for sixteen years in the shelter of suburbia and, as then-Kathy Klein had known, was never one to give the world the finger. He would, at most, veer. And that's what he did. He ran away from camp and headed home.

For all the thought he'd given to moving in with his dad, it didn't occur to Philip to stay at Jerry's apartment alone. That would have meant occupying the emptiness. His mother's house was also empty, but it was an anticipated vacancy. He'd lived there alone before, often for weeks at a time, as she and 'Eduardo' or other post-divorce boyfriends travelled. At such times—for some legalistic reason, he still only stayed at his dad's on weekends—as desolate as the house might feel, he convinced himself that he was enjoying a rare freedom. He was an independent teenager, answering to no one. He could come and go, throw parties, cook what he wanted or take himself out for burgers or matzoh ball soup. Then his mom would return, take up her place in the elbow of the sectional couch, legs stretched out on the vinyl cushions, and, as he poured her goblets of Chablis or large icy glasses of tonic, recount her adventures. "I was made for the worldly life," she'd explain, still buzzing from the excitement of Manhattan or Venezia or Madrid. "I'd never say anything negative about your father, but he always, it must be said, reserved the choice parts for himself."

Now, though, her house was empty, but there was no freedom in it. His mother was somewhere in Mexico. She'd offered to return, but he knew she didn't want to. He didn't want her to, nor did he want to be responsible for her unhappiness. It took him many days to reach her. He was in a wild state, sad and panicked. When he wasn't sleeping, which was most of the time, he was trying to think himself out of his predicament. He raged at the thought of Jody with Jack, at the bullshit brainwashing of Friedkin, at the pervasive lies of musicals and suburbia and family. He woke in sweat from dreams of his father's body, rotting on mounds of bones.

By the time Philip located his mother, she was ensconced in San Miguel de Allende with her boyfriend, and he was sleeping in his cousin Mitchell's room at his aunt Phyllis' house in Des Plaines. Phyllis' heartbreak over her only brother's disappearance was exacerbated by the rage she felt at her former sister-in-law's negligence. Phyllis had long shared Jerry's belief that Judy was

171

an incompetent, self-centered mother. In her arsenal of Judy stories, the most pointed was this: "Judy's parents wanted to be buried side-by-side. She had them cremated. Sold their cemetery plots. Bought new carpet. Planted a lousy tree."

It was true. Judy's parents died less than a year apart. She got away with it because her father, the second to die, was incapacitated from a stroke some years earlier and so never knew of his wife's fiery fate. Before her father had even died, Judy sold their pricey plots at Chicago's Montrose Cemetery and used the money on wall-to-wall shag for the house she'd won in the divorce. "My folks wanted it that way," she'd told the incredulous Phyllis. "They wanted me to have a better life after they were gone and never cared about being buried there."

"Never cared to the tune of the seventeen or eighteen thousand dollars they spent on those graves," Phyllis would conclude.

Now Phyllis was determined to take matters into her own hands. She offered Philip a home with her—her children had both gone away to school. She also hatched an alternative plan: Philip would join her son Mitchell in Washington State. He would live with Mitchell and Mitchell's girlfriend Amanda at their group house in Olympia, Washington, and finish high school there, while they acclimated to life after college.

"I'm not going to tell you what to do," she told Philip. "This is a miserable thing that's happening, and you're going to have to find your way through it. Trust me, I know."

Philip listened to Phyllis with heightened attention. Phyllis knew from loss, as his father would have said. She'd been eleven when her and Jerry's mom died, while Jerry was in Germany. Phyllis had been shuttled from relative to relative after the fact, until her father found his footing and remarried. Not a happy marriage, that second, brief one, and Phyllis spent most of her adolescence with her own aunt and cousins, on her dead mother's side. Phyllis' kindly husband died young and suddenly—out jogging—when the kids were still in middle school. And now this: the living loss of a brother she loved.

"I know you know," Philip said. "What do you think I should do?"

"Well, personally, I think it's inexcusable that your mom didn't get her *tuchis* back to Chicago the minute she heard your dad was in trouble. But who am I to say? Judy is Judy. You know it; I know it. And she's your mother."

"I don't want her to come back. I don't want to live with her."

"Then don't. I'm sorry it's come to this, but don't. Stay here and let her stay in Mexico. Or we'll put you on a plane to Washington, and Mitchell will look after you. Not that you need looking after." Independence was the best defense, Phyllis believed, and she'd learned it the hard way.

Philip spent most of the next few days at his mom's house trying to decide what to do. He wished he could talk all this over with Lila, but he couldn't. The thought of speaking to anyone from camp after his disgraceful exit was almost as humiliating as the thought of spending another year with his mom and returning to Niles for school. He prowled from room to room in his house, picked clean of anything of value that might tempt burglars during Judy's long absence. He made his mind up in the rec room, or maybe the rec room made up his mind.

It had been, in his early childhood, a basement play space, as well as a sort of living room to the small wood-paneled bedroom where one or another housekeeper slept. It had been his parents' play space, too, a venue for the kind of cocktail parties at which middle-class moms and dads could almost convince themselves they were "swingers." Had it always been this creepy? The bamboo bar in the corner was stocked with glasses of every size and shape, including a set of tin tumblers in metallic rainbow colors. There was a Hulu-dancer lamp with a grass skirt and Christmas light boobs. And, to extend the theme of titillation, one wall still held a larger than life pin-up for the game, "Pin the Breasts on the Lady," though its proximity to the dartboard meant it was now pricked full of holes. The books, likewise, were circa 1960s suburbia—Leon Uris, James Michener, Jacqueline Suzann, early Philip Roth in paperback and Leo Rosten's Yiddish books, among other collections of party (and potty) jokes. Philip couldn't stomach the place anymore. It was a mockery. He knew so many kids with practically identical houses—houses made of ticky-tacky, as the song went—houses that smiled over perfect lawns while all kinds of horrible things happened inside. Horrible people lived in them.

His mind made up, he gathered what remained of his things, adding them to what was already in his footlocker and duffel bag from camp, and locked the door behind him, determined never to step foot in the house again.

When Philip finally spoke to his mom, he let her do the talking. She railed against his father. "He has no concern for anyone but himself, never has." She went on for a long time. She was angry at Jerry, justified by the court's discovery that he'd been a cheat and a liar all along. "And now he's savaged my one chance at happiness."

"Aunt Phyllis says I can stay here," Philip finally said. "That way you won't have to give up your trip."

"I couldn't," Judy said, after a pause. "It would be too much for Phyllis, and you need me. Oh my poor baby. What did you do to deserve such a father?"

"I'll be all right," he said, not saying anything about running away from camp. "We weren't going to be together this year anyway, and I need to get ready for college."

"But Phyllis has so much on her hands..." Judy said, trickling off.

Philip always knew what his mom was thinking. She was trying to reconcile letting another woman mother her son, while she stayed away. It wouldn't work for her, he knew. It would look bad.

Philip used her hesitation to try out Plan B: a year with his cousin in Washington State. "We thought of another idea, and frankly I like it better. I could live with Mitchell in Olympia. There's a great school there, and he has room in his house. It'd be like I was at college, which is what I wanted anyway. You always said independence is the goal of parenting."

"You have been wanting more freedom," she conceded. Even through the crackly phone lines, he could feel her try to justify the move, to let herself off the hook. "But I should really be there to see you through this hard time."

No, he thought, mortified. "'Travel is the best doctor,' you said so yourself... Look, Mom, I know you love me." Philip could almost feel his mother's sigh of relief.

"You're right!" she said brightly. "It's a great idea, a great plan."

Philip kept his mouth shut. He didn't want to scotch it at the finish line.

"But what will you do for money?" she asked, suddenly worried.

He knew she'd ask, and he knew better than to tell her about the Traveler's Cheques from Jerry. He'd prepared a lie. "I made a lot at camp. Bernie gave me a bonus. Plus I have a few hundred dollars in savings." And the truth: "Aunt Phyllis said she'd pay for my flight. Mitchell needs the company, she says."

"Well, of course, I'll pay her back," Judy said (and believed). "I still have some money from the sale of your grandparents' condo. Not much, but I could help. And they left you a little something for college."

"That'll be good."

"Well, okay then," she said, decided. "But remember, I love you and if you ever need me, I'll be there in a jiffy."

"I know, Mom."

No, Philip never disappeared. He sealed the deal in a single call with his mother and relocated shortly after, leaving nearly every familiar soul behind. He threw himself into a new school, SAT prep and, the second year, college applications. He made himself a responsible member of a houseful of self-styled back-to-the-land post-grads with musical inclinations, all six years older than he was and almost as lost. His mother made a couple brief, highly theatrical visits with her Mexican tan and expat air. They visited area colleges.

He was accepted into Evergreen State and plunged into the dark. He eked through his final semester in high school, spending stretches of days in bed, despite Mitchell and Amanda's kindly urgings, and nearly lost his job stocking produce at Safeway. He rallied for freshman year.

It is difficult to explain what happened next, except as a kind of self-disappearance. He continued to fulfill the outward form of being a college student. He read books. He spoke with other students. He went to classes but showing up took all his effort. He grew scared when the mouths of lecturing teachers appeared rodent-like. He became timid around girls (who insisted on being called women) at school. He avoided friends and classmates, often skirting the campus after spotting someone in the distance. Philip involuted.

Mostly what he felt was nothing. He wanted nothing. He began a program of philosophical self-abnegation, giving away 'worldly possessions', eating less-than-enough of a macrobiotic diet. He gave up coffee and alcohol. He eschewed anything that might project ego into the world, including acting, singing or dancing. He preached (inwardly at least) a communalism that meant dissolving one's self into the community. He practiced Tibetan meditation. To his mind, he was centering himself in a psychotic, troubled world, searching for stillness. He was, in fact, doing whatever he could to deaden the storms inside him.

"You pulled a Franny," his wife Paula would say years later, referring to the Salinger character who incessantly repeats a Jesus prayer to herself, masking her nervous breakdown as a quest for enlightenment. Philip's self-disguise was that of the unmasked man, peeling back the inauthentic selves he had accumulated, removing the hardening layers between world and 'essence'. He didn't know it at the time, but he was joining a brotherhood of lost souls in that part of the country, latter-day-hippie isolates, mistaking loss of presence in the world for purity, wandering through their lives in a state of global depression masquerading as mellow.

It was easy to escape notice at Evergreen, where, as they liked to say, the radical fringe was the center. He created his own interdisciplinary course of study, melding Eastern philosophy with the analysis of mid-Twentieth Century alternative educational theories and a history of American labor unions. "Don't ask," he'd say, when, as the decades went by and conversation turned to college majors, someone would, inevitably, ask. His advisor was an old school pothead with a rigorous intellect and zero sense that Philip was anything but normative among the freaks of Olympia. It was easy to float away, even from one's self.

He couldn't entirely numb himself. There was no way to meditate into submission his furies after he learned that Jerry had returned, that, in fact, he'd never gone away at all, except to a federal work-release prison downtown. His rage would spike, and he would call his father, now home, in the middle of the night. Philip would shout and cry, then he'd hang up, swearing to cut Jerry out of his life forever. He tried. He would pursue inner peace at all costs. Until months had passed and the furies tracked him again. He would call again and make his violent point to Jerry by remaining utterly silent on the line.

He paced and fasted and failed to sleep, until his physical condition and rapid-fire redundant diatribes began to worry his cousin Mitchell's attentive wife Amanda. Mitchell wanted to write Philip's behavior off as the necessary post-collegiate struggle to orient to the real world. (Mitchell was having such a struggle himself, as Amanda had gotten pregnant with their daughter.) But Amanda, more empathic and solid, took Philip in hand, dragged him to the doctor, who diagnosed dehydration, anemia and, probably, clinical depression, and had him immediately hospitalized.

If Amanda saved Philip's life, his students pulled him out of the mire, though it was a long time before he felt the change. He had begun student teaching while he was still in school, and though he had the impulse to throw himself into it, he resisted wanting even that. Still he became known as a friend of the weird, someone who would never rush a problem child, who could, intuitively, find a way to make even the most ordinary, boring crap seem a little marvelous. The classroom, in which he began as a helper and which consumed more and more of his limited energy, was the place Philip could show up: a place of presence.

Meanwhile, a social worker from the hospital got him into a therapy group and suggested meetings for something called Adult Children of Alcoholics, a twelve-step recovery program not for addicts but for their grown kids. He found the ACOA rubric reductive and wasn't sure it fit him, but the stories told in anonymity around the circles of chairs in church basements and community centers heated Philip up, got him feeling again. He attended religiously for a couple of years.

At a meeting in San Jose, he found himself miraculously reunited with Melly Barber, the robust, effusive survivor of multiple addictions, and a sight for his sore, longing eyes. "Hey, Sweet Boy," she'd greeted him, coming up casually from behind.

When one of the teachers at Olympia High recommended Philip to a friend in Northern California looking for a semester-long sub for a social studies teacher on an emergency personal leave, Philip got the job. On the spur of the moment, he packed his very few things, said a grateful, teary goodbye to his guardian angels Mitchell and Amanda, and transplanted himself in San Mateo.

Philip prepared for his classes around the clock. He took his students troubles home with him. He dedicated himself, as if to save himself. He took a series of language intensives and became nearly proficient in Spanish. The effort paid off. He began to work more easily with bilingual populations, as long as he didn't mind being the butt of their teasing for his stumbles. Teaching occupied him. It was the one thing he could always focus on. Through it, he began to surface.

It was 1982, and within a few months he had met his future wife Paula, then studying to become a social worker, through an English teacher at San Mateo who had gone to Occidental College with her. Philip wound down his attendance at ACOA meetings but, with Paula's encouragement, sought personal counselling, and landed his first job at Watsonville High School.

"Tell me about camp again," Paula would say when he couldn't remember details from the years after he'd fled Friedkin. It was as though the tape on which he'd recorded his life since then had been demagnetized.

"You're either crazy or a patient saint."

"I want to know." And he'd populate their dates with the people he'd known in his mythical homeland. Paula knew the way to help him shine.

Paula had a fierce desire to have children and, while Philip never refused, he used every passive stalling tactic in the book. By the time they'd been together for four years, his postponements had pushed them to the edge of their relationship. "I know you work so hard for your kids at school," Paula finally told him, "but I can't trade them for kids of my own." This was as close as she got to an ultimatum. He felt the threat.

He spent long hours on the phone with his cousin Mitchell, who now had a six-year-old and a toddler of his own. "You're never ready. That's the amazing thing. It's tidal. Unstoppable. It carries you away."

"I don't want to get carried away," countered Philip.

"Bullshit. You've been wanting to be carried away since you were two. You just don't want to love anyone too much."

"Thanks, Doc," Philip said.

"That'll be five cents please," Mitchell laughed.

Philip's gradual acquiescence was, ultimately, mooted by Paula's difficulty getting pregnant or, once pregnant, carrying a baby for more than a few weeks.

Paula's anguish brought them closer, though, and as Philip's compassion for his wife deepened, he began to feel more dimensional. Paula saw the change, felt that his love for her had more blood in it. It didn't fill the space she'd reserved for children, but it gave her hope. After several years of failure—and the discovery of an experimentally treatable quirk of blood that made her womb inhospitable to its own offspring—they managed to make it through the whole of the first trimester of a pregnancy.

It was 1989, the year Jerry Rosen would die, and Philip was about to return to Chicago for the first time in fifteen years.

Chapter 42

Philip prepares for the trip the way a pilgrim would for a long trek. He has to make himself ready spiritually as well as physically. Packing is easy; he'll only be gone four days. His internal baggage, though, gets shifted around numerous times, as if the right fit can't be found, as if he's carrying too much for the available space. His own anxiety amazes him.

"What is it?" Paula asks him. "You worried about the speech?" She knows better.

"It's a talk," Philip says. "And no."

"You nervous about the flight, the weather?"

"I grew up in Chicago. February in 1989 is no more threatening than February in 1974."

They are walking their evening walk around Almaden Lake. Their "sweet talk walk," as Paula calls it, and because they know it will change, because they know that pretty soon they'll be pushing a stroller around the perimeter and dragging a distracted or reluctant toddler along its paths, they cling to the ritual of their bike ride out to the lake after work and their hand-in-hand circum-navigation in the gathering dusk. They found the lake when they rented their first place in San Jose in '84. ("Yes, I know the way," he'd told his mother when he'd first informed her they were settling in the South Bay, and she'd started to sing the Bacharach song about San Jose. Now it was his mother's line, on her annual visits, including the one that has just, thankfully, ended.)

Philip and Paula are walking and playing that game they play, their version of twenty questions, where Paula gently fishes for answers to a question she already knows the answer to. Philip, in all his mock reticence, feints and parries until she hits home—touché—at which point he spills the beans. This time, though, for a change, Paula has it wrong.

"Uh, could it be your dad?" she asks.

"That would make sense," Philip says, "but no. Believe it or not, an hour with Jerry, during which he finds out he's going to be a grandfather, seems like a piece of cake compared to everything else. He loves you. What he knows of you. He'll think it's detente and his second chance…"

"And maybe it is…"

"Yeah, second, third, twelfth. Maybe. But no, it's not my dad."

"Hmm," Paula intones. "What then?" She stops on the path and faces him. He suddenly finds the surface of the lake compelling, though he can't help but smile. She throws her strong, graceful arms around his neck and says, "Tell your pregnant wife."

He smiles bigger and puts his hands to her ever-so-slightly blooming waist. Why is he forcing her to draw him out? She's the one who spends her mornings puking and shaking. She's the one whose body, carrying a single bean, after years of 'process failure' is making like a hothouse, all sunlight and glass, both fragile and impermeable, perspiration air. Why make her guess? Just tell her.

"I can't believe I'm going to see Lila."

"It's wonderful. What could be more wonderful?"

"It's terrifying."

"Tell me," Paula says, as she steps back and, curling her fingers up in his, begins to walk again. She knows better than to crowd him during revelations, grand or infinitesimal. She excels at this, modulating space, creating just the right amount of room, the right distance for intimacy and separation. She will be the world's most natural mother, he believes. She will understand grip, and she will understand release, connection and remove. He understands none of it. He clings too hard or runs too far. He remains stationary when afraid, paralyzed between retreat and flight.

In the classroom, he strides, proud and alert, as in that acting exercise where his own high school class thought him a lion. That's who he is again when he teaches. That's who he'll be when he gives his talk to the breakout session within a breakout session at the secondary school educators conference in Chicago: high school teachers; subcategory: history and social studies teachers; sub-sub category: history and social studies teachers who also teach English; sub-sub-sub: all who teach in multiracial settings, in small cities, in working-class communities. In this sub-sub-sub-sub-corner of a super-small sub-category, he'll be a star, a confident lion giving a paper on his experience teaching Shakespeare to the children of migrant workers, cleverly entitled: "Will to Live: Toil and Trouble in the Fields." And in that teeny tiny super-sub-context, nested within other larger ones like a village of Russian teaching dolls, he'll receive a distinction—a small distinction, he makes it clear to everyone who presses—for teaching, a wee certificate and resumé blip that is the slight, happy outcome of a secret nomination from his own principal.

"Tell me," Paula says again.

"It's all so small and so big at the same time," he says. Paula waits and walks. Their arms swing as they move. To her, Philip is a miracle of talent and a mystery of lowered expectations. Over the seven years they've been together, she's seen him grow into himself or, as he would put it, grow back into himself, a little at a time, as though he'd been previously growing into someone else altogether. She's seen him 'show up' to love her. "It scares me, like Lila knows things about me I don't know. Like there's too much to atone for. She must be so old."

"You love her."

"I haven't seen her in almost fifteen years."

"The return to Anatevka."

"You can't go back."

"You have to. You have to go back."

"Did I ever tell you," Philip says, "that when they did *The Wizard of Oz at* Friedkin, they changed the ruby slippers line from 'there's no place like home' to 'there's no place like Kansas?'"

"Why would they do that? It's a terrible line."

"They didn't want the kids getting homesick in rehearsal. They didn't want to use the word 'home' over and over."

"Now, you're clicking your heels together, and you're going to wake with Auntie Lila at your bedside..."

"And you were there, and you were there...and I wish you would be there."

"I wish I would, too." They walk.

"Last time I saw her—"

"What?"

"Nothing."

"I know. A long time ago."

Philip can't find words.

"Nothing to atone for," Paula says.

He tries: "You're standing on the dock and on the deck of a ship at the same time. The boat pulls out."

"You wave to yourself?"

"No, that would be like growing up—waving your young self off on a grand adventure. No one waves. You just watch yourself recede. You can't stop it."

"I know. It's a terrible dream," she pulses his hand. This is his nightmare, watching himself slip away. Paula always thinks of Joni Mitchell's song about Amelia Earhart. "A ghost of aviation, she was swallowed by the sea, or by the sky." She thinks she understands; she read the books as part of her social work training and practice. She's read the book of Philip. But Paula comes from a family of sisters. She comes from a clan of natural tension and too-closeness. She knows about being absorbed by the energies of others, fighting control and fighting for it. Being swallowed, disappearing completely—sea or sky—this is still a riddle to her.

"You'll get on the plane. You'll get off the plane. You'll meet your cronies, give your speech—talk! You'll get your award—uh, certificate. You'll go see Lila. It'll be great. You'll go see your dad. It'll be weird and brief. You'll come home. That simple. I'll be here. You'll go back to work. We'll have a baby—finally. You'll live happily ever after."

"Hippie-ly ever after."

And he does get on the plane. And the ride is horrible. Turbulent. A baby screaming behind him, another kid vomiting in the next aisle, the father scrambling to change his clothes while wiping up the viscous eruptions of half-digested egg and yogurt with the wet towels the stewardess rushes to him. Is everyone on board having the same experience, or has it been staged solely for him?

He lands at O'Hare and finds the conference meet-up table, where he shakes hands with half a dozen other secondary school teachers, mostly a little older and a good deal more weathered than he is, serious types in rumpled, ten-year-old fashions with frayed collars and ties opened to mid-sternum or, for the women, flared pantsuits and synthetic silk-like blouses. They have dressed in a

180

confusion of meanings, uncertain whether this is a workingman's holiday or a meeting with the school board, no longer clear whether to present themselves as young Turks, seasoned veterans or ageless compassionates. All complicated by the need to bundle in their warm best against the late winter Midwestern freeze (spring break indeed!). Their scarves dangle and their bulky parkas hang open, their hoods fringed with polyester fur. This is the year the Berlin Wall will fall, and the world will see that American teachers and the Soviet bloc chic wear the same kind of yesterday's clothes.

In the shuttle bus, he lets himself dwell on the sight of passing houses and frozen, snowy lawns. The sky is so close to the ground. His body breathes fully, as he sinks into the familiarity of the landscape. This is how buildings are meant to look. These are the colors of brick, this is the size of a lawn, the shape of a picture window, the grid of alleys. This is how big the sky really is, its proper relation to buildings and earth. For all of California's oceanic beauty, for all the forested splendor of Washington State, none has felt as natural and right as Chicago, whose geography puts him instantly at home.

Fifteen years, he thinks, marveling at the way his body has, in this place, clicked into place.

* * *

The conference goes well. Approximately thirty people attend his talk on the final morning, and they applaud him vigorously, a couple making a point to congratulate him afterwards, one speaking vaguely about publication in a journal he advises. Philip feels good in front of the small assemblage and believes that he not only has something to say, but that he has mostly found a witty, moving way to say it. The truth is he loves his kids, loves teaching, and, while he wishes he had the internal motor and chutzpah to be a real activist, pounding down doors and making the world a better place, he's almost convinced he's doing some good, even if only one kid at a time.

He goes back to the hotel to get the bag he's checked with the concierge. He takes the El from downtown Chicago to downtown Evanston and trudges along eight blocks of slushy sidewalks to the condominium building where Lila lives. The butterflies in his stomach feel more like rabid squirrels, and he decides this is a fool's errand, that he should let the past be past and head to the airport. If taxis trolled this small city the way they do a few miles south, he might do it, but there are just regular cars, utilitarian Midwestern sedans, crunching slowly through the snow-chunked streets.

Lila's building is a five-story orange-brick condo complex, built in the late 'sixties, fronted by a circular drive and a bus stop. Nothing distinguishes it, and it shocks him that such an ordinary place can be so unsettling. He is stumped for a moment, looking down the panel of buzzers for one that says Friedkin, but, of course, she's listed here as Sahlins. He knows how the kid on the plane felt, puking up his breakfast. "Okay, Rosen," he tells himself, "you're a 32-year-old man. You're going to be a father. This lady runs a summer camp. You will survive." He presses the buzzer.

He doesn't know what he expects. They had spoken briefly, warmly on the phone. They'd made a date for his visit. Does he expect to step back in time, to open the door of her condo and be transported to Friedkin's or the room above the dining hall where he'd seen her wailing on her knees, clawing at the mantel behind which her mother's photo had fallen. Does he expect to be greeted in the dark by a crone in the musty room where she's waited since 1974, gathering cobwebs like Dickens' Miss Havisham?

Whatever he anticipates, he is greeted with a solid embrace by a vigorous seventy-six-year-old woman in a floral babushka, orange blouse, and black slacks that could have been the ones she'd worn to class in Showboat. She squeezes him to her, pulls back to study him, and squeezes again. "Philip Rosen," she says, as if by saying his whole name, she has conjured him out of air. "Philip Rosen."

He thaws in the warmth of her greeting. He remembers everything about her. "You look amazingly the same," he says.

"I was about to say the same thing of you," she offers, "but you were always so intent on growing up fast that I didn't want to insult..."

"Time is a fiction," he says, instantaneously fluent with her.

"A mirage!" she replies with glee, folding him again in her arms.

* * *

"When I was a girl, this was how we drank all our tea. Always tea, even in the bookstores and restaurants." She motions him to sit. A spoon in each glass, she pours tea. "The spoon takes the heat," she says.

Lila reaches for a little jelly jar on a Lazy Susan in the center of the table. She lifts the silver top and, with the jelly spoon, flicks two dabs of raspberry preserve into each glass. They watch it drift to the bottom. Taking a pair of scissors from a ceramic pot on the counter, she snips a straw in two, and spears a half into each glass. "You want to do like this," she says, positioning the straw against the bottom of her own glass at the place where the jam is thickest. "Drink through the fruit for the sweetness." She demonstrates. "My father would hold a sugar cube between his teeth instead of jelly and a straw." Her tea is too sweet. She made it that way for Philip, never uses more than a dab for herself. Not like Papa, a regular sugar tooth he was.

"I wish I'd known your father," he says. "I remember Gramma Della so well." They set down their glasses of tea, and she tours him along the walls. The walls are a portrait gallery of camp family and blood family, from this century and, apparently, another. Lila carries the dead with her, he thinks, but she works every minute of her life for the future. He passes photos of people he knew in childhood and people who had died years before he was born. Lila stops at a photo of herself and Sylvie, each on one of their mother's arms. Della, maybe forty, beams through thick glasses, her dimples deep and adorable. "I guess nothing was going to stop you three," he says.

"She wouldn't have let it. She looks like a cutie-pie, but she was Muhammad Ali."

Philip asks her the expected questions about camp: how it's changed, how it's still the same. He asks about Max and how he died.

"Slowly and suddenly at the same time. The longest three months of my life and altogether too fast. It was devastating. It still is. Eleven years and yesterday." This is Lila, he is reminded: every feeling she has—every feeling in the wide world—plays across her face. There is no filter. She is emotional conduit.

"He was a great guy," Philip says.

"You know," Lila tells him, "he thought the same of you."

Philip doubts this information, doubts whether Max even gave him a moment's thought, but he takes it in. He turns away from the portraits and takes in the rest of the apartment. It is cluttered but neat as a pin, home to an industrious, fastidious soul.

"So you're a teacher!" she says, as if the sun had just come out after a season of eclipse.

"No," he says. "You are. I'm the sorcerer's apprentice."

"Modesty is verboten here," she insists, "at least from you." She hits him with her high beam, all-seeing eyes. She draws him out, asking the most specific questions about his students, about his classroom, about the parents and their involvement. She wants to know what texts he uses, and how much time he spends with each. How do the Spanish-speaking kids do with textbook English, with Shakespearean verse? Does he teach from song lyrics? When they read history, do they identify as American or Mexican? How do their parents identify?

Philip is startled by a realization of the obvious: Lila is a teacher. Her life has been teaching. She is a master teacher asking him questions about his methods because she still has more to learn.

He describes the laborious satisfaction of teaching a mix of history, literature and current events to mostly immigrant kids at Watsonville High. He understood, almost from the start of college, that this was what he wanted. He never veered. "Can you believe it? I'm already Mr. Rosen. I'm going to be that geezer who teaches the same class for 30 years. 'Man, can't that old guy think of nothing better to do?'" he says, with a slight Spanish lilt. He clearly loves it.

"I knew it," she says quietly, almost to herself.

"You should have seen the *Fiddler* I directed with the kids," Philip continues. "Tevye was this doughboy kid named Octavio. He was amazing. Their parents were a little confused at first, but it was phenomenal. It turns out there are a lot of Mexican fathers out there trying to deal with their daughters growing up and leaving home. I wish you could have seen it."

Although his manner is subdued, she can detect the spark, the ardor of the young actor he had been.

"You stopped acting, though?"

He smiles. "Tony was the pinnacle. What could top that?" After a pause he adds, "I wasn't cut out for acting. That intense, constant emotional delving. Paula's yoga classes are about as deep as I can go. I lose my shit in Chair Pose. Don't tell her I told you."

"My lips are sealed," she winks, holding herself back from grabbing him by the hair and kissing his face.

They talk for two hours about their lives and work, about politics and art. They talk about everything but the past, the hole of Philip's past. But that doesn't matter. They find each other fascinating, like people who grew up together, sharing more than they can get to. They talk about Sylvie and Bernie, still going strong, and Lila says, "I wish you had time to see them. They'd be so happy. They'd be so proud."

"Next time," he says.

"Make it soon," she scolds.

"Sure. But please, don't tell them you saw me. I mean I wouldn't want to hurt their feelings, for them to think I chose you over—"

"We chose each other," Lila says with a smile. He looks down, a slight nod. "I won't lie to them, but if it doesn't come up...I wouldn't want to hurt their feelings," she adds.

He hesitates at the door. He is excited by their conversation and Lila's closeness. He wants to say something important, wants to sum up this flush of feeling. As ever, she seems to know what he's thinking. She says, simply, "Don't stay away so long next time."

He begins to cry. Lila holds him and holds him.

It is too perfect. Lila walks him to the elevator after many minutes embracing him like this and, as the elevator opens, an elderly man steps out. He greets Lila as if he knows her only by sight and says, "Is this your son?"

Lila and Philip respond instantly. They both say, "Yes."

* * *

Jerry is waiting in a faded blue Mercedes about ten years old, directly in front of the apartment building, motor and heat running. Before Philip gets to the passenger door, Jerry has it open for him. "Get in," he says, leaning across the seat. "You can't be used to this cold anymore." Philip tosses his shoulder bag in the back and plops down in front. He is struck by the pleasant smell of old leather, or maybe it's leather polish—the car's own smell. Jerry leans over once more and kisses Philip's cheek, and the young man's hand floats to his father's shoulder. Before Philip can say anything, Jerry is back at the wheel, putting the car into drive and rolling down the street.

"Welcome to Chicago," Jerry says. "The city has missed you."

"It looks so the same," Philip says.

"That, my boy, is the charm of the Midwest." Jerry smiles, with Midwestern charm.

The city looks the same, but Jerry doesn't. Philip has only seen him a few times in the past four years, and he still hasn't gotten used to his father silver and gaunt. Jerry is sixty-three, but he looks a lot older. Also, he looks handsomer, with the roundness gone, without the gin bloat. Heart surgery must have its upside, as he looks healthier old and sick than he did young and plump.

Philip is still buzzing from his time with Lila and, if Jerry were anyone but Jerry, he'd launch into the story of their re-meeting, his amazement and release.

He remembers he's just been crying and turns his face to the window. He pictures John Dillinger, played by some character actor in an old movie. "No one gets out of Chicago alive," the mug says.

"How's my favorite daughter-in-law?" Jerry asks.

Philip is still back in the doorway with Lila. He doesn't want to start on this yet. But the clock, he knows, is ticking. "She's been a little sick," he says.

"Sorry to hear that. She's a sweet one, that Paula. I know you know. You have good taste."

"Thanks, Jer," Philip says, droll.

"No, I mean it. I've always felt that we share—not the good taste; God knows I haven't had the best record—but a real romantic streak. You probably don't know this, but I've always been only too willing to throw everything over for a woman. It's the thing I've cared most about, my relationships, other than you, of course."

"Hmm," Philip intones.

"I'm not saying you threw anything over for Paula. She gives you life. Don't think I don't see that. She's a good one," Jerry's nervous, but Philip doesn't flag it as nerves.

They're headed for O'Hare with about enough time for a drive-thru hotdog. He may as well do this. "She's actually been kinda pregnant."

Jerry brakes. The car skids a little on the slick street. He checks his mirror and pulls over, stops at the curb. Philip notes the location: Main and Crawford. "That's wonderful news," his father says. "Congratulations, Philip."

Obviously, Jerry wants to throw his arms around 'the boy', as he still thinks of him. He restrains himself. "Wonderful news," he says, through wet eyes. "I'm so happy for you."

"Thanks. We're pretty happy, too. It's been a long time coming—"

"You should pardon the expression," Jerry says, because he is Jerry.

Philip ignores the joke. "It still feels touch and go, but she's nine weeks in, and the doctor says all's well."

"You're going to be a terrific father," Jerry says, full of feeling. "I know you're already a great teacher. You're going to be terrific."

In spite of himself, Philip is happy for the prediction. "Thanks, Dad. I don't know."

"I do," Jerry says, starting the car up again, "and maybe you don't know this. I mean things haven't always been so perfect between us...but at the end of the day, your kids are everything. I mean, you are the thing—the person—that I'm the proudest of. I hope you know that. I'm very proud of you."

"Thanks, Dad," Philip says, hoping his gratitude will end Jerry's sentimental outburst.

"The way you've turned out. Paula. The teaching. You gotta know that."

"Dad—"

"And pride isn't taking credit. I don't. The credit's yours. I want you to know that."

"Okay, okay. Enough already."

"Sure, sure. You should just know is all."

Jerry drives. "Flipper junior," he muses, keeping the rest of his thoughts to himself. He points as they drive, "They closed that school. Baby boom's over. Not enough kids... And remember that? Milt's first Stereo Palace was there." He chortles a little, "Thank God it's Fridays now."

Philip lets out a laugh puff.

"Does it look very different?" Jerry asks. "How long's it been?"

"No. It hardly looks different at all. How can that be? Fifteen years, and it looks the same."

"You were young," Jerry says. There is nothing for Philip to say.

Jerry was the one who was supposed to flee Chicago, but he's the one who stayed. Mom followed the sun, and Philip just got away. Jerry stayed, in spite of himself, and so he knows every block of every street. What memories he has, he has from here. Does that make it home or prison, Philip wonders?

Jerry turns into Wolfy's. He gives their order into the squawking box and pulls to the window. The hot dogs steam. They pop when you bite the skin, and Philip thinks he has maybe never tasted anything so good. The fries are caked in salt, and Jerry passes on them. Philip has a milkshake and, pulling it in through the straw, he's thirteen again, sampling a vanilla shake from the burger place as he carries takeout through the alley home.

At the airport, Philip reaches for his bag and says goodbye.

Jerry stops him with his deliberate words, "I meant what I said. I'm happy for you, proud. I love you very much."

"I know," Philip says. He's not sure what to do next or what to say. He's holding the bag in his lap. He figures it will be a long time before he sees Jerry or Chicago again, especially now that the baby's happening. His father will ask to visit and, sooner or later, they'll invite him, suggesting a nearby hotel for his stay. Maybe they'll take the chance to leave the baby with him one night while he and Paula go to dinner.

Jerry thrusts bills into Philip's hand. "Buy something for the baby," he says. He plucks some more money from his wallet. "And buy that lovely lady something to keep her feeling beautiful. You'll be glad you did."

"Thanks, Dad."

"And remember what I said."

"I will," Philip's hand is on his door. "I love you, too, Grampa," he says.

He hasn't planned to say this, and he doesn't know that he means it. It's a fortunate phrase, though, since this will be the last time he sees his father. Jerry will never babysit his granddaughter, will never know whether or not she made it because he will die days before she is delivered into the world. Jerry will check himself into a hospital just as he checked himself into prison. He won't let anyone know where his is. On the third day of tests, an aneurism in his stomach will tear, and he'll go quickly. He will have given a lot of thought to his son Philip's life and to what Philip told him the last time they were together. Jerry will choose to believe that Philip was being truthful and not merely giving him the good lie.

Chapter 43

Dear Aunt Phyllis:

I'm sorry that Paula and I won't be with you tomorrow for Dad's funeral. I know you understand that it's truly a choice between life and death. The good news is everything's over but the impatience. Paula's 'greatly improved' as they say on doctor shows, and it won't be long before our still-unnamed daughter-to-be joins us, and Paula can finally get the hell out of bed. Anyway, I'm certain you understand and thanks for that.

It can't be fun, doing a sister's work and a son's. I know that all the details—the planning and mourning, the burying—should be mine to attend to. Please know how grateful I am. You've backed me up so often, so completely. I wish I could back you up for once, that I could catch you. I also wish it were easier for you. In fact, I wish it had been easier for him, this life, but it wasn't, sad to say.

Yes, I'm sad he's dead, and I'm sad about his life. Sad even though I missed so much more than I was there for, maybe sad because of that. Sometimes, I think the effort it has taken to stay away—to keep him at such an enormous distance—is proportionate to the effort it took him to keep at such an enormous distance from himself. Do you know what I mean? Of course, he survived things I can't imagine, hard as I try (and I have tried). But that self-distancing takes work. It saps a life's energy. (We talk a lot about energy out here in No Cal.) It did, I believe, for him. And keeping him at bay (or Bay Area) has me a bit ragged.

Anyway, all to say, I wish I were there with you, and I don't wish it. I mostly wish things were different, and that dad and I hadn't done such a mighty job of passing each other like ships in the night—his a battle-scarred PT boat, maybe, and mine a negligible sunfish.

I'm taking your advice (for once) and faxing you some words (below) to be read at the funeral. Paula sends her love to you, and she sends her sorrow. You know, the few times she met him, she liked him a lot. She saw his many charms, which makes me think that if we'd had more time, we might have found a way (even tentatively) back to each other. But time is what we didn't have, so here we are. Or here we are, and there you are. In a better world, our here and your there would be just the same. Then we could tackle this together.

Much love, your grateful nephew,
Philip

September 17th, 1989
Dear Family and Friends,

Sadly, it isn't possible for me to be with you all today, to celebrate my father's life and grieve his death. My aunt Phyllis suggested that I send some words instead, a eulogy from afar. Please accept these words in his memory with my gratitude for your being there to honor that memory. I'm especially grateful to Phyllis for making my dad's funeral happen. She has been our family's rock for ages, and here I am, leaning on her once again, just when she could probably use someone or something to lean on.

I've asked one of my oldest friends, Katherine Klein, to read this for me. She threw my father and me a lifeline that allowed us to reconnect. Without her, I might have missed knowing him these past few years. Without her, I can't imagine what.

A eulogy, as I understand it, is a way of paying tribute but also a way of sharing the sacred in spirit when it's no longer possible to do so in body. It derives from an early Christian Eucharistic practice of sharing a portion of consecrated bread with those who weren't present at communion. Please, excuse my pedantry, but I'm a teacher and, well, academic ways die hard. I say this because I want to find a way to the spirit of the man who was my father, Jerry Rosen. I want to find a way and to share with you what I find.

It's not an easy enterprise. As you probably know, he barricaded that spirit well—with humor, with cynicism, with aggressive charm, with silence. With that brash, hacking laugh of his. Also, I doubt he thought in terms of spirit. The world was very concrete for him, very real. He had little interest in God or any of what we in Northern California call 'spiritual practice'. He did, though, visit synagogue once a year to say Yizkor for his mother. He had a romantic streak, a search for love that has a spiritual side. And he knew something about awe, which for him, unfortunately, was more horrible than magnificent. I stood beside him in Yad Vashem in Jerusalem one day in the early seventies, surrounded by photos—and I suspect memories—of death camps, and I saw him overcome, silenced. As for religion, I learned quite early that he believed in, precisely, nothing.

Things weren't easy for him—his mother died young, his war experience was horrific, he saw marriages fail, went to prison, lived with the alienation of his son. Things weren't easy for him, and so he did what we all do, in one way or another: he sealed off much of what was best in him. I wish I could enumerate the thousand times I saw that best part—the loving, striving, vital spirit part. But I can't. If, at moments, the spirit of Jerry Rosen broke through the hard casing life baked around him, I mostly missed it.

We are marked by what we witness—our lives are defined by it. At least, my father's was. We are also stamped, maybe equally, by what we miss. The things others see that we fail to see. The clues dropped, the opportunities blown. And so, in memory and words, we try to piece together the life we failed, by accident of history or character, to witness. For me, the life I spend the most time trying to piece together, to imagine my way, actor-like, to the inside of, is Jerry Rosen's, my father's.

I wish I could be with you to hear stories of him—to see him through the eyes of his friends. I have no doubt that we knew different men, and I'd like to meet the one you've known. While it's my job, in a long-distance eulogy, to share his spirit after the body is gone, what I really wish is the chance to hear you evoke him, to taste the bread of communion you all bring to the table. (Some image for a nice Jewish boy, no?) I wish, too, I could see him surrounded by grandchildren, a gray old grampa, telling tales of the 'old country' that is Chicago. Or reminiscing with his sister, my aunt Phyllis, creating a family history for us to soak in.

What I can tell you is this: one day when I was sixteen and he was forty-nine, he drove from Chicago to Swallow Heart Lake, Wisconsin, where I was at summer camp. He came to tell me about his legal troubles, to tell me he was headed to prison. Before he could explain what had happened, though, he began to cry. He tossed back what seemed like a couple dozen glasses of scotch, and he told me—through tears, as they say in the stage directions of plays—about his time in the war, his part in the liberation of the camps in Germany. He had never talked about it before. He told me something that I suspected, and now know, was impossible—that he had buried the bodies of Anne Frank and her sister.

I was overwhelmed. I'm sure I didn't take in half of what he told me. But I saw him. For that moment—and I've replayed it a thousand times—I saw my father, Jerry Rosen, as he had been and as he was. I saw tenderness. I saw loss. I saw a man who had been in over his head as a boy and was in over his head as an almost-fifty-year-old man. A man who tried to think five steps ahead of everyone else but who, all at once, couldn't do it. I saw his wish to have done something loving, maybe even historically so. It was, almost but not quite literally, the last time I saw him.

Was the man I saw the real Jerry? Are we who we are at our most vulnerable or at our most guarded? In our hearts or in the masks we wear? I suspect this sounds rhetorical, but understanding it about him is, to me, urgent. His experience is my legacy, and his partialness is my mystery, my puzzle to complete.

I would wish my father, in death, the wholeness that he failed to find in life. I would wish this—I do—except I don't believe it's possible. I don't believe—as he didn't—that anything happens after death, except right here. I believe that we complete each other right here, or we don't. Children complete their parents; lovers complete each other; friends offer connection and some small completeness. Even as a people, as citizens of cultures within a larger world, we add up. We make something bigger than our small solitary selves. That's the hope anyway, and yet it doesn't often happen. Too often, we end as we begin, separate and partial—incomplete.

For me, the grief I feel at my father's death is magnified by my sense of how very separate and partial he was. A terrible thing to say about your father, I know, but there you have it. He wouldn't want less than the truth, and I won't dishonor him by serving up less.

Someone I once loved very much told me that we make a world from freaks, from freaks who do kindness to each other. I take this to mean that we are all partial or, in the eyes of others, freakish. I take it to mean that we can choose to do kindness or we can choose to do violence, that we can go our own ways or link our strange, fragmented selves together. In this version, this vision, these links are the way we—freaks all—forge a better world than the one we came into.

My father might have agreed. (He was, after all, a good Jewish-atheist-liberal.) But he still would have called it bullshit. We don't connect. We aren't kind. The world doesn't get better.

My final wish for him, then, is that we prove him wrong: life is not separate and solitary. We can find each other. We can make our world better.

What we can't do, and, as I write to you about my father, Jerry Rosen, I know this more powerfully than ever—what we can't do is unbury the dead. We can't dig up the dead and tell them all those things we should have told them. We cannot disinter them and make amends or peace. We can't remake them out of bone and ash. We can't remake them at all.

We can only—and this is hard enough—remember. Please help me remember my father. I have so little of him. Help me remember him as you do. Write down any stories you have about him and send them to me. Anything at all, however small, however fragmentary. Help me get to know the man I missed.

My aunt Phyllis called to tell me he'd died. I'd spoken to her only days before when she phoned to check in on Paula and me. I thought she was following up, but she said, "Dad's dead." It took me a moment before I realized she was talking about my dad. Jerry. Later, it hit me that her phrase wasn't accidental. He was, in fact, a father to her, too—eight years older, someone to look up to, someone who looked after her. This wasn't a story; it was a gift. A blast of light.

She told me something else too, and I've been trying to make sense of it. At the end of the war, during his first days in the camps, he went crazy, suicidal. He drank himself unconscious and, you could say, cracked up. This much I knew. But what she added, I didn't know. He had never mentioned it.

The Army offered him a Section Eight. Immediate discharge for having lost it, for being mentally unfit. He could go home, just up and leave. However, Phyllis tells me, he turned the offer down. He stayed. Chose to stay, to finish the work he'd started, the work that threatened to kill him, that did, in some real way, kill him. He didn't run. He didn't flee. He chose—God knows why—to stay in that hell and keep shoveling.

Thank you, Phyllis, for introducing me to the man who stayed. I never knew him, and now I do. Thank you, dear Katherine, for caring enough for long enough to lead us out of the cold and back to each other. And thank you all for whatever else you can tell me about him.

I will light my candles. I'll visit the synagogue once a year, as he did for his mother, and listen to Hebrew words I don't understand sung to a music I can't follow. I'll dig out a picture of a younger him—laughing—and frame it for my shelf. I'll recite Kaddish in translation from some West Coast hippie poet. I'll do my ritual best to piece him back together and keep his memory alive. But, please, help me fill in the blanks.

Acknowledgements

Many people have contributed to the life of this book—by reading it, offering kindness, or buoying my spirits during the long years it's taken to find final form. I can only thank a few of the most important here.

My wife, Karen Hartman, was the first and last reader, the best and always reader. My gratitude and love for her is on every page. My brilliant writing group—Gordon Dahlquist, Liz Duffy Adams, Joseph Goodrich, and Honor Molloy, who did a master-class edit of an early draft—were with me on this ride long after we dispersed. Some years ago, more than forty-five New Dramatists playwrights signed a letter to buy me sabbatical time from my artistic director work there, in order to begin this novel. Their effort failed, but the vote of confidence got me launched and kept wind in my sails. Another letter, written by a sister of my youth, Jan Cooper-Nadav, drew deep and loving connections between our summer camp history, the lives we've lived since then, and the story I wanted to tell; I've carried it with me and re-visited it when I needed fuel.

Others have helped in numerous ways: thanks to the whole team at Austin Macauley and to James Morris, my guide there. Gordon Edelstein opened his home as a writing retreat, as did Melissa Leo. Neil Steinberg, Steven Gore, Julie Marie Myatt, Adam Langer, Linda Healey and my brother Paul London gave me notes and encouragement. Darrah Cloud, who shares my obsession with our mutual hometown, and Anna Fogelman were key readers who said all the right things. The prodigious Kia Corthron not only gave great notes on the manuscript, but saved it with her eagle eye. Another camp sister, Janice Gaffin, to whose mother this book is dedicated, gave me still more reason to finish. I thank the whole Harand community for being family to me, especially Sulie Harand Friedman and Pearl Harand Gaffin, who led me to myself.

I have recast pieces of my father's life for this novel, and in a way it's a love letter to him. By extension, it's a love letter to my own sons, Guthrie and Grisha.

CPSIA information can be obtained
at www.ICGtesting.com
Printed in the USA
LVHW080053310320
651615LV00007BA/215

9 781528 950671